# THE ISOLATED SÉANCE

*Also by Jeri Westerson*

*The Crispin Guest Medieval Noir series*

VEIL OF LIES
SERPENT IN THE THORNS
THE DEMON'S PARCHMENT
TROUBLED BONES
BLOOD LANCE
SHADOW OF THE ALCHEMIST
CUP OF BLOOD
THE SILENCE OF STONES *
A MAIDEN WEEPING *
SEASON OF BLOOD *
THE DEEPEST GRAVE *
TRAITOR'S CODEX *
SWORD OF SHADOWS *
SPITEFUL BONES *
THE DEADLIEST SIN *

*A King's Fool mysteries*

COURTING DRAGONS *

*Other titles*

THOUGH HEAVEN FALL
ROSES IN THE TEMPEST

* *available from Severn House*

# THE ISOLATED SÉANCE

## Jeri Westerson

**SEVERN**
**HOUSE**

First world edition published in Great Britain and the USA in 2023
by Severn House, an imprint of Canongate Books Ltd,
14 High Street, Edinburgh EH1 1TE.

severnhouse.com

*British Library Cataloguing-in-Publication Data*
A CIP catalogue record for this title is available from the British Library.


ISBN-13: 978-1-4483-1074-6 (cased)
ISBN-13: 978-1-4483-1075-3 (e-book)

*All Severn House titles are printed on acid-free paper.*

Typeset by Palimpsest Book Production Ltd.,
Falkirk, Stirlingshire, Scotland.
Printed and bound in Great Britain by
TJ Books, Padstow, Cornwall.

# Praise for Jeri Westerson

"Everything a reader could want in a Victorian mystery: dastardly deeds on dark London streets, cockney squalor, upper-crust skullduggery, a hint of the supernatural, even a stalwart sidekick named Watson . . . Sly Sherlockian fun"
Steve Hockensmith, author of the Holmes on the Range mysteries

"Jeri Westerson is at the top of her game"
Louis Bayard, bestselling author of THE PALE BLUE EYE, on *Courting Dragons*

"The Tudor court as seen through the eyes of wily Will Somers, Henry VIII's jester, comes to vivid life in this sparkling mystery"
C.W. Gortner, bestselling author of THE TUDOR SECRET, on *Courting Dragons*

"Devotees of Alan Gordon's Fools' Guild mysteries will welcome this promising series"
*Publishers Weekly* on *Courting Dragons*

"Familiar historical figures seen from a different viewpoint add spice to the mystery"
*Kirkus Reviews* on *Courting Dragons*

"An appropriate end to Westerson's series. Long-time fans will be eager to see if Crispin can triumph over the past, and anyone who enjoys medieval mysteries can follow it easily"
*Library Journal* Starred Review of *The Deadliest Sin*

"Westerson's acclaimed series mixes historical detail with a deep dive into the character of a flawed but honorable hero"
*Kirkus Reviews* on *Spiteful Bones*

"History, mythology, and mystery mix in a rollicking adventure"
*Kirkus Reviews* on *Sword of Shadows*

# About the author

**Jeri Westerson** was born and raised in Los Angeles. She is the author of the CRISPIN GUEST MEDIEVAL NOIR mysteries, the KING'S FOOL Tudor mysteries featuring Will Somers, three paranormal series and several historical novels. Her books have been nominated for the Shamus, the Macavity and the Agatha awards.

www.jeriwesterson.com

*To Craig, who solves all my ills.*
*Without a Calabash churchwarden pipe.*

# ACKNOWLEDGMENTS

I would like to thank my editor Sara Porter, my many whip-smart copyeditors, Senior Brand Manager Martin Brown in Marketing, Sales Director Michelle Duff, and all the good people of Severn House and Canongate for giving me and this new series a chance. Your help and confidence are very much appreciated.

*'No, it's not quite so bad as that. It is the unofficial force
– the Baker Street irregulars.'*

Holmes to Watson in *The Sign of Four*

# GLOSSARY

**Barrow boy** – a person who sells wares from a pushcart.

**Bogtrotter** – offensive term for an Irish person.

**Brown betty** – a round-shaped teapot with a deep brown glaze, made and used in England to this day.

**Bumbershoot** – umbrella.

**Coppersticks** – police truncheons.

**Costermonger** – a person who sells wares, particularly fruit, vegetables, or cooked food-on-the-go, from a pushcart or wagon.

**Crawlers** – destitute women who are usually too weak to beg on the streets and spend their time in a twilight in doorways.

*Cuir bouilli* – boiled leather to create stage armor or storage cases.

**Damme** – exclamation: damn me. Pronounced 'dammy.'

**Dossing, dosses, doss house** – a 'doss house' is a common lodging house with several beds to a big room for nightly rental. 'Dossing' is finding anyplace to spend the night.

**Doxy** – term for prostitute.

**Esse** – a particular brand of iron cook stoves still manufactured today.

**Fauteuil** – upholstered chairs where the wood of the arms and legs is exposed without cushioning.

**Fireplace fenders** – a brass enclosure around the front of a Victorian fireplace to prevent logs from rolling out of them and into the room. Some are more elaborate, being taller with cushioned seating atop them.

**High-striker** – a carnival or funfair game where a person strikes a button with a mallet to make a striker rise on a measuring post in order to prove the person's strength by ringing a bell at the top.

**Hob** – a shelf, projection or grate in the back or side of a hearth to keep food warm. Later British usage meant the burner on a cooktop.

**Knifeboard bench** – seating on the top of horse-drawn omnibuses, particular to the trolley-type carriages popular in London from

1875 to 1895. So-called for its resemblance to a utensil for sharpening knives. Enough room for about eight riders sitting back-to-back.

**Knocking shop** – house of prostitution.

*Lion Comique* – a type of music hall popular entertainer making fun of the upper classes in pantomime and song, made popular by Alfred Vance and G.H. MacDermott, among others, described as 'a Lion of a Comic.'

**Lorgnette** – a pair of spectacles with a handle to make it easier to hold it in front of one's eyes.

**Nomades** – same pronunciation as 'Nomad,' but with nineteenth-century spelling. Itinerate groups of British Isles people. See Travellers.

**Pastiche** – a work of fiction that imitates the style, characters and themes of another work of fiction, in this case the Sherlock Holmes stories by Sir Arthur Conan Doyle.

**Pepperbox revolver** – any number of small handguns with multi-barrels instead of a revolving cylinder. Small enough to fit in a lady's purse, like a Derringer.

**Penny dreadfuls or penny fiction** – lurid tales of crime, romance or the supernatural, printed cheaply and for a penny each, and then later for a ha'penny each in the early nineteenth century, sometimes later appearing in book form.

**Pitches** – market stalls.

**Pixilated** – crazed, bewildered; in the manner of pixies confusing the unwary.

**Punter** – customers, or marks; those who are tricked by con artists.

**Romany** – formerly also termed 'Gypsy,' the latter term now considered by some as derogatory, although some Romany still describe themselves by this term. Permanently wandering people, originally from India (their darker complexions were mistakenly attributed by Europeans as Egyptians, hence the origin of the corruption 'gypsy'), but now more commonly thought of as Eastern European stock, though today Romany or Romani or Roma people are from all parts of the globe.

**Street Arabs** – street urchins; boy pickpockets, etc. (From *A Study in Scarlet*, written in 1887 but set in 1881, where we first meet the Baker Street Irregulars. Watson describes them as 'half a dozen of the dirtiest and most ragged street Arabs that ever I clapped eyes on.')

**Travellers** – itinerate groups of people, similar to Romany but mostly Irish or Scottish, living like but not mingling with Romany.

**Wagtail** – a prostitute.

# ONE

## Badger

*London, 1895*

'We sat around the table in the unused room,' said the possible client. His speech was better than Tim Badger's, more like a tradesman, though he said he was a valet. His clothes certainly looked the part: fitted coat, waistcoat, hair parted down the middle but a little windswept. No mustache or beard, but he was in want of a shave.

'Go on,' said Tim. Conscious of his own ill-fitting suit with its threadbare elbows and the loose threads at the cuffs, he glanced over his shoulder for reassurance from the stoic face of his partner Benjamin Watson, whose shaded eyes never left the client's. His brown suit was little better than Tim's, stretched as it was over his stocky frame.

The client's eyes roved uncertainly over the dim room. Wallpaper was peeling off the wall by the door. There was a rusty stain on the plaster in the far corner that made a crack that traveled the length of the ceiling from one side of the room to the other. And above the fireplace, the whole wall was blackened by coal smoke. Not one piece of furniture was in perfect order, with a torn cushion here, a repaired chair leg there. Tim could see it all on his face. The man was beginning to wonder what in the world he was doing there in a shabby room in the slums of London, hiring these nobodies to save him.

'Describe the scene,' Tim hurried to say. 'Please.'

The distraction seemed to work, for the man faced Tim again and resumed his narrative. 'None of us wanted to be there. The room felt close, stuffy, especially because of the burning incense.' He sneered in disapproval. 'It made everything a bit smoky, even though the window was open, though the drapes were shut. Only the single oil lamp hanging above us lit the table – the rest lay in shadow.' He paused, thinking. 'Erm . . . It's a small room. Paneled wainscoting with plate rails. A mirror on the wall beside the fire-place. A brass candlestick on the mantel.' He shrugged. 'That's all. It was empty but for the table and chairs. No pictures. No fancy things.'

'How many were in the room?' pressed Tim, standing at his own sooty mantel, holding the unlit pipe to his face, but neither lighting it nor putting it to his lips.

'There was five of us, including the madam or medium, whatever you'd call her. She had rings on her fingers and gold earrings under wild hair. Looked like her neck needed scrubbing.' He shivered. 'I suppose she was a Gypsy.' This did not seem to rouse the interest he'd hoped for, and so he continued, counting them off on his fingers. 'There was her, me, the housekeeper, the housemaid, and Mister Quinn. Then she told us to touch the planchette. You know. That thing that skates along the spirit board. Well, I don't think any of us but the master wanted to touch it, but we did. She told us to concentrate. On what, I'd like to know. "We must reach into the spirit world to talk to your business partner," she said.' He shivered again. 'I don't mind saying, the whole thing was queer.'

'Interesting,' Tim decided he should say, waving the pipe. 'Go on, Mister Brent.'

'Well, she said something like, "I call to Stephen Latimer across the spiritual plane," or some such nonsense. And damme, that plan-chette moved along the board by itself! I don't believe in those things, Mister Badger, but it did give me a fright. Especially when the maid shrieked at it. But she was always in a state. Like a mouse, she is. Well, then the madam went on with, "Is it you, Mister Latimer? Tell us." And blimey, but that planchette jerked and skidded over the board *again*, landing on "Yes." Even the master, Mister Quinn, gasped at that. But then Mister Quinn, quite agitated by this time, demanded, "Ask him what I want to know!"

'The madam scowled at him. "We must take our time, Mister Quinn," she said. "We cannot hurry the spirits of the dead."

'"He'd better dashed hurry," he said in a state. "I've been searching a fortnight since he died." He even yelled to the ceiling, "Give it up, Latimer, you scoundrel!"

'It upset the madam terribly. Mister Quinn growled something at her again. He's the one who wanted this séance in the first place, but he seemed barely able to tolerate it . . .'

'A question, Mister Brent,' said Tim. 'Just what is it the master wanted to find?'

Brent shrugged. 'He never told us. Then the maid, almost in tears, said, "Oh sir, listen to the madam. I don't want no ghosts getting angry at us." And I thought she had a point until the house-keeper told her, like she always does, "Silence, girl. You do what you're told."

'The maid simpered a bit as the madam continued. "Mister Latimer," the Gypsy woman said, "come to us. Tell us the information."

'When the master yelled again, "Spill it, Latimer, you swine!" the planchette moved *again*, sliding across the board to where the letters were. A-T-I-C, it spelled. And the master got worked up again and cried, "What are you talking about, you fool? There's nothing in my attic!"

'And that's when the oil lamp went out. Then someone jarred the table. The maid screamed. The housekeeper slapped her. There was a sound of stumbling, movement. And across the room, a silky mist began to appear. The maid screamed again. Even Mister Quinn yelled.

'I got up from my seat, stumbled to the fireplace, and struck a match, blinding everyone for mere seconds and freezing them all to the spot, before everyone turned to the master slumped back against his chair. A letter knife stood up in his chest and there was blood.' He swallowed hard. 'He was dead.'

Thomas Brent then took a deep breath and eagerly looked up. Tim got the uncomfortable feeling that Brent expected him to solve it right then and there.

Trying to seem professional, Tim asked, 'And where exactly were *you*, Mister Brent?'

'I was standing at the fireplace. That's where I got the matches.'

Watson was about to speak with finger raised and mouth open, when he seemed to think better of it, curled his finger down and leaned back in his chair once more.

Brent sidled close to Tim and thumbed behind him at Watson. 'Do we have to have this blackie in the room? These are personal things I'm telling you.'

Tim blew out a long breath with barely constrained patience. 'That, Mister Brent, is me partner, Benjamin Watson, and no better man there is in an investigation. His skin color is of no concern of mine, nor should it be of yours. I beg you to have a better care in what you say in his presence, for I will not abide any form of intolerant speech, sir.'

Brent turned and looked over his shoulder at Watson again. Face dark as coal, hair close-cropped to his head, except where he parted it on the left side, he was a man with some heft to him and presence, with wide shoulders, chest and beefy arms. He seemed to be a stone statue, saying nothing, nor twitching his face one iota.

'All right, then,' Brent muttered unapologetically.

'Did you see anyone, Mister Brent?' Tim continued, pushing on.

'Did the door open?' asked Watson suddenly.

Brent turned from one to the other. 'I didn't see anyone. It was dark. The light had gone out and it wouldn't light again. So I lit the candle.'

Tim leaned an arm on the mantel, still clutching the unlit pipe and posturing with it. 'What do you make of the strange glow in the room?'

Brent shrugged. 'I don't know. It was odd, is all I can say about it.'

'Did it come from the lamp? Had you ever seen it before?'

'No one was allowed in that room. It wasn't ghosts, if that is what you're trying to say. I don't believe in them.'

'Then why were you there, Mister Brent?'

'I'm Mister Quinn's valet. And footman. And driver. And everything else he needed a man for. I was the only man in his employ at the house. He *told* me to be there. Told the maid and housekeeper, too. None of us would have been mixed up in such nonsense otherwise.'

'But isn't it true, Brent, that you were blamed for the murder and have been on the run since?'

'How . . . how did you know that?'

'Simple, really.' Tim gestured with the pipe. 'You've got shaving soap on your collar and patches of stubble, which indicates a slap-dash shave. You've got a tear in your trouser leg – new – that you haven't had a chance to repair, and your fingers are scuffed and scratched as if making a hasty exit . . . out of a window, possibly.'

Tim slid his glance proudly toward Watson in time to see the man roll his eyes.

'That's . . . amazing, Mister Badger! I knew I was right all along in coming to you, sir.'

'There was also the notice in the *Chronicle*,' Watson said, *sotto voce*, hiding it under a cough. Then, leaning forward, elbows resting on his thighs, he asked, 'But why?'

'Why what?' Brent didn't seem to like speaking directly to Watson.

'I want to know why you came to us . . . instead of Mister Sherlock Holmes.'

Tim gave him a warning look, but, as usual, Watson ignored him.

'Well . . . truth to tell . . . I did go to him first, but he told me he hadn't time to take the case. And to come to you.'

Tim pulled up short and nearly dropped the pipe. He stared at it and placed it on the mantel. Composing himself – pulling taut his patched waistcoat and clamping his hands to his tatty coat lapels – he postured once again. 'I see. That was good of Mister Holmes to send you here. He and I are colleagues, after all.'

'Yes. Well.' He glanced around the shabby room once more. 'I can't be clapped in gaol, Mister Badger. Once a man like me gets nicked, there's no hope. And I didn't do it.'

'Of course not.' Tim picked up the pipe again, opened the lid of the chipped tobacco jar on its wobbly side table, and dipped in the bowl of the pipe. He inexpertly shoved the tobacco down into the bowl with his thumb and turned again to the mantel to pinch a match from a wooden cup, striking the match on the scuffed and repaired sole of his shoe. Touching the flame to the tobacco, he sucked hard on the pipe as it slowly drew. He then tossed the match behind him into the fireplace, leaned an elbow on the mantel again, stuffed his other hand in his pocket like any country squire, and puffed on his pipe.

Watson watched the whole performance, shaking his head slightly with open mouth before he took a breath and leaned toward Brent again. 'How did the spirit or that madam spell "attic" again?'

'A-T-I-C, like I told you. Just like . . .' He frowned and said no more.

Watson thought for a moment. 'And how would *you* spell attic?'

'What the deuce difference does it make?'

Watson paused before he sat back. 'Nothin'.' He crossed his arms over his chest and did what he did best: stare with hooded eyes.

Brent turned back toward Tim. 'Will you take the case, Mister Badger? Will you find the real culprit so that I don't get arrested for it?'

Tim pulled the pipe away from his lips and coughed. The toxic fumes seemed to rumble uncomfortably in his belly. He didn't feel so good. 'Quite, Mister Brent. We'll take the job. How will we find you, should we need to ask more questions? I assume you are going to your nearest bolthole?'

'That I am. I'll contact you every other day, Mister Badger, if that's in keeping.'

'Very good. I don't suppose Mister Holmes mentioned a retaining fee?'

'Oh. You mean . . . you want money?'

'Just a small fee to retain our services. We'll be so busy with other work . . .'

Brent gave the room another perusal.

'It will take our valuable time, you see?' said Tim. 'A man must be paid for his time.'

Brent thrust his hands into his trouser pockets. 'Well, er, how much, Mister Badger? I haven't got much, being that I had to hastily leave my situation.'

'A shilling will do.'

'A shilling? I don't have as much as that, Mister Badger.' He pulled his hand free of his pocket and in his palm lay four ha'pennies. 'But I can get more for you later.'

'Naturally. That will do for now, Brent.' Tim cocked his head at Watson, and a silent exchange ensued. With a frown, Watson grudgingly leapt from his seat and took the money.

Still coughing, Tim escorted Brent to the door. 'We shall see you soon, Brent. Keep your head down.'

He no sooner closed the door on him than he leaned against it and coughed helplessly.

'You look green, Tim,' said Watson.

'Ruddy pipe,' he choked.

'What did you expect? You never smoked a pipe before.'

'That shag . . . it's awful. It's like smoking hay that's been shat on by a team of oxen.'

Watson slapped him in the back to help the coughing. 'And what's the idea, making me fetch the money? I told you I was not going to pose as your servant. Proud and equal, is what you said. It's what we agreed on.'

'It's your money too,' he gasped, eyes watering and lying against the door. 'Gawd. Get rid of that pipe, for Heaven's sake.'

Watson took the pipe from the mantel and knocked the burnt tobacco on to the coal.

Tim slid slowly down the door to the floor. 'I don't know how you smoke them cheroots. It's all an abomination.'

'It takes practice. But why do you suppose Mister Holmes wouldn't take his case?'

'Get me some beer, will ya?'

'Get it y'self.'

Tim lifted himself from the floor and dragged his feet to the curtained alcove of their pantry. He grabbed the near-empty jug and poured the beer into a clouded glass. He downed it and leaned heavily against the pantry shelf. 'I think I'm going to be sick.'

'Do it out the window. I don't want to smell your sick all night.'

Tim rested his hands on the sill, but there was a crawler sleeping in the narrow space between his building and the next, and he soldiered through it instead, breathing deep of the outside air, though that was barely fresher than a room full of tobacco smoke.

'Why wouldn't Holmes take the case?' Watson asked again.

'Why do you care?' Tim asked, coming back in and resting against the wall.

'Because I don't like it, is why. Don't it seem like the kind of case Mister Holmes would take?'

'Maybe it's as Brent says. He's too busy. Wants to give me a chance, his old Irregular.'

'Seems dodgy to me, is all.'

'You know what they say about looking horses in the mouth.'

'That's *gift* horses.' Watson sighed, looking at the coins in his palm. 'We're never going to make money at this.'

'We got four pence.'

'No, we got four *ha*'pennies. That's *two* pence.'

'Oh. Right.'

'You look less green. Feeling better?'

'I'd feel better with a pint of bitter.'

'You'll get nothin' for tuppence.'

'We . . . we could share one.'

Tim watched Watson's face skew from angered to defiant to resignation. 'I'll get you a bloody *half*,' he muttered. 'And oi! Forget the pipe. Smoking ain't for you.'

'You're right. You're always right.'

Together they went around the corner to their local and ordered a half each. They sat at a scratched table in a dim corner. The weak flutter of gas in the sconce above them flickered its light. Most of the regulars were there – wagtails with tatty shawls taking a rest from walking the streets, working men with dirty faces slouched over their gins, other men and scoundrels in furtive conversation.

Watson drank his mostly down before he set the glass on the table, but kept his hand on it lest some drunkard got it into his head to steal it out from under him. 'Whatcha want to go and smoke a pipe for anyway? Because the guv'nor did?'

Tim felt foolish now for his attempt with the pipe, for the truth of it was just as Watson had said. Holmes did it. Why couldn't he? 'Aw, lay off, Ben. Can't I preen a bit, getting a decent client for once?'

'I think if the rozzers have him down for it, he probably did it.'

'Nah, Mister Holmes wouldn't have done that to us. He's a right proper gentleman.' He lifted his half glass, studied the dark beer for a moment, simply whetting his thirst, before taking a large dose of it.

'He spelled "attic" wrong.'

Tim smacked his lips and set the glass down. 'Why are you still on that?'

'Because the ghost wouldn't have got it wrong. The madam wouldn't have got it wrong. Who knows what went on at that séance?'

'Well, me lad, that's what we're hired to find out.' He clinked his glass to Watson's and smiled.

'Then what next?' said Watson. 'Talk to them others at the séance? We'll have to find that madam as well.'

'I wonder if we *will* be able to find her. Sure as you're born that Mister Quinn hired her.'

Watson wiped the beer from his lips. 'Now what would a gentleman know about hiring a medium? It's got to be one of them servants what knows.'

'Sounds like a perfect job for a chimney sweep, hired by the master before he died.'

Watson gulped another swallow of his beer. 'You want me to go by m'self.'

'You're the one what knows how to be a chimney sweep, not me.'

'Ain't that convenient,' said Watson into his glass.

# TWO
## Watson

With his brushes and rods over his shoulder – and a little extra soot on his face and shoulders just for authenticity – Ben tramped down Gower Street in Bloomsbury toward the Quinn house. Clean and bright terrace houses, looking like picture books on a bookshelf, all stacked neatly together. The street was clean, too. None of the garbage in the gutters one found back in his part of town. None of the smells either. Maids regularly brushed and cleaned these porch steps. Coppers, no doubt, made this one of their beats to keep the riff-raff out.

Ben glanced behind him to make sure he had no rozzers on his tail. He cheerily tipped his hat to the ladies and gents along the avenue as he walked. And because he was attired as a sweep, they were friendly back.

He found the right address at last – a middle-class house made of brick, with a nice, black-painted metal fence surrounding the step-down to the kitchen entrance below the front stairs.

When he knocked at the front entrance, a maid opened the door, startling upon seeing him. 'What do you want?' she said in an expression somewhere between haughty and frightened.

He tipped his hat and smiled. Ben knew he wasn't a bad-looking bloke. But white women generally didn't treat him as anything but a servant, and one to be watched at that.

'Good morning, miss. I'm here to clean the chimbleys.'

She narrowed her eyes, her hands still firmly clutching the edge of the door. 'I don't know nothing about no chimneys being cleaned today.'

'I got me orders from Mister Quinn not more than three days ago.'

She turned her arm just that much to show the black armband. 'The master died *two* days ago.'

'No! That's a shame, that.' He pulled the dented gray topper from his head, pressed it to his breast, and bowed. 'I give my blessings to all in sorrow in this household.'

She started to close the door. 'So, as you can see, we won't be needing the likes of—'

'Then you are in *sore* need of your chimbleys cleaned. The room to lay him out in, at least. When I'm hired to do a job, I don't skip out on it. It's me honor at stake, you might say.'

He donned his hat again and sidled ever so slowly toward the door. When it didn't look as if the maid would surrender the doorway, he simply pushed forward, pretending he had been given permission.

She stuttered and made a bit of a fuss. 'I . . . I didn't give you leave . . .'

'Blimey . . .' he said, reaching under the brim of his hat and scratching his head. 'Quinn. Isn't that the gentleman what was killed here . . . during one of them séances?'

He stood in the foyer on its black-and-white tiled floor, looking about. It was just what he expected from a terraced house on this street: arched entries to parlor, morning room, and to a back stair. A table in the center with a dish for calling cards. There were none. One would expect there to be *some* for a death.

'It's none of your business . . .' said the maid, rushing toward him.

'I read it in the paper.' He shook his head. 'What a shame. I'll wager you didn't know nothin' about it, being the maid and all. And right here under your roof.'

She seemed to calm from her earlier fluster. 'That's all you know.' She glanced over her shoulder and drew her voice down to a whisper. 'I was right there in the very room.'

'No! That's horrible. You was in the room?'

'I was. And the master making us all sit for that terrible spirit conjuring. That's what comes of devil work.'

'He made *you* sit in on it? That's a terrible thing.'

'Ain't it?' She clutched at something from the pocket of her apron. Ben thought it was likely a cross at first, but when her busy fingers moved over it again and again, he could see instead that it was a rabbit's foot.

'So what happened?' Ben felt the smile inside. He'd done it again. At first, they were frightened of him. He was a burly fellow, just a little on the stout side but tall with wide shoulders, and a beard. Intimidating, he admitted, and most weren't used to talking to a black man, but with a little beguiling and a cheery attitude, he got them to talk. He knew there was nothing a young housemaid liked to do better than to gossip to a stranger. More experienced housemaids and ladies' maids knew better than to speak out of turn, but this girl was ripe for the pickings.

She sidled closer. 'We was sitting there. And I don't mind saying that I was terrified. That ain't nothing a Christian woman should be doing.'

'Oh, miss, I agree wholeheartedly.'

'I don't mind the occasional tarot card or palm reading. That's different.'

''Course it is.'

'But this was calling to the dead. You must never call out to the dead. The dead might linger.'

He shivered at the thought. Even though he wasn't one to believe in ghosts. It was just the idea of the thing, he told himself.

'And there we were,' she went on. 'That madam talking in a scary voice, and her a Gypsy, I reckon – and you can't trust *them*, now can you? We was there and she was talking to some spirit and our fingers were on that spirit board and I was ready to jump to me feet and run, I was that frightened.'

'I wouldn't blame you if you did.'

She stopped and truly looked at him. He knew how to lower his chin, to look up at her with a soulful expression, and she offered a shy smile, all the while stroking the rabbit's foot. 'That's kind of you to say.'

'It's God's truth, innit? Then what happened?'

'All of a sudden, there was a cold wind, like the coldest snowy street in winter, and the lights went out. I screamed. I couldn't help m'self.'

''Course not.'

'And when Brent lit the match, the master . . .' Her large eyes

filled with tears and her lip trembled. 'The master was dead,' she
sobbed, bringing her apron to her face. 'Murdered!'

Ben shook his head again. 'Gor. Murdered. That's a sore thing.
And during a séance! Crikey. Who in the world would know how
to hire a medium, I wonder?'

She wiped her reddened nose with her apron and shrugged.

'Couldn't be the master,' he offered.

'It couldn't be.'

'Could it have been someone else in the house?'

Her pretty eyes grew wide. Her wet cheeks glistened. 'I don't
know.' She dropped the rabbit's foot into the apron pocket again
and smoothed the whole thing down.

'Wilson!'

She hastily swiped her hand over her cheeks. 'Blimey, it's the
housekeeper, Mrs Martin.'

'Was she there too?'

'We all were. It was horrible.'

The housekeeper bellowed her name again. The housemaid gave
him another smile and her eyes – clear now of tears – gleamed a
little, looking him over. 'I have to go. The parlor's in there. He's
in there too,' she whispered the last, pointing to a double door. He
had only enough time to touch the brim of his hat before she was
gone.

Housemaids. They always cooperated eventually.

Ben knew he had to hurry. He pushed open the sliding doors
and there was the man himself, all laid out in an open coffin set
on two trestles hastily covered with a cloth. He was decked out
in a dark suit with a dark waistcoat. The room smelled faintly of
flowers that had gone off. Not a lot of flowers in abundance at
that.

Quinn had called for this séance, apparently anxious to find some
information his deceased business partner had not given him before
he died. What was that information? And *where* was it? Brent had
said it was something about the attic.

'Or more accurately,' he muttered to himself, 'the "A-T-I-C."'

He'd have to discuss these questions further with Badger.

He tipped his hat to the dead man and quickly found the stairs
in the hallway behind an arch on the other side of the room, and
hurried up to stand in the narrow passage on the first floor. His eyes

rose to the ceiling. Did he have time to investigate the attic? No, best use his time to look over the séance room.

Looking down the passage of closed doors, he reasoned it had to be one of these rooms. He stuck his head in one at a time.

First one: bedroom for the master. He closed that door and quickly opened the next. Bathroom, complete with tiled walls, floor, and a large bathtub with clawed feet. Odd. A pedestal sink stood opposite with an oval mirror above that.

Closing that door, he opened to a second bedroom. All the looks of a nursery with its painted walls, but without a bed or crib. Brent had not said there were children. The wife died some years ago. He and Badger would have to go into Quinn's history.

The next door revealed an empty room . . . so this last one was probably it.

He stepped inside and looked around the small, empty room. He sniffed and detected the faint odor of . . . incense? Yes, it smelled not so much like a church with its incense – and he was no pope Catholic, after all – but it was more like a . . . a fancy knocking shop. Not that he was a patron of such places. But the incense smelled . . . cheap.

It was a smallish room. No guest would be put in there. Might have been for the nanny that they hadn't needed. Possibly why there were no personal furnishings, no photographs, no knick-knacks. Just an oil lamp hanging from a chain from the ceiling, a mirror next to the fireplace, a candlestick on the cloth-draped mantel. No bed, but there was a round table in the middle of the room with chairs pushed away from it, one tipped to the floor.

Ben approached the table. 'So this is where it happened . . . where he died.' No tablecloth was there. 'Probably needed some scrubbing.' And the thought of it made his stomach squirm. That had to have been a lot of blood. Not just on the tablecloth, but the chair, and the rug beneath it.

He laid down his brushes on the table, put a hand on it to steady himself, and crouched to look below. The rug looked newly cleaned, mostly directly underneath the table.

Which chair was it? He hadn't thought to ask.

He looked around at the dark floral wallpaper, high wainscoting with a picture-hanging rail with no pictures.

He studied the wainscoting and ran his hands over it. Solid. But there was something peculiar about this room. He couldn't put his finger on it. And even as he thought about it, a cold chill rippled up his back.

'Gor,' he whispered. Did he feel something? Like a . . . No! Not a ghost. He didn't believe in them any more than Brent did.

Still . . . there was a cold spot. Right where he was standing.

In a room that held a séance . . .

He raised his head to the window. *Must be a draught*, he decided, and walked to the single window. He pushed the heavy curtains aside. The window was barred, but he flicked the lock and pushed up the sash. It moved easily.

'What are you doing there?'

He spun and saw a slender woman, as stiff as a corset with a lace cap on her head and wearing a black wool dress, standing in the doorway. She was staring down her long nose at him.

He dragged his hat off his head again and gave a curt bow. 'I thought I'd start up here. That way, I wouldn't be underfoot. Just making sure the fresh air can get in. It's dusty work, this.'

'I don't know what you think you are doing, man, but you have no permission to be here.'

'The master hired me—'

'The master is dead.'

He put his hat over his heart. 'So the maid told me. And sorry I am for you all. But he hired me, promised me my fee, and I've come to do the job.'

'Mister Quinn has never hired any workers for this household in the entire time I have worked here, and that, young man, has been for twenty years. *I* am the one who hires laborers, and I never hired *you*.'

'He said his name was Mister Horace Quinn, he was a rather large gentleman with gray mutton chops, and he give me this address. That seems satisfactory to me.'

'Well, it isn't satisfactory to *me*! Now. I have told you to leave. Must I get a policeman?'

Ben sagged and put his hat back on. 'Well. That sounds final, dunnit? I'll, er, just be on me way.'

He gathered his brushes and rods from the table, touched the brim of his hat, and sidled past her and her scowl through the doorway and then down the stairs. He didn't like the look on that housekeeper. She might call a policeman on him just out of spite.

He hurried down the steps and retreated through the kitchen. The housemaid – Wilson was her name. He wished he had caught her Christian name. She wore a sorrowful expression as she watched him leave – and up the stairs he went to the street, feeling lucky he had escaped without trouble.

He glanced back up at the face of the house. Its windows now seemed grim under his scrutiny, as if they wanted to keep their secrets. The window in the séance room faced the street and he stared at it. Remembering the strange coldness he had felt, he shivered. Feeling foolish, he decided he wouldn't tell Badger about that particular bit, and trudged back to the dirtier streets of the East End near Fleet Street. The bricks on these terraced houses were not scrubbed and clean-smelling, but dark with soot, and the streets and alleys stank of piss. Stragglers – with bleary, faraway looks – sat along the curb, too weary to lift their dented cups high to ask for charity. Ben dropped a farthing in the closest one, and looked back at a little girl in rags, her feet bare and black as soot. She had a bundle of rags in her hand, probably a doll someone had cobbled together for her of cloth too shredded for anything else. She watched him walk for a long way. He suddenly wished he had a scrap of bread to give to her. Little wonder he and Badger didn't get many clients. Who would come down here, looking for a detective, of all things?

He reached their flat and trudged up the rickety steps, minding the missing one. He hated to fail, and this venture had only been marginally successful. What would happen if he returned with Badger to interrogate the household? Probably best he didn't. Keep the mystery about the two of them. Though it was true Badger had taught him various disguises, he'd still be a black man – or woman, though that had to be quite the emergency for him to don a dress and shave his beard again. They would still look twice at him, and they wouldn't do so if he were white. And there was no amount of pancake make-up that would hide that fact.

He reached their door and pushed through. Badger had spread papers all over their table. His fingers were stained with ink, as he haphazardly scribbled with a discolored wooden pen. There was even a streak of ink across his brow where he pushed back his unruly dark hair. Ben huffed a chuckle of affection deep in his throat. That was the Tim Badger who had convinced him five years ago to become a confederate of his in this scheme of detecting; the man who was engrossed in his tabulations and maps and plans, his sole concentration on the work at hand.

When his friend looked up with widened eyes and a ready smile at Ben's return, Ben knew – despite their many setbacks and scrapes – that it was all worth it. Or at least . . . someday would be.

'You're back. What did you find out?'

Ben ran his hand over his face, fingers grooming his close-cropped beard. He made it to the hearth, picked up a poker, and jammed it in the grille to move around the few pieces of coal. 'I found out that the housekeeper is a pinched old bird who don't like black men poking about, and out I was tossed.'

'No! Bloody hellfire.'

He cracked a smile. 'But not before getting into the séance room.'

'Ben Watson! You are my little miracle. What was it like?'

Even thinking of it he shivered. 'I don't mind saying, something was queer about that room. I . . .' No, he wasn't going to mention the cold spot. 'It's just . . . something. And the housemaid. At least she was forthcoming.'

'They always are under your twinkling eye.'

Ben preened, casting a glance at himself in the cracked mirror over the hearth. 'They do twinkle a bit, it's true.'

'And? What did you get out of her? Besides an invitation to come calling.'

'More's the pity we didn't get that far. But she did verify what Brent told us. So as far as that goes, it's the truth. She didn't know who hired the medium. She didn't think it was Quinn. It wasn't her, and by the look of that housekeeper, Mrs Martin, I don't think it was her neither.'

'We'll have to talk to Quinn's business acquaintances. Maybe he got a recommendation.'

'True enough.' He counted aloud on his fingers all the points they had to discover, about the information Quinn wanted out of Latimer, about Quinn's business, his home life and past, and, of course, who hired the medium.

Badger nodded, writing out the points on the corner of the large map-sized paper before him. Each corner was held flat by – respectively – a cooking fork, a clothes iron, a shoe (Ben's), and a heavy decorative finial they had found inside their rented wardrobe.

'So what have you got there?' said Ben, inclining his head toward the paper.

'Just drawing the room and where everyone was sitting so's I can fix it in me mind. See here.'

Ben stood behind him and looked over his shoulder. 'Nah, Tim. Give that pen over.' He took the pen from Tim's fingers and dipped it in the inkwell. 'This is where the hearth is. And here the window.' He carefully scratched the places over the thick lines his friend had drawn. 'And here the door to the room. The room next to it . . .' He pointed with a stubby index finger. 'This was a nursery, and the séance room was probably the nanny's room, but neither of them was used.'

'Ah.'

'The séance room didn't have no ornaments at all, no pictures; no nothing but the hanging lamp, as Brent said.'

'Hmm. That is odd. And this is where the window is?'

'Yes. I even opened it.'

Badger shuffled papers and pushed a larger sheet over the others. 'I made a careful drawing this morning of the street. You know how I like to keep the whole of the thing in my mind . . .'

Ben leaned on the table, scanning the drawings. He was always amazed at Badger's skill. The man had many talents and could have employed them to greater reward in many professions, but chose – in all opposition to common sense – to concentrate on this most difficult of tasks, that of a private detective. That was all right for Sherlock Holmes, who seemed to possess a preternatural ability to ferret out criminals, but as for Badger . . . well. He tried. And he did stumble upon the right clues now and again, but at present he wasn't as efficient as he might have been. Even with Ben's help.

Ben bent over the papers and scanned them one last time before he straightened. 'We'll have to get into that attic and look about for that information, whatever it is.'

'Why would it be in the attic?' Badger brooded.

'That's what I been asking m'self.'

'Didn't Brent say that Quinn railed that it *wasn't* in his attic?' Badger began rolling the papers into long scrolls. 'I think it's worth a try looking, just the same. It's a shame you didn't have a very long inspection of the house. That only means I'll have to do it tonight.'

'Tim, what do you mean, "tonight"?'

Badger smiled that dangerous smile of his, the one that got them into more trouble than Watson liked. 'I'll have to break in.'

# THREE
## Badger

'You see,' said Tim, 'I think the best course is to get to the roof of the house next door and make our way into the attic. See how they connect?' He gestured toward the houses along the darkening streets. On either side of them, the terraced houses looked down, shoulder to shoulder, like disapproving soldiers. Faint light shone through the parting of curtains, or down below in the kitchen windows under gaslight. Lamplighters were busy with their ladders, going one by one, up the street and down, to light the way as darkness slowly encroached under a lingering mist of fog and soot.

'"Our" way? You're talking about housebreaking, Tim. I want none of that.' He kept his voice down. It seemed the thing to do as the streets themselves became vacant of people.

'Now see here, Ben. You know it's to discover what we have to find to solve this.'

'All I see is lawbreaking. And how much the rozzers would love to toss you in gaol. And me as well, for that matter.'

'Come on, Ben. It's got to be done.'

'Can't you just present yourself at the front door and *ask* to look about?'

Tim screwed up his mouth and glared at his friend. 'And just who would *I* be? I don't get to throw about the name of Sherlock Holmes. I'm just me, Tim Badger of Shadwell. Who's going to let *me* in?'

'You've done it before,' he said sullenly.

Tim patted his friend's shoulder. 'And so I have. But not to a house such as this. And you said so yourself, I'd never get by that housekeeper.'

'Yes, she's a mastiff, for certain.'

'So my idea is to break into the attic, quiet-like, and search around. And if I find . . . whatever it is . . . then I won't have to get into the rest of the house.'

'But you will. Because how did someone stab Mister Quinn in the chest with a letter knife? There wasn't time. Think about it. The lights went out, the match was lit, and he was dead.'

'Remember,' said Tim sagely, 'them that tell these tales don't always get it exactly right. They each see something different.'

'I'm the one that told you that!' rasped Watson, looking over his shoulder for anyone lingering on the street.

They hurried down the pavement as the light faded, he and Watson talking furtively. They dodged the pavers' wagons with their bubbling hot cauldrons of tar as they stopped work for the day; digging out the old, uneven cobblestones and replacing them with new granite stones.

Tim liked very well this idea of breaking in. It reminded him of his early days on London's streets, before Mister Holmes made him a Baker Street Irregular. Before he had got some respect for himself. After all, if a gentleman like Mister Holmes could see something in him other than a thief and pickpocket, then he had a future ahead of him. And now was the time to make that future happen.

'Look, Ben, you stay as watch on the ground, then, eh? And then Bob's-your-uncle, I'm in and out. Easy.'

'That's what *you* say,' he muttered.

Tim gave him a smile and a wink, moved round to the side and began searching up and down the walls for a good foothold that wouldn't be noticed from the other houses. The corner downspout looked like the best spot. He had to climb a short iron fence, but that gave him a leg up and, when he grasped the boxy spout with its lead bands, he was able to scramble up quick. Up he went like a squirrel up a tree, getting new handholds on the stone lintels over the windows. When he got high enough, it was a simple matter to haul himself over the top and onto the slanted roof.

He lay there and gingerly peered over the side, searching for Watson among the shadows. There! The man was his signpost.

Off he went, dodging brick chimneys and iron vents. A low wall ahead – the wall of the next house – made no encumbrance as he slipped over it. Two dormers emerged from the fog. One had to be the attic, but he had to make certain it wasn't the attic *room* that the housemaid slept in, and when he got up to them and, on his toes, looked over the side of the roof, he saw Watson leaning against a lamppost and lighting his cheroot.

Looking through the window of the first dormer, he could see it was a dark room with objects in it all a-jumble. Not the maid's room then. With a small knife, he worked the blade into the window lock, swore when he broke the lock, and pushed up the sticky sash with difficulty. He could move it no more than halfway, but he reckoned that was enough. He pushed his head through first and slid his slim body to the floor with a bump that made him wince. He lay flat and still, breathing shallowly of the musty air and listening hard to the floors below. When he had waited for at least a full minute – and this he could tell, being as quiet as he was, for he could hear the clock on the lower floor chime – he finally began to move again. He rose and unhooked the bullseye lantern from his belt, the one he'd nicked from a copper some years ago. He lit the candle and closed the fisheye lens over it before scanning the room with its weak light. Trunks – a fair few – and hat boxes, folded canvas to cover God-knew-what, various vases, some cracked, some not, and a profusion of empty, open crates with wood wool spilling out of them.

He peered into these and moved the wool about, mindful of the lamp, but saw nothing. As he scanned the walls, he noticed a four-foot-tall wooden sculpture of a blackamoor with a fan. He crept toward it and shone the light on it up and down. *Watson would love this*, he mused, thinking of his dignified partner. The man would never be caught dead in its muscle-defining *cuir bouilli* garment, carefully carved on the figure's torso, with its frilly tasseled skirt, the artist's idea of what an African tribesman looked like. Not that Ben Watson had ever seen Africa, nor ever would.

Tim chuckled and moved the lamp's light until it lit upon a chest of drawers. 'Bless my soul!' he whispered. He pulled on the top drawer but it was locked. He set the lamp down on a small table opposite and removed the ring of skeleton keys from his trouser pocket, holding them tight to keep them from jangling. He measured the size of the lock and chose a smaller one, thrusting it in and manipulating it in the lock till it clicked.

Carefully, he slid the drawer out and riffled within. At first, he thought it was filled with kerchiefs, but on pulling out one of the items, he discovered it was a baby's gown. He pulled out others and found more gowns, silky with lace. *Ben said there weren't no babe in the nursery.* He turned the gown this way and that. *Could be it died. Poor soul.* He returned the garment to the drawer and proceeded to use his skeleton key to unlock the one next to it. More baby clothes. He sighed, looking at them. So many died as babes where he grew up. Including his own brother and sister. Maybe that's why he survived. There was more to eat with fewer mouths to feed . . . though he wouldn't wish such on any mother.

He moved to the other drawers down the chest and could not find anything of any value that Mister Quinn would have been looking for from a business partner. Certainly no cash box or hidden jewelry. He even took the drawers out and checked beneath them for secret hiding places. No letters or documents. What the bloody hellfire had Quinn wanted?

Retrieving his lantern, he turned it all around the attic room and didn't find anything else. He jimmied open the trunks and found only a lady's clothing, likely the missus that was long gone.

'Well, don't that beat all,' he muttered. This had been a futile search. And just as he was thinking of looking through the rest of the house, he heard a sharp whistle on the street.

*Watson?*

He tiptoed to the window and looked down at the lamppost . . . but he wasn't there. That could only mean one thing . . .

Faintly, he heard a creak on the stair. Damn!

He lifted the conical cap off the top of the lantern and blew out the candle. Curse it for still smelling like lit tallow in the room! He waved his hand, trying to disperse the smell as the floorboards creaked closer to the door.

*Time for a hasty exit*, he told himself, and crept lightly toward the window.

He had one leg over the sill when someone with a lantern reached the attic. He could see a seam of light along the bottom of the door . . . when a hand closed over his leg hanging out the window.

He yelled.

'I have you, my lad,' said the voice. That no-nonsense tone could be no one else but a constable. Tim looked up at the dark figure with the custodian helmet, just as the other copper opened the attic door.

'Have you got him?' he asked.

'I've got him,' said the rozzer on the roof.

Tim's heart sank.

# FOUR

## Badger

T im squinted through the bars of his communal cell. He touched the tender spot on his mouth where, last night, the constable tried hard to remind Badger with his fist that Tim was the lawbreaker, and not the great detective he thought himself to be.

Leaning against the cold iron bars, he wondered how long it would take Watson to discover where he'd got to. Of course, he must have seen his capture and rabbited out of there. He hoped. What did it matter? Watson had no way to get Tim out. Who knew how long he'd be in the nick this time?

Pipe smoke. Among all the smells in the cell, from the chamber pot to the drunkard lying in a pool of his own sick, he didn't expect to smell that particular brand of tobacco here. He straightened. Ever before that voice spoke in its low, cultured tones, he knew immediately who it had to be.

'Well, Badger. Not the most propitious beginning to a career.'

He whirled about, and there was the Great Man himself on the other side of the bars. 'Mister Holmes!'

Sherlock Holmes puffed on his briar pipe, his sharp nose looming over it like a gargoyle perched on the roof of a cathedral. His eyes were hooded when he slid his gaze toward Tim.

Tim sighed in his relief . . . but, at the same time, the heat of mortification washed over him. The last thing he had wanted was his old guv to discover him in gaol.

'It's not my fault, sir,' he said quickly.

Holmes chuckled. It escaped his lips as curls of smoke. 'Never fear. I had no doubt of that. I'm certain your enthusiasm manifested itself into incautious behavior.'

'It did that, Mister Holmes. No mistaking.'

'Which is why I have talked it over with Inspector Stanley Hopkins to have you released, no charges. Ah. Here is the gate-keeper now.'

Over Holmes's shoulder, Tim heard the clinking of keys. The big-bellied copper came up to the door, eyed Holmes with an enquiring brow, and fitted a key in the lock. The other bleary-eyed prisoners rose with hopeful expressions. 'Badger only,' said the sergeant, threatening with his truncheon toward the others. They moved back against the wall of the cell. Tim gratefully slipped through the slim opening before the man could change his mind.

The policeman nodded toward Holmes. 'He's in your custody now, Mister Holmes.' Spinning on his heel, he let the ring of keys fall to his considerable waist as he stomped away.

'Thank you, Mister Holmes!'

'Hadn't we better leave this place? It is less than conducive to a complete recitation of the facts.'

'Lead on, sir.'

Tim noticed he was of a similar height to Holmes these days, and had that same lean figure, and so following closely on the man's swift strides was not as challenging as it had been when he was a youngster.

But when they left the precincts of the police station, there was that confounded woman again.

'Mister Badger!' she cried. She lifted her gloved hand with its pencil. In her other hand was a notebook.

How had she found out about his capture?

She pushed forward, nudging Holmes aside. Tim was worried the guv would be affronted at her rude behavior, but Holmes's expression was nothing but amused.

'Pardon me,' she muttered with but a scant glance at Holmes and with no apology in her voice. 'You were arrested for housebreaking, Mister Badger,' she said with a feral smile. 'What have you to say to the readers of *The Daily Chronicle* for that and how it relates to your supposed business as a "private detective"?'

Holmes snorted and stepped out of the way, pretending to fiddle with his pipe.

'"Supposed"?' Tim didn't like the way she said 'private detective' with a sneer. He slapped on an injured expression, as he'd seen on

Holmes many a time. 'My good woman, you're making assump-
tions without the facts.'

'Then care to share the facts, Mister Badger? Wait, I'll help you.'
With index finger, she riffled through her notebook and consulted
it. 'Last night you were caught housebreaking into the Quinn residence at 49 Gower Street, Bloomsbury, where it is known by this
reporter that you contracted work from the felon Thomas Brent,
who is sought by police for the crime of murdering his employer
Mister Horace Quinn, resident of the very same house.'

'As a point of correction, Miss Littleton, Thomas Brent is not
a felon. He is only wanted by the police for *questioning* about
certain details. He ain't—' He cleared his throat. 'He *isn't* to be
arrested. I'm sure *The Daily Chronicle* readers would like the
most *accurate* reporting, not the more sensationalized version of
events.'

She flashed a smile, and Tim thought it was most becoming on
her pert face, surrounded as it was by a cloud of auburn curls.
'That's where you're wrong, Mister Badger. They greatly enjoy
sensation. But as a female reporter out to do her best job, I *personally* seek the truth. And the truth of it, Mister Badger, is that you
are a criminal, fobbing yourself off to the public as a . . .' She
laughed, jostling the bright curls propping up her smart, jaunty hat
with its feathers.

Tim suddenly didn't think that smile was all that pretty anymore.

'As a *private detective*,' she went on merrily. 'Comparing yourself
to the Great Sherlock Holmes? How absurd.'

Holmes leaned in. 'I beg your pardon—'

'Just one moment,' she said rudely, shouldering him back without
a glance. She flapped her notebook in Tim's face. 'I have enough
on you to send you to Fleet, my man. I've had my eye on you for
a long while, Tim Badger.'

He postured. This was wasting his time. 'Miss Littleton, you've
got it wrong. As usual! And I will prove it to you at some point in
the future. But in the meantime, I've got work to do.'

'More housebreaking?'

He frowned. His instinct was to tell her where to shove her lies,
but with Mister Holmes standing there, smirking, he merely raised
a brow. 'No. If you don't mind, I need to consult with Mister
Sherlock Holmes.'

'Oh, of course you do!' she crowed. 'I'm sure he'll give you the time of day.'

Holmes finally pushed his way past the reporter, seeming to make certain to knock into her shoulder. He raised his hat. 'Pardon me. You must be Miss Ellsie Moira Littleton of *The Daily Chronicle*. Charmed to make your acquaintance.'

'And who is this, Mister Badger? Yet another accomplice in your crimes?'

Holmes chuckled. 'Oh indeed, Miss Littleton. An accomplice, surely. *My* name . . . is Sherlock Holmes.' He snickered again, touched the brim of his hat, and scuttled around her, taking Tim tightly by the crook of his arm, and steering him away.

Miss Littleton sputtered, and Tim was of a mind to keep *that* picture of the rude woman in his mind, but there wasn't time to look back when he was pulled hard by his guv.

'Let us find a refreshment room, Badger. I'm certain you must be hungry after your night in gaol.'

'It would be much appreciated, Mister Holmes, but . . . er . . .'

'Don't worry, Badger. My treat.'

They had their tea things in front of them. Holmes did not eat, but he ordered *for* Tim; some cold meats, a pork pie, bread and butter, and suet pudding, it being after eleven by then. Ravenous, Tim tucked in. He preferred a beer to wash it down, but he was trying to learn the ways of a gentleman, and devoured Holmes's manners and preferences as much as the food.

He slurped his tea between bites as Holmes watched him with lidded eyes. 'How are you getting on, Badger? Besides the occasional detour to Her Majesty's accommodations.'

He was about to wipe his face with the serviette, when he noticed a man at a far table, dabbing his lips under his mustache with *his* serviette, and Tim did his best to imitate him. 'Well, Mister Holmes, in all truth, it's a bumpy road. Me and my Watson are doing our best, but it's hard finding clients. And I'd like to thank you, sir, for piloting Brent our way. We're much obliged to you.'

Holmes waved his hand. 'It was nothing. I had no time for it.'

Tim leaned in and spoke quietly. 'Is that really true, Mister Holmes? I mean, it was probably a trifle to you. You could have solved it in a blink. Maybe you've already solved it?' The last he said perhaps a bit too hopefully, trying to measure the man's face, but he was as inscrutable as a stone statue.

'No, Badger. I have not solved it. As I said, I am too preoccupied with other arrangements. But as to your clientele, perhaps your lodgings aren't conducive to inspiring some of the more . . . genteel patrons.'

Tim shook his head and, with his mouth still full, offered, 'That's a sore thing, Mister Holmes. Me and Watson, well. We don't make much. Can't afford much.'

'Don't worry about that, Mister Badger. I have found suitable lodgings for the two of you. Your share of the rent will only amount to, say, a crown a week.'

Tim choked. He put his serviette to his face and hacked into it. Holmes reached over and slapped his back.

Tim grabbed his cup of tea, knocked it back, and set himself to rights. 'Mister Holmes,' he said, recovering. 'I've never heard of no decent lodgings for a price like that. We pay twice that, and it's rough, sir.'

'As I said.' He had propped his hands on his stick for the whole of the meal, and swiveled his head about, no doubt taking in details of each of the refreshment room's patrons. 'Don't worry about it, Mister Badger. The remainder of the cost will be dealt with.'

Tim's jaw dropped and he quickly clicked it closed. 'Now Mister Holmes, I can't allow you to do that. That ain't . . . *isn't* right, sir.'

'Nonsense. Do you think I always charge a fee for my services? And how do I live, do you wonder?'

'I . . . I don't know, sir . . .'

'Of course not. I am not in the vulgar habit of sharing my personal affairs with even my closest acquaintances. Suffice it to say, I shall not want if I chose to spend my money as I please. And to further put your mind at ease, I consider you an investment, Mister Badger. You and your very clever friend, Mister Watson.' The corner of his mouth flickered with a smile, as it always did when he mentioned Badger's partner's name. 'In other words, Badger, I want you to succeed. As your success rises, so shall your rent.' He took a card from his waistcoat pocket and slid it across the table. 'This is the address.'

'Mister Holmes . . . I have no words, sir . . .'

'Then don't try to speak them. Do your job, Badger, and all will be well.' He watched Tim eat for a few moments more before he asked, 'Tell me, Badger, what do you know about the people in this room?'

Tim smiled. It was the old game they used to play. He hadn't known at the time – when he was much younger – that it was devised to hone his skills at observation. He swallowed and dabbed at his mouth again. Scanning the room, he took in the patrons. 'Well now,' he said quietly, not wishing to alert any of them, even though they were far enough away not to hear him. 'There's an older man in the corner there, by the window behind you, sir. The slim one with the pince-nez. His suit is clean and well-tailored, but it's cut in an older style, so I'd say he's a working man. I perceive dabs of ink on his fingers and he eats hastily, as if his time is dear. I believe him to be a clerk.'

'Working where?'

'It would have to be close by, wouldn't it.' He stared hard and then noticed white hairs on his coat near the hem. 'Law courts. He works for a barrister. He's got wig hair on his coat.'

Tim looked up and noted the minuscule smile on Holmes's face. 'And another,' was all he said.

Tim glanced to his left. A young man, also in a decent suit, sitting across from a woman a little too rouged, wearing too many frills of lace and ribbons. She appeared to be wheedling him about some-thing, and he kept shushing her, looking anxiously about. 'That's a man with a mistress,' he said with a chuckle. 'And she ain't being too subtle about it, much to his chagrin. He isn't from this side of town. His suit is from Croft and Sons in Camden. I recognize the trim of the coat. There's a bulge in that coat pocket. Probably a gift, but he hasn't given it to her yet and he looks as if he's having second thoughts.'

'How do you know he is married, but not to that young lady?'

'His shirt's starched and white, as is his collar. His suit is brushed and cared for. But the woman with him has a somewhat disordered use of ribbons and buttons. One button on her dress is broken in half. Her ribbons are not in neat bows. It wasn't this woman who cared for that man's clothing.'

The man rose, leaned over, and quietly admonished her. He swiveled his head, left coins on the table, and hurried out, keeping his hand in the pocket with the bulge.

'I suspect his wife will get the gift after all,' said Tim.

'Interesting and detailed assessments, Mister Badger. Quite entertaining, in fact. And completely wrong on all counts.'

'Eh?'

'The man with the ink-stained fingers works in a bank. I noted a tally book just peeking from his waistcoat pocket when I entered this establishment, with the name of the bank on it. The white hair you mistook for a barrister's wig is from a dog. There is more hair on the leg of his trousers. I'd say the dog in question stands approximately two feet high. A breed with short, curly hair. White, of course.'

Holmes lazily gestured toward the table Tim had identified as having a man and mistress. 'The man works as a theatrical agent. Did you notice the spectator shoes? He was not in cricket garb, therefore he is a man of the theatre, used to going about in flash attire.'

'But how could you know he was a theatrical—'

'While you were eating, I overheard snippets of their conversation. The woman who is rouged and be-ribboned is an actress. Before I heard them speak, I noted the bits of powder sprinkled on her shoulder, the kind worn in theatrical entertainments. He was trying to entice her to perform in a particular theatre that she seems disinclined to accept. A program from the theatre in question lies on the table between them. The parcel in his pocket is of no consequence to their exchange.' Holmes smiled. 'But you did get the cut and proprietor of his suit correct.'

Tim gawped. His face flushed hot with embarrassment.

Holmes rose, taking his hat and gloves from the windowsill where he had set them, then donning the hat and slipping on the gloves one at a time. Grasping his cane, he bowed slightly. 'Practice makes perfect, Badger. Work on my method. And do finish your meal. You'll need the strength to continue your investigation.' He turned to depart but stopped and angled his head back toward the man. 'I assume you are making the necessary enquiries of the servants?'

He fiddled with the silverware. 'Not as yet, sir.'

Holmes offered a brief and mischievous smile. 'May I recommend you get to it?' He nodded again, and strode away with a swift gait.

Tim sat unmoving, chastened. He'd been certain of all that he observed . . . but he only had to turn slightly to spy the program on the table that he had completely missed, and the powder from her make-up that dusted the breast of her gown. The man who sat behind Mister Holmes did, indeed, have white dog hair on his trouser leg. *I should have caught that*, he berated himself. He jumped too fast to conclusions. He always had.

Sitting a while longer in his embarrassment, he scanned the others in the room and tried to make better assessments: looking at the contents of their tables and deciding what they could and could not afford to buy; what they wore, down to their shoes and the soles of them if he could see them; what their hands and nails looked like . . . and promised himself to do better.

It wasn't long until the sting wore off and he stared down again at the card he was still clutching in his fingers. He took up his cap. 'Thank *you*, Mister Holmes,' he breathed, 'for . . . *everything*,' and darted out of the shop as if he had stolen something.

# FIVE

## Watson

B en paced. He'd done nothing for hours. He had no money to bribe or bail out Badger, and he knew of no one he could ask for the money. Certainly not Tommy the Shark. He loaned money, all right, but he'd exact due payment whether it was coin or your arm.

It had taken some time for him to settle his mind, and finally, with much trepidation, he had sent word to Mister Holmes. He hadn't known if it had been too audacious a thing, what the man would do, what he *could* do under the circumstances . . . or if Badger even really knew him at all. But he had to take the chance.

Was it all for nothing? Was Badger finally snared for good?

Ben was just getting up the courage to go to the police station himself when he heard someone stomping up the stairs. 'Oh, Jesus,' he murmured. What if those were coppers coming after *him*?

He scrambled to the window and had the sash halfway up before Badger strode into the room.

'Tim!' he cried. He ran for him and wrapped his arms around the man. 'How did you ever get out?'

'Easy, my lad. Nothing to it, like I told you.'

'But the coppers . . .'

'Oh, they put the finger on me, no mistaking. But Mister Holmes got to me this morning and out I came, quick as a wink. No charges at all.'

'Thank God! I was hoping he'd do something, but I never dreamed of that.'

'You contacted him? Why, of *course* you did!' Badger slapped his back with a wide grin.

Ben noticed some bruises on his friend's face but decided not to mention them. He'd heard what the nick was like, even though he'd never been in himself.

But now that Badger was safe, Ben's mood darkened. 'Didn't I tell you that was an empty-headed idea? Didn't I warn you—'

'Oi, Ben. I'm here and safe and I've got a lot to report. But first, the good news, me lad! Come along. Is there anything in this godforsaken hovel that you need?'

Ben looked around at the tatty chairs, the broken tables, the sooty mantel. 'What do you mean?'

'We've got new digs, my friend. Pack your things, all them smelly alchemy bottles and beakers and your chimney-sweeping tools. Pack your other coat and shirts, even if they're drying on the line.'

'What do you mean? Tim, what have you gone and done?'

'Not me, my friend. Our benefactor!'

Ben couldn't believe it as he packed his goods into a crate and loaded it onto his cart, while Badger explained what had happened. Mister Holmes, their benefactor? For all this time, he scarce believed that Tim even *knew* Mister Holmes, that maybe his friend was a little too fond of telling tales. But this seemed to prove it, once and for all.

Especially when he followed Badger to Dean Street on the outer edge of Soho. Terraced houses of brick and stone, not tenements neither. The brick wasn't dark with soot, but seemed to be cleaned regularly, and the window frames gleamed white, without chipped paint. An enticing pavement, clean and smooth, ran along the avenue. Perhaps not as high-class as Belgravia, but it would do for the likes of them. Plenty of merchants and clerks lived along streets like this.

No men with sandwich boards, no doxies or crawlers in doorways. It was a proper street.

Ben looked up and down the lane. Dean Street and Shaftesbury Avenue. 'This can't be right,' he kept muttering. He elbowed Badger as they both stood before 49 Dean Street. St Anne's Church stood across the lane and a pub – the Lion – graced the corner. But the thing that nearly knocked Watson over was the painted sign next to their door. It read – in gold letters – 'Badger and Watson, Private Detectives. Enquire at Number 49b.'

'Gor . . .' he breathed.

'Blimey,' whispered Badger beside him. 'Will you look at that! This . . . this had to be planned for some time.'

'I think I'm dreaming,' murmured Watson. 'Or I'm dead.'

'You ain't dead yet, me lad. This is it. This is where we truly begin our lives, Ben.'

Ben began his tabulations in his head. How much would they need for proper furniture? They'd have to get themselves back to St Andrew Street to a broker's shop to get some second-hand frock coats and hats, and to a cellar shop for new boots. They couldn't go around in the coats and caps they presently wore. Oh, they'd be good for disguises, but not for meeting clients or hailing cabbies – if that was on the table. Maybe Wardour Street had some decent chairs for clients. But it all took coin. Coin they didn't have.

'Well,' said Badger, 'we might as well go inside. Our names are on the shingle.' His smile was back, and he punched Watson's arm.

Badger ran up the two steps and stood before the door . . . and then didn't seem to know what to do from there.

'You don't have a key?' said Ben, climbing respectfully up the steps one at a time.

'Er . . . no. So . . . maybe we just . . . ring the bell?' He grasped the handle and turned it. The bell rang harshly on the mostly quiet street.

'Who's gonna open the door?' asked Ben, when they both heard footsteps and the door was flung open suddenly by a stern-looking woman. Her dark reddish hair, salted with gray, was piled up like a bulging crown atop her head. Her nose was small but sharp, and her mouth was equally small but well-shaped and not striated by wrinkles. Her slender frame wore a dove-gray dress, buttoned from the belt at her waist up to her neck, with a white lace collar, and

he noticed she did not wear a starched apron, so she wasn't likely
a housekeeper. The landlady?

'Do I take it I am making the acquaintance of Mister Badger and
Mister Watson?'

Ben was taken aback by the Irish accent. Usually Irish women
were housemaids, but this woman was definitely no maid to be
bossed about.

With his usual aplomb, Ben snatched the hat from his head and
bowed. 'You do indeed, my good woman. I am Ben . . . er . . .
Benjamin Watson, and this my associate, Timothy Badger.'

'Very good, then. I'm Mrs Kelly, your landlady. Mister Holmes
was quite specific that I was to help you with meals and the maid
with the cleaning.'

'M-maid?' squeaked Badger.

'Murphy. She'll be flittering about and you are *not* to molest her.'
She emphasized this with the shaking of her finger in their faces.
'Do you understand?'

'Yes, ma'am,' they said in unison.

'Well then. Your baggage . . .' She looked down the steps and
wrinkled her nose at the cart and crates. 'I see. I'll have Murphy
take the boxes around the back . . .'

'Oh, I'll take the crate,' said Ben. 'It has my chemistry things.'

'Oh yes. Mister Holmes warned me that this might be so. Well
then, come in, gentlemen.'

Ben exchanged an anxious glance with Badger before they both
stepped over the threshold and up the stairs, along clean and well-
kempt carpets to a shiny black painted door with a transom window
marked with the letter 'b'.

The more they saw, the more Ben's breathing quickened. He
grabbed Badger by the arm and silently asked. Badger looked back
with an equally flustered expression and shrugged.

Mrs Kelly unlocked the door and then offered two latchkeys to
them, one for each. Sheepishly, they took them. Opening the door
and standing at the jamb, she gestured them through.

It wasn't lavish, but it was clean and the furniture in the sitting
room wasn't torn or too old-looking. There was coal in the grate
and dark green drapes on the one window. They walked in and stood
on the worn oriental rug, both seemingly afraid to touch anything on
the few tables.

Bookshelves were situated on either side of the modest fireplace, and they appeared to be filled with scientific books, journals, books of philosophy and annals of crime.

Ben forgot all about his crate downstairs as he walked like an automaton to the bookshelves, running his trembling fingers over all the spines.

'That way is *your* room, Mister Watson. It's the larger one, as Mister Holmes talked of your alchemical experiments, so there is a table within for such and a cabinet for your what-nots. Mister Badger, over there is *your* room. The bathroom is down the corridor. There is a bell on the mantel that will bring either myself or Murphy.'

She turned to exit when Badger called her back. 'Mrs Kelly . . . I . . . we . . . Surely Mister Holmes explained that we . . . we can't afford your services, or that of a maid.'

She gave an efficient smile. 'Mister Holmes made allowances for that. You mustn't worry, Mister Badger, Mister Watson. It is all taken care of.'

'And . . . the furnishings . . .'

'All taken care of. If that's all? Or will you be wanting tea?'

Badger stared back at Ben, and it was Ben who was forced to shake his head. She turned away but just as quickly spun on her heel. 'I almost forgot. Will you gentlemen please look in that box? The one there on the little table.'

Ben exchanged a wary glance with Badger before he reached for a carved box on a side table. It seemed a bit worn, well-loved perhaps. Not new, surely. Ben lifted the lid and quickly slammed it down again. 'Er . . .'

'Did you find it satisfactory?' she asked.

He darted his gaze about the room before leaning toward Mrs Kelly and whispering, 'There's something wrong.'

She frowned and trod purposefully toward him. 'Something wrong?'

He pointed to the box. 'There's . . . there's coin in here.'

Relief flooded her face. 'As there should be, Mister Watson.'

'But there must be some mistake. This isn't ours.'

'Mister Holmes left strict instructions. He allowed you a few coins to get started with.'

Ben stared down at the suddenly terrifying box. Badger slowly

approached and studied it from side to side. 'But . . . why?' asked
Badger.

'Well, as Mister Holmes explained it, there is a need for some
small amount of money for two young gentlemen. For cabbies, for
. . . well, bribes, so he says, and . . . if I may say so, more suitable
attire.' She looked the both of them up and down with tart
disapproval.

Ben wiped his hand down his tatty coat. 'Oh. I see.'

'Will there be anything else, gentlemen?'

'No, Mrs Kelly,' he said, voice squeezed. 'That's . . . that's more
than I can take in at the moment.'

She strode out of the sitting room and closed the door behind her.

They stood in silence for what seemed like hours. Until Badger
stumbled to the mantel and ran his hands over the painted wood.
'Gor blimey,' he muttered.

Ben breathed deep and opened the box to stare at the coins again.
It wasn't a king's ransom, but it was more than they had ever had
in one go. 'Why do I feel like *I'm* housebreaking?' he said.

Badger couldn't stop touching the things on the mantel, even
though they were certainly second-hand. 'Because we never called
so nice a place "home" before.'

Ben wore a stricken look. 'Tim . . . how will we ever pay Mister
Holmes back?'

'Ben, I think the best we can do is not think too hard about it
right now. We've got a job to do, a client to serve. Now, sit over
there and I'll tell you what I found last night.'


# SIX

## Badger


Watson had eased himself in a chair, one that wasn't
scruffy and losing its stuffing. Tim looked around
the room with a certain amount of pride and then at
the coin box. Yes! This would do nicely. It was just what they
needed. Holmes had surmised that they wouldn't get any further

while operating from their old lodgings or wearing their present clothing. A clever codger, was Mister Holmes.

With a sudden swagger to his walk, he strode to the chair opposite Watson and sat, moving his backside into the cushion. No springs poking at him, no unsavory smell emerged. He leaned back with his hands on the chair arms. 'This will do,' he said, happily.

Then he noticed what was on the small table beside him. Calling cards fanned in a pewter dish. 'Bloody hellfire, Ben. Look!'

Tim picked up one of the cards and passed it to Watson. A finely printed card that read just like the sign by their door: 'Timothy Badger and Benjamin Watson, Private Detectives. 49b Dean Street, Soho.'

'Your guv thought of everything,' Watson breathed. He sat back, staring at the card and fiddling with his cap. 'I suppose I need to apologize.'

'You? For what?'

'Well . . . I scarce believed you even knew Mister Holmes. I mean . . . really! *You*, working for *him* . . .'

'I wasn't no valet. I was a street Arab, a pickpocket. That was the type of boy the guv wanted to work for him, one who could listen and spy at keyholes, things a man like him couldn't do. There was a rag-tag lot of us. His Baker Street Irregulars, he called us. I told you all that.'

Watson shrugged. 'But I didn't believe you.'

All those tales he had told to Watson, and he'd just regarded them as rubbish? 'I'm hurt, I am.'

'Now Tim, you do have the art of . . . er . . . embellishment . . . when a tale is told. You must admit.'

'Well . . .' Tim rubbed the back of his head. 'I reckon so. But now you know it was the truth.'

Watson's wide eyes took in the room again. 'God's truth.'

Tim snapped his fingers at the dazed man. 'Oi, lad! Harken. So, I got into the attic—'

'Truly?'

'Why d'you reckon I was nicked? Anyhow . . .' He scooped some of the cards into his waistcoat and handed a few to Watson. 'I got in and had a good look around. I could find no riches, no strong-boxes, no container of jewels. The only thing I found in the chest of drawers was old baby clothes. And women's clothes in a trunk.'

'So there *was* a baby.'

'Yes.' Tim nodded solemnly. 'God rest the little tyke.'

'So nothing that Quinn might be looking for?'

'How could it be? It was just clothes. I even looked for false bottoms. I saw nothin' in there worth a ransom. No documents, no letters. And besides. It was his own house. He could turn it over anytime he wanted.'

'Yes. That's odd, innit?'

'Right enough. Maybe it wasn't *his* attic we was to search in. Probably old dead Latimer's. But that house is likely cleaned out by now. Mister Holmes suggested we learn about the people left in the Bloomsbury house. The housekeeper and housemaid.'

Watson seemed to grow a smile. 'I reckon I can talk to that maid.'

'She must be young and pretty. You can talk to her, right enough. You'll learn the color of her mother's bloomers in no time.'

Watson's smile grew wider. 'That leaves the shriveled fig for you.'

Tim's face fell. 'Thanks.'

Watson settled in the chair and leaned forward. 'But Tim – and what Mrs Kelly so promptly put to us – we need to get ourselves some proper clothes. It won't do to even try to get to that house and talk to the housekeeper if we don't look like gentlemen.'

'You've got the right of that. Wardour Street? There's a bloke or two what owes me down there. And with Mister Holmes's benefi- cence . . .'

They both turned their eyes to the magical coin box. Neither of them wanted to move first. But in the end, they both got to it at the same time.

Watson admonished him not to take too much. He well knew Tim could easily drink it all away, but for some reason, a little voice in Tim's head – which sounded half like Mister Holmes and half like Watson – told him to put aside all that drinking time in a pub and finally get down to business.

They cut down St Anne's Court from their new lodgings to Wardour Street, only a short distance away from Dean Street in Soho. They both managed to get decent frock coats without patches, waistcoats that matched, and trousers with a good line. They also each got themselves tweed suits for most of their investigating. As for hats, Watson preferred the bowler, whilst Tim took up the homburg, along with two boaters, one for each of them.

Slightly worn, but nevertheless softer leather boots completed the ensemble, and Tim even managed to wangle a pocket watch with a long chain to swag on his waistcoat. He was all in brown tweed, whilst Watson favored the dark gray. When they observed themselves in the spotted mirror in the shop, they were both satisfied at the outcome.

With their old clothes and extra shirts packaged in brown paper under their arms, they made their way back to Dean Street, where they acquainted themselves with their rooms, hung their extra coats and trousers in their barren wardrobes, their shirts and undergarments in the wardrobe's drawers, and met again in the sitting room.

'I think it's best we get to it and see that we befit all that Mister Holmes has done for us,' said Watson.

'I agree, mate. So. I'll go talk to Pruneface and you talk to the housemaid. I mean, there's no telling how much longer they'll be in that house with the master gone. Say, I'll see if I can find out Quinn's solicitor's name and get out of the geezer who the heir is. Then we can go talk to *him*.'

'And how are we going to talk to the solicitor? Us?'

'We'll show him our calling card. And act arrogant, like other men of business. Like we belong. Because we do. Look at us, man.'

Ben turned to the window, where his reflection was plain to see. Tim stood beside him. 'Now you're a man who looks like he knows what he's doing.'

'Yes. That's a good rule to live by,' said Watson. 'We aren't no one's servants no more, are we? We'll "sir" them, of course, but they can't dismiss us like we're bootblacks or stable boys. No more of that. We'll talk to lawyers and rozzers like we're their equal.'

Tim's smile widened. 'That'll be something, won't it?'

'But it's how it's gotta be. Think like we're gentlemen,' he said, tapping his own temple with a forefinger.

'Gentlemen. We're gentlemen.' He stood taller.

'So. Once you get the housekeeper out of the way, I can talk to the maid.'

'Good plan.' They shook on it.

They agreed to arrive at the house on Gower Street from different directions, so the housekeeper couldn't spy Watson.

When they reached the Quinn residence, Tim skipped up the steps, stared at the black wreath hanging on the door, and rang the bell, just as Watson appeared around the corner, lingering at the painted iron fence near the lower kitchen door, reading a folded newspaper, like a man waiting for an appointment.

The door swung open, and the housekeeper – severe face and all – glared at him. 'Yes?'

Tim tipped his new hat. 'Good day . . . Mrs Martin, is it?'

'Yes. What do you want?'

He presented the card from his waistcoat. 'I am Mister Timothy Badger, a private detective. If I may, I should like to ask you a few questions regarding the murder of Horace Quinn.'

She stared at the card. 'What is a "private" detective? Are you with the police?'

'I work closely with them, madam. I do the work they cannot spend the time on, getting all the little details. If I may come in . . .'

*The moment of truth*, he thought. Would his tone and clothes finally give him the access he desired?

She huffed an exasperated breath. 'Oh, very well! I suppose you shall be wanting tea.' She spun on her heel and went inside. Badger turned to Watson and gave him a thumbs up before he disappeared over the threshold, closing the door behind him.

As he passed the parlor with its doors halfway open, he saw the coffin on its trestle. 'First, madam, may I pay my respects?'

She looked at him surprised before she shrugged and rang for the maid.

Tim stepped into the parlor. He wasn't fond of looking at dead bodies. Not by a long chalk. But in this business he knew it must be done. The few jobs they had before this had only involved finding vandals for certain shopkeepers and even recovering a stolen item or two. None of them had involved murder, but he reckoned that murder was the best-paying kind of job.

He swiped the homburg off his head and cradled it in his elbow. He surreptitiously peered over his shoulder and found that Mrs Martin was nowhere to be seen. *Quick now*, he told himself.

Mister Quinn wasn't looking good, nor smelling good, and the flowers around him looked to be wilting. Not a man with a lot of friends or relations, was Mister Quinn. Not a man well-loved, at any rate, for there were precious few flowers and even fewer calling cards. His pale hands lay on his chest. His waxy, white face had the unmistakable slackness of the dead, and his eyes had been mercifully closed. Those few flowers arranged in vases around him got Tim to thinking. *Was* he such a rich man? The house looked stuffed with the objects of a rich man. There were crossed lances on the wall, a shield that looked African, some long curved ivory tusks under the photo of an elephant, and other mementos that seemed to be from a man who had spent time in the army. Lancers? Zulu wars?

There were other accoutrements about the room that spoke of a man who did not want for funds . . . but they looked of an older style, as if from another era. Even the room, though good enough, didn't seem to be as luxurious as it should have been, lacking the rugs or family pictures or other little things that made a house a home. Badger well knew a man's fortunes could turn on the smallest of circumstances.

He realized with a smile that he was deducting, using Mister Holmes's method. For in his perusal, he could say at once that Horace Quinn might have enjoyed some prosperity once, but that it was fleeting. Bad business decisions? Loss of wife and child (and where were the pictures of them?). A combination of melancholy and poor choices? He couldn't quite say yet. Like Mister Holmes, he wouldn't guess. He'd have to *know*.

He stood over the man in his coffin for but a moment. Quinn wore a somber suit with a plain white shirt and collar – neither particularly new – buttoned up all the way to his black tie. Badger gathered himself before getting up the nerve to reach inside the coffin, balancing his hat on the edge of it. He breathed out of his mouth, as the corpse was getting ripe. Grimacing as he unbuttoned the man's coat, it revealed a gray waistcoat and then a shirt. He spread it, pushed open the chemise beneath it, and looked for the wound . . . and there it was. A slice that would never heal. Right below the sternum and into the heart. *That was mighty accurate for someone*, he mused. From a letter knife? In the dark? It seemed like an awfully big cut for that.

There was little else to ferret. It was already cleaned, of course, so he buttoned him up quick and set him to rights. He snatched up his hat and backed away, leaving the parlor. By then Mrs Martin had returned with a tray. He feared she meant to take it into the parlor with smelly old Quinn, but he sighed in relief when he followed her instead to a drawing room that was warm with a coal fire.

She poured. 'Do you take sugar, Mister Badger?'

'Yes, please.' He took the offered cup and saucer and sipped, realizing he hadn't eaten since Holmes had bought him his very late breakfast. He took a biscuit from an oblong plate and munched it. It was stale.

'What is it you wish to know?'

He quickly dispatched the biscuit, took another sip of tea, and set the saucer down. 'Tell me, madam. Just for the record. What is your Christian name?'

'Amelia Martin.'

'Right then. And how long have you worked in this household?'

'I have worked for Mister Quinn for twenty years.'

Now that he got a close look at her, it wasn't that she was very old. She wasn't. Mid-forties, perhaps. But she was buttoned up, and that gave her the air of someone far older. He made a note of it in the back of his mind to use later for himself when he donned disguises, as Mister Holmes had done.

'And how was he as a master?'

She sat straight-backed, her shoulders never touching the chair. 'I hardly think that is a proper question.'

'Ah, but much must be ascertained to get a full picture of events.'

'I think we well know the full events. Thomas Brent killed the master.'

'And why should he do such a thing?'

'He was always a bit wild. Didn't seem to know his place. Taking on airs above his station. He and Mister Quinn had arguments.'

'Oh? And why would Mister Quinn put up with such guff, if you'll pardon the expression? Why didn't he sack him?'

'That, Mister Badger, has always been a mystery to me. I have to assume that Mister Quinn thought it too much of a waste of time and expense to train a new valet. Mister Quinn was a man of habits, and he didn't like change.'

Tim took up his cup and saucer again and snatched another sip. 'The night of the murder. This séance.' He set the saucer on his knee. 'That was a queer thing to do, wasn't it? Or did Mister Quinn indulge in that particular diversion often?'

It never wavered, that iron back. 'As far as I knew, this was the first time that Mister Quinn ever deigned to participate in such a practice.'

'Seems like a certain amount of desperation, don't . . . er, doesn't it?'

She said nothing.

'You don't approve.'

The slight lifting of an eyebrow was the only movement on her stiff body. Possibly even stiffer than Quinn's. 'It was not for me to say.'

'But he got you to sit in on it?'

'Yes. It was . . . most distressing. I am a Christian woman, sir. I believe the Bible specifically condemns those who would commune with the dead.'

'That it does. Why did he insist the household participate?'

She shook her head. Not a wisp of hair dared to get out of place. 'I have no idea. Perhaps the medium insisted there be more people.'

'About that medium.' He edged closer. The teacup rattled on the saucer. He had forgot it was still there, perched on his knee. Setting it down on the table, he slid to the edge of his chair. 'Who hired the medium?'

'I'm not certain.'

'Could Mister Quinn have hired her?'

'I can't imagine he would have known how to do so.'

'If you had been asked, would *you* have known?'

She suddenly shot from the chair and paced before the glowing grate. 'As I said, I do not have any truck with such things. Especially a Gypsy in the house. Merciful heavens. I don't trust that lot not to rob us blind.' She had been rubbing one hand over the other, and abruptly stopped her pacing to stare at Tim. 'And only last night, one of them broke into the attic. That's what comes from inviting Gypsies into your home.'

Tim's collar suddenly felt tight. He adjusted it with a finger.

'Though it was probably that Brent fellow,' she volunteered, continuing to pace again. 'No doubt he knew all sorts of unsavory people.'

He grabbed the saucer again. 'Why do you say that?'

'He was more than a valet. He served as Mister Quinn's footman, as well as his driver. He dealt with those on the streets and such.

That was, of course, when Mister Quinn still had a carriage. That was one of the first things to go.' She seemed to realize she had said too much and stopped talking.

'Were funds a problem in the household?'

'This is a better question to be put to his solicitor.'

'But as the housekeeper, you surely must know what the household budget was. I mean, to pay the greengrocer and butcher . . .'

'There was enough, but no more than that, as far as it concerned me and my job.'

He measured the woman, so stiff, so austere, and decided that *he* wouldn't have liked working for her. 'Do you think Thomas Brent capable or even desirous of killing Mister Quinn? I mean, from a purely monetary viewpoint, to kill your master is killing the goose that laid the golden egg, as it were.'

'As I said. They had arguments.'

'His position in the household . . . and killing him so publicly. Does that make sense to you, Mrs Martin?'

'Very little about that young man made sense to me.'

Tim drank more tea and licked his lips. 'When was he hired?'

'Five years ago.'

'By an agency?'

'Yes. Mister Quinn saw to it personally, of course. It is not for the housekeeper to hire the valet.'

Tim set down the saucer and took a notebook from his coat pocket. He licked the point of his pencil and began to scribble notes. He asked the agency name and wrote that down as well.

'Mrs Martin, do you think . . . I mean, it's quite a stretch . . . but do you think your housemaid here could have done it?'

'Jenny Wilson? She hasn't a brain in her head, that child. She's always forgetting her duties. The stupid girl even forgot to fill the oil in the lamp in the room where the séance took place. So there's the answer to the little mystery as to why the light suddenly went out, though the newspapers would make more of it than there was.'

*Ah,* thought Tim. *One mystery solved!* 'But might she be harboring a motive to do such a deed?'

The housekeeper pondered for a moment, looking down at her feet. A small watch on a long chain hung from her neck and she closed her spindly fingers over it as she thought. 'Well . . . there was an . . . incident. I don't like to tell tales.'

'Of course not, madam.'

'She's such a stupid girl. I told her that when the master was in his cups to leave him be.' When she glanced at Tim, he was all propriety; sitting up straight, giving her his full attention with slightly raised brows and his chin held high. 'She . . . confided in me that Mister Quinn . . . apparently he . . . but she was able to get away and so it was never mentioned again.'

'Oh, I see. And do you believe her? That this happened.'

'I'm very much afraid that I do.'

Tim scribbled it down in his book, set the book down, and grabbed his saucer once again. With teacup nearly to his lips, he remarked, 'Mrs Martin, were you here when the baby was born?'

She stopped. Her whole body became even more rigid and she stared wide-eyed at him. 'We *never* discuss . . . *that.*'

'But were you here?' he said firmly.

'It . . . it was a month before I arrived.' Her body seemed to liquify and become more human in its movements. She sank into her chair again, her back not quite as rigid as before. 'I understand the mistress had a miserable time of it, both her being in a family way and the delivery. She didn't last long. And then the baby . . . the baby died too. The master was inconsolable. Or so I have been told.'

'My sincerest sympathies, madam. Does, er, Mister Quinn have any other heirs?'

'I believe there is a cousin in Dartmouth. A letter has been dispatched.'

'Would you know the name of Mister Quinn's solicitor?'

'Miles Smith, Tottenham Court Road.'

'Thank you.' He rose. 'Oh, one more thing. Just what was it Mister Quinn was trying to find out at this séance?'

'It wasn't any of my business.'

'Of course not. But . . . I take it a business partner had recently died and he was trying to find information of some sort?'

She snorted in disgust. 'Imagine using the summoning of spirits for such a thing. They used the same solicitor. Why not ask him?'

'Quinn didn't?'

'Not that I could tell.'

'And the name of this business partner?'

'Stephen Latimer. He died a fortnight ago.'

'Thank you. Mrs Martin, how long will you continue in service here?'

She smoothed out the wrinkles in her gown as she rose. 'I have no idea. One can hope that the heir might keep me on, but at this juncture, it is all an unknown. The solicitor will read the will tomorrow after Mister Quinn's funeral.'

'I see. Well . . . I hope the best for you then.' He set his hat back on his head and realized he had forgot to get himself a pair of gloves. 'Thank you for your time.'

'You *will* find Thomas Brent and bring him to justice?' she said, following him to the door.

'It is my hope to find justice for *Horace Quinn*, madam. Good day.'

He stood on the steps and looked back at the closed door. A good deal more could certainly be had by being able to ask questions firsthand, he mused. He pulled taut his waistcoat and brushed off invisible dust from the shoulder of his coat. And a man could certainly stand taller in a fine suit of clothes. Others measured his character by them as well.

He wondered how Watson was getting on in his new suit.

# SEVEN
## Watson

Ben trotted down the steps to the kitchen entrance and rapped gently on the door with the back of his knuckle.

The pretty maid answered and he gave her a smile. He warmed when she smiled back with a coy lowering of her chin. 'You're back,' she said.

'That I am, miss. And here's my calling card.' He brandished the card and presented it to her. She took it with a crease to her brow and read it slowly.

'Are you Badger or Watson?'

'Ben Watson at your service.'

'You're a detective?' The frown grew deeper. 'You're not a chimney sweep.'

'Dear lady, I am both, and more. I've done work as a sweep, a smith, a chemist's assistant, a milkman, a cobbler's apprentice, even a funfair performer . . . and now a detective. I am here to investigate the death of your employer.'

Her pretty mouth formed an 'O' of surprise and her widened eyes gleamed. 'Truly?'

'Indeed. Let me in? I could use a cuppa.'

Still staring at the card with both hands clutching it, she backed away from the door and moved thoughtfully to put the kettle on the hob. The worktable in the center of the room was dusted with flour and scraps of dough. Ben inhaled the beginnings of a pie baking in the large Esse taking up residence within the roomy and ancient kitchen hearth.

She finally surrendered the card back to him, then prepared the Brown Betty and placed a cup and saucer before it, with a sugar bowl and a chipped jug of milk on the worktable.

'What's your name, lass?'

'Jenny Wilson,' she said. 'I never talked much to a black man before. The greengrocer down the lane, but no more than a "good morn" and such.'

He kept his smile. 'I'm really no different from other blokes.'

'But you are. You've got a nice smile. One might even call it . . . pixie-like.' She giggled at her own boldness and bit her bottom lip.

He sat at the table and set his bowler aside, petting his beard. 'I've got no reason to frown. Now, my girl. Jenny. Let's talk about the death of your master.'

She rested her hand on the side of her face. 'So horrible,' she said quietly.

'Indeed. But now . . . it seems everyone thinks it was Thomas Brent, but no one can truly say for sure, it being dark and all. What do *you* say?'

She used the edge of her apron to grab the copper kettle's handle and brought it to the table where she carefully poured the steaming water into the Betty. 'It *was* dark. You couldn't really see a thing. I never thought it was Thomas till Mrs Martin started saying it. No wonder the poor man hopped it.'

'Why would she think he done it?'

After setting the kettle back on the hob, she pulled out a chair and sat opposite him, preparing his cup. 'Thomas and her, they never got on. Like cats and dogs, they were.'

'Do *you* think he did it?'

She shook her head as she poured the brew into the cup and slid it toward him. 'I don't know. I don't like to think such things about people I know.'

Ben drank the hot beverage, feeling the sense of renewal that a good cup of tea could provide; something he hadn't had in a long time with the few leaves he and Tim could afford from the tea monger. 'Jenny, do you think you can take me up to the room, proper this time? None of my creeping about in the house now. Now that you know I'm working with the police to investigate.'

Her eyes grew wide. Ah, she was a sweet-looking lass, and no mistake. 'Yes, I can do that. I just want to . . . want to make sure Mrs Martin is out of the way.'

Ben reassured her that she was busy with his partner, which surprised Jenny Wilson, but she motioned for him to follow her. Watson grabbed his hat and set it on his head again. They took the back kitchen stairs, up past the ground floor to the first floor where the bedrooms were.

She went directly to the séance room and paused. 'It was in there.'

He didn't wait for her. He opened the door himself and stood in the room. And once again, he got a chill at the back of his neck. He whirled around and looked behind him, but he saw nothing that could cause it, except for the open door. Jenny peered in at him with wide, dark eyes.

'This was the nanny's room,' he said.

She stepped closer to the threshold but didn't cross it. 'It was?'

'Yes. Long before your time, I'm sure.' He looked the table over. 'Show me where you were sitting.'

She hesitated.

'It's all right, Jenny. Nothing will harm you while I'm here.'

She seemed to gain courage from that and hurried in and stood at the table near the window. 'I was sitting here.'

'Next to the master?'

'Oh no. Mrs Martin sat there.' She pointed to the left of her. 'Mister Quinn was sitting with his back to the door, facing the window.' She raised a finger to her mouth and gnawed on it a moment. 'Over there, facing Mister Quinn, with her *back* to the window, that's where the medium was. And Thomas had his back to the hearth, next to the master.'

'He was next to the master?' Ben strolled to the other side and sat in the chair. And as if he was holding an invisible knife, he turned and mimed jabbing it into an equally invisible Quinn. *He could have done it*, he mused, frowning. But it would have been awkward.

'But he couldn't have,' she said, distress plainly brushed across her face. 'Because he was lighting the lamp.'

Ben stood. 'Like this?'

'No.' She now looked perplexed. 'From over there.' She pointed to the place the medium sat.

'Why did he move there?'

'I don't know. When the lamp went out, we were all a-jumble. There's matches on the mantel next to the candlestick. Maybe that was why. He had to light the candle because the lamp wouldn't light. I sprang up from my chair and stood against the wall there.'

'Why?'

''Cause I was scared. And I heard a noise. And I just wanted to get away.'

'What kind of noise?'

'Like a . . . like a ghost noise. Like a whoosh. Like some spirit.'

'So you were there and Thomas was there. Where was Mrs Martin?'

Jenny bit her lip in thought. 'She was just there. Where she was always sitting.'

'And what about the medium, the Gypsy lady?'

Her restless hands worried at her apron, hand in the pocket likely fingering that rabbit's foot. 'I don't know. I wasn't looking at her.'

'She talked to the police, though.' He suddenly wished he could read the police report and wondered vaguely if they could sneak into Scotland Yard and . . . No. That was foolish.

'Oh no,' Wilson went on. 'She was gone long before they showed up.'

'Wait. She didn't stay?'

'If I were a Gypsy woman and there was a murder, *I* wouldn't stay.'

He supposed she was right. 'She probably high-tailed it the moment she reckoned what was going on.'

Jenny Wilson had taken out the rabbit's foot and was stroking it with her thumb. 'Except that the door was closed.'

'Eh?'

'The door was closed from the moment we were all here. The Gypsy lady said it was better for the spirits, or some such. And it was closed until I opened it to go fetch the police. And I didn't hear no one open or close it, neither.'

'I see. Can you think of any reason Thomas would kill Mister Quinn?'

She shook her head, her hand once again lying on the side of her face, her eyes darting as if seeing it all again. 'I shouldn't say.'

'What shouldn't you say?'

'Oh, sir . . .'

'Ben.'

Her lashes were like wide-open fans over her rounded eyes, fans like those ladies on the stage at the music hall had. 'Ben,' she said softly. He liked the sound of it. 'Well . . . Thomas was in a proper fit. The master swindled him out of some money he owed him.'

'Eh? Mister Quinn? Why should he do that?'

'It's what Thomas told me. "Swindled" him, he said. Those were his words. Thomas did a special job and Mister Quinn promised to pay him and then when he done it . . . Thomas, that is, Mister Quinn told him that he wouldn't pay him.'

'Do you know what this "special job" was?'

'He never said.'

Ben tapped his lip with his finger and then looked up. Again, he was caught by her eyes. He sidled closer. 'And the old missus. Anything ever get her back up? Did she have a reason to do him in?'

She looked back over her shoulder and got in closer. 'I heard that the master promised her an annuity and took it back. Took back the offer.'

'You don't say! Where'd you hear that?'

'Well . . . I overheard her say it to the housekeeper next door. Oh, she was fuming, she was. Even nastier to me than usual for a fortnight.'

'Swindled the valet, done the housekeeper out of her retirement. Not a nice man was Mister Quinn. What about you? What did he do to you?'

Those wide eyes suddenly filled with tears. It was a natural business to simply enclose her in his arms. 'There, there, lass. He's gone now. He can't hurt you no more. You don't have to say.'

'Thank you, sir,' she said in a small voice. He liked the feel of her in his arms. She smelled of plain soap and a little soot in her cap.

She pushed away and straightened herself, swathed her hands over her cheeks to wipe the tears away. Oh yes, Ben could just imagine what it was that Quinn did to make her cry, and his fury at the dead Quinn suddenly rose in his chest. What a lecher! This sweet girl. She wasn't a flirt. Ben knew a flirt when he saw one, and she wasn't it.

He walked to the window, cast open the curtains, and examined the frame, the glass. In his hasty perusal from before, he had not noticed the small bits of mud left on the sill. 'Jenny, dear, can you fetch me two envelopes?'

'Envelopes? Whatever for?'

He turned his head and gave her a full-blown Ben-smile. 'It's for my detecting.'

She slowly smiled back, curtseyed, and ran off to get them. He could hear her tromping down the back stairs.

He unlocked the sash and lifted it. When he leaned out, he noticed the sill was wide, as were the moldings around the window. Wide enough for someone to stand there. Looking around the room, he grabbed a chair from the table and pushed it up to the window, whereupon he climbed onto it to step out onto the sill. He had to crouch, but he was able to do so easily. And the window to his left – the one to the nursery – was easily accessible with the same wide sill.

A shriek. He ducked to spy the maid standing in the doorway. He climbed back in and jumped down off the chair. 'I'm all right. Don't you worry. You got the envelopes?' He strode toward her – since she seemed frozen in the doorway – took them from her hand, and proceeded back to the sill to gently sweep the dried mud into one of the envelopes. He gently turned in one of the envelope's corners. 'Do you recall if the windows were closed or open during the séance?' he said as he worked.

'I . . . I don't know. The curtains were closed.'

'Very well, then.' He thought he remembered Brent saying that the window was open but the curtains were drawn. He mused on that as he tucked the envelope into an inside coat pocket and turned to her. 'There was mention of a glow or some such during the séance. Did *you* see it?'

'I did. I think . . . I think . . . it was Mister Quinn's spirit leaving his body.' She thrust her knuckles into her mouth, stifling her gasp.

That pulled him up short. 'His . . . his spirit?'

'Yes. It had to be. Or it was Mister Latimer, the dead man.'

'Where did you see it?'

She made a vague wave toward the wall with the fireplace. 'Over there.'

Ben turned to the wall and waved his hand over the wallpaper next to the fireplace. 'Here, maybe?' Then he waved his hand over the mirror.

'About there, yes.'

His gaze darted here and there, assessing, before he gave up. 'We should probably be heading back, Jenny. But one more stop.'

He entered the passage and went into the nursery, marching directly to the window. When he examined the sill, there was no mud there.

He led the way down the back kitchen stairs, but when they reached the kitchens, Mrs Martin was there again, glaring at them.

'And what are *you* doing back, young man?'

He pulled the card from his waistcoat. 'I'm Benjamin Watson, private detective investigating—'

'*You're* a detective?'

'I am indeed, my good woman. I believe you were engaged talking to my partner and colleague just now.'

Her mouth drew open but nothing came out. He touched the brim of his hat with a slight bow. 'Thank you, Mrs Martin, Miss Jenny, for all your help. One more question. Is there a back garden?'

'Yes,' said the housekeeper, face still frozen in shock.

'I'll leave by the garden, then, if it's awright.'

The housekeeper, without further words, led him to the garden door, and he trotted nimbly down the stairs, tipping his hat as he went. 'Good day to you.'

Once outside, he walked around the house, staying close to the walls, eyes scanning the loose earth. The murder was days ago and it had rained. He had no hope of finding footprints, but he decided to take a sampling of the dirt by the house anyway and sprinkled it in his envelope. He folded that one in half, and stuffed it, too, into his coat.

He left by a gate and had to walk around to the streetside pavement where he met Tim, who was smiling.

'Pub?' said Badger.

Ben patted the envelopes in his pocket. 'Good idea. We'll talk there.'

# EIGHT
# Badger

They sat in the Lion on the corner of Shaftesbury Avenue and Dean Street – their new public house – and huddled close at a table, each with a pint in their hands.

'So here it is,' said Tim, looking at his notes and including what Watson had reported. 'They all had a motive to kill him. Mrs *Amelia* Martin because he rescinded his promise of an annuity, Thomas Brent because Quinn "swindled" him out of money for a job he did for him—'

'And we've got to find out what that was,' put in Watson.

'And then Murderer X possibly at the window, once you do your chemistry with that soil.' Tim smiled slowly. 'Look at us. We're finally sounding like a couple of detectives. Cheers, mate.' He clinked his glass to Watson's, then went back to his notes. 'Swindled Brent out of his money; and dear little Miss Jenny Wilson, he tried to have his wicked way with her while under the influence of the demon drink.' He picked up his glass and took a swallow. 'What a household! They all done it, or at least wanted to.'

Watson shook his head in disgust. 'What is London coming to? Murder on every corner.'

'Crime, me lad. It means more fees for us. To crime!' He raised his glass, and Watson reluctantly followed suit.

'Crime is nothin' to cheer on,' muttered Watson.

'Ah, you know I don't mean it that way, Ben. It's going to be there anyway. Might as well make a shilling or two, eh?'

Watson nodded, sipped, and then set down his glass on its wet ring on the table. 'What's our next move?'

'We need to talk to the solicitor and then find out the job Thomas Brent was supposed to do. Tell you what. I'll meet you at Tottenham Court Road and we'll go see that solicitor together. Say . . . in an hour's time.'

Watson stared into his beer. 'How you gonna find that rogue Brent?'

Tim wiped his lips with the back of his hand. His hat was propped back off his forehead. 'I need to do some deducting, is what.'

In Shadwell in the East End, Tim asked his usual squints if they'd seen Brent – the drawing of his face was in all the newspapers – but no one had seen him, even when he greased a few palms out of Mister Holmes's stash. He reckoned the best way to discover it was to get it from the horse's mouth, but he'd neglected to get the whereabouts of Brent's bolthole before he'd gone to ground. Over their pint in the pub, both he and Watson had tried to pin the murder on Brent as they went over and over their notes, but neither of them could seem to do it, without any explanation as to why they preferred another for it. They both had a gut feeling about it, and if *both* of their guts spoke to them, then they'd best listen. *Of course, with more information, that could turn on the head of a pin*, he decided. No use ruling him out altogether and be found wrong all this time. That wasn't good for business at all.

The narrow street, with its crowd of houses tilting toward one another across the path, made a shadowed passage, and slowly vanished under gray-shrouded fog easing in over the rooftops. He wrinkled his nose, remembering well the smell of the place like a latrine. He was raised on these same streets, knew them well. Too well. And he was heartily glad to move on from them. Funny how the least little civilizing of a man – a new suit of clothes, a new flat that wasn't rat-infested, with a servant or two – could make a man turn up his nose at his former life. Of course, that had happened fourteen years ago, when that slender gentleman in the Ulster tweed coat had approached him on these very streets and asked if he'd undertake a job that would be to his liking. Oh, Tim had laughed at first. What was this toff trying to tell him? And him flashing his coins in his twelve-year-old face. 'All you need do, my lad, is spy on a gentleman,' he had said in his own gentleman's tone. 'Tell me where he goes and when, and get that news back to me as fast as your feet can carry you. Back to me on Baker Street.' It sounded mad. But there was the coin. And it was easy, wasn't it? And when Tim had done it and done it well, that same gentleman had asked if he'd like to do more of it, and he was to ask his friends on the street if they'd like to do this work too. And it wasn't until years later that Tim realized that it wasn't so much that he and his fellow Irregulars were good at their running and hiding and climbing over walls. But that their kind – the poor, dirty street urchins – were all but invisible. No one bothered with them, no one noticed them, no one saw them, even as they lay sick in the streets. Even as some of them died there.

*Well, not again. Not ever.* He pulled his tweed coat taut at the lapels and was nearly upended when a similarly invisible street *man*, sitting in a doorway, with his long legs thrust out in the lane, made Tim's tread stumble. 'You nearly ditched me in the mud, my good man,' said Tim, dusting off his coat of imaginary mud.

The man had a red nose and red cheeks under a layer of soot. His beard was grizzled and unkempt. One eye was covered with a patch of leather, stitched all around it in red thread; the other was topped by a truly enterprising bush of a brow, arching over the bloodshot eye beneath like a thatched roof. A clay pipe hung from the man's lips, with the most acrid of tobaccos burning within it. A dented and hopelessly scuffed topper shadowed his face.

'It's you what needs to look where you're going. You got two good eyes, haven't you?' His voice growled with an undertone of a wheeze that spoke of inhaling the soot and filthy fog of London all his life.

Tim suddenly felt badly for the bloke, with his ratty coat and old shoes, where one of the soles was pulling away from the upper, letting in the mud and cold. He touched the rim of his homburg with a curt smile. 'No harm done.'

But as he tried to make his way around him, the man got shakily to his feet. 'For tuppence, I'll tell you where that rogue you are looking for is.'

Badger stepped back and measured the man down his nose. 'And how would you be knowing—'

'Heard you talking to them lads, didn't I? You're looking for that Thomas Brent what done in his master in Bloomsbury, eh?'

'I might be.'

'Let's see the tuppence.'

Tim knew this game. He'd played it often himself when he was in a similar state as this street gent. Claim you have information since you were following the punter and overheard him, offer to help for a few coins, then, once the coins were in your pocket, either lead him around till he was topsy-turvy as to where he was, or simply hightail it the moment the brass landed in your palm.

If this was the case, Tim didn't have the heart to mind. He reckoned he owed it to his fellow man in a worse-off situation. After all, this was him once.

He dug into his trouser pocket for his small purse and took out the coins. Instead of throwing them to the ground as other so-called 'real' gentlemen had done, he put them into the man's dirty palm, each line etched with grime. Those fingers closed over the brass and made a fist. He smiled, with several blackened teeth. 'He's down St Giles, in a cellar room by the bootblack.'

'And how do you know I'm not a copper out to arrest him?'

'I can tell. You don't smell as bad as them.' And then he cackled a laugh at his own joke, coughed and hacked, and then spat into the mud. Of course, Tim realized the joke could still be on him, going all the way to St Giles and never finding Brent. He'd take the chance.

'Much obliged,' he said instead, touching the rim of his hat once more. It didn't hurt to show another man respect. There was something he saw in that one eye looking back at him that said the man appreciated it.

He walked on and got a funny feeling, as if he'd seen that man before. Foolish, really. He'd known so many like him over the years. Still, he looked back, but the man had vanished.

St Giles had many streets offering old clothes for sale; the stalls hung with them, waving in the dirty breeze like lethargic sails on a ship in the harbor. His nose reminded him it was also the place for fishmongers, and not quite fresh produce at that. He imagined buying old clothes here and never getting the stench of day-old fish out of them.

His eyes scanned the lane, trying to see past the barrow boys selling their cheap wares from their carts, and wagons pulled by large, sluggish horses, with their broad shoulders and muddy fetlock feathers.

He took in the many pitches and stalls; a pawn shop with a rusted sign above the door with its three tarnished brass balls; an old furniture shop with a dirty window; a boarded-up shop with a faded, painted sign. And there, finally! A bootblack near a corner. He had his wooden box with his shoe-blacking tools for a gentleman to rest his booted foot upon. Behind him, along the sill of an empty shop, he had bits and bobs of things he was selling to supplement his shoe-shining trade: worn books, a few chipped jugs, a plate or two, and flowers in a sugar bowl.

Tim looked for it and found it. Behind the bootblack was a fanlight at street level, with bars in front of the cracked glass. And when he looked further under the bits and bobs, there was a stairway down to a door. He made his way there, giving a greeting to the bootblack, and trotted down the steps. The door's paint was peeling off, but it still looked substantial enough to keep a robber out. He knocked, listened, knocked again. 'Tom,' he said loudly enough to be heard through the wood, 'it's Tim Badger. I need to talk to you.'

Silence.

He waited and listened harder. A scuffing of a shoe.

'Brent, it's me.'

A key turned in a rusty lock, and then the door opened a crack. Tim could barely see a single eye staring at him from the darkness within. He pushed the door open, throwing Brent off his feet. Tim quickly closed the door behind him. 'I told you it was me.'

'How am I supposed to know? How'd you find me?'

'I'm a detective, ain't I?'

Brent's eyes traveled over Tim's figure. 'You look like a toff.'

Tim couldn't help but pull proudly at his lapels. 'A businessman must look like he means business. And here. My new lodgings in Soho, in case you need me.' He handed Brent a calling card. The man stared at it with a frown.

'I just have a few more questions for you. You doing awright?' He looked around at the dingy interior. He'd lived in plenty of places like this; wallpaper sagging off the walls, mouse holes in the corner moldings, broken windowpanes with pieces of wood or rags doing the job of keeping out the cold, and dark as could be with a cold hearth. 'Have you eaten?'

It had only been a day since Tim had met him but, of course, Brent had been on the run two days earlier. Brent's eyes were set in dark hollows and his hair was wild and unkempt. He shook his head.

'Bless you, man. I'll fetch you something to eat. But first, I have questions. Your Mrs Martin thinks you done it.'

'That dried-up old bird.'

'But Miss Jenny . . . well, she doesn't know.'

He shrugged.

'You've got motive.'

He leaned hard against the wall, arms folded tight over his chest. 'What does that mean?'

'It means you had a reason to kill him. What was this job he had you do that he cheated you out of paying for?'

'That? *That's* what made you think I killed him? I thought you were working for me.'

'I am, Mister Brent. But I have to know that you're innocent. And I believe you are. But in order to find out who had a better reason to kill Horace Quinn, I have to eliminate you. So be quick about it.'

He sighed. When he sat, his entire body sagged. He looked tired. Tired of life, tired of hiding, tired of this whole business. 'Mister Badger, that man was a horror. I don't know who killed him, but maybe he done the world a favor.'

'That isn't what I asked, man.'

'What was I doing for him that he couldn't spare half a crown for? I done just what he told me. I broke into Mister Latimer's house.'

'Stephen Latimer? Quinn's dead business partner?'

'Yes. He wanted me to find something.'

'What?'

'A strongbox. And I brung him the only strongbox I could find.'

Tim didn't like the taste of this. Didn't like that it would give the police something else to blame on Brent. Slowly, he asked, 'Was this before or after Latimer died?'

He scowled. 'After. I didn't kill him, neither.'

A wretched feeling squirmed in Tim's belly. He hoped it was

just him feeling sick at how badly Horace Quinn treated the people he was supposed to take care of, the people close to him who worked for him. He truly hoped it *wasn't* that he was beginning to think that Brent was guilty.

'But that wasn't what he wanted?'

Brent shot from his chair with renewed energy. He ran his hand up his arm. His clothes were looking grubbier, like he'd slept in them. He probably had done. He had left the Quinn house with nothing but the clothes on his back, Tim reckoned. 'It wasn't. Got cross at me. I did what he asked, risking myself. Said he wouldn't pay me after all since it wasn't what he wanted and I wouldn't go back to look again. Ungrateful bastard.'

'Steady there, Brent.'

'Well, he was! But I didn't kill him. I needed that job.'

'Who hired the medium?'

He shook his head and huffed in disgust. 'What a fool thing that was.'

'It wasn't you?'

'No. How would I know how to find one? Go to the Gypsy camp outside of the city, I reckon. But I didn't. He never asked me to.'

Tim pushed the homburg back off his head and scratched his hair, mussing it. 'Looks like *no one* hired her. Did she just walk in the door?'

'I don't know.'

'Ever see her before?'

'Do I look like I truck with Gypsies?'

'Awright. Look, here's some coins. I reckon you need them more than I do now. I'll go out and get you a pastie and some drink. I'll be right back.'

Brent looked down sorrowfully at the few coins and didn't move, even as Tim opened the door.

'Lock it after me.'

Badger waited until he heard the key turn in the lock. Weren't their clients supposed to pay *them*? Ah well. The money comes and the money goes. He reasoned that he'd just waste it on drink or gambling anyway. All work and no charitable giving . . . 'will make Watson and me poor boys,' he said with a sigh, before he rose up the steps . . . and ran into Ellsie bleedin' Littleton again.

# NINE
## Badger

Her bright eyes darted toward the door below stairs he had just left behind. 'Is that where Brent is hiding, Mister Badger? I'd like the exclusive, if I may.'

He walked toward her, forcing her to walk backward. 'That ain't – *isn't* – Brent in there. I do have to do my detecting, you know.'

Suddenly, she stopped and looked him over. 'My, my. You almost look respectable.'

'And *you* don't.' He pushed past her, hoping she'd leave Brent alone if he looked as if he didn't care. His hopes that she'd leave *him* alone crumbled when she came up behind him.

'That wasn't a very polite thing to say, Mister Badger.'

He didn't spare her a look. 'I haven't seen *you* being particularly polite, Miss Littleton.'

'It isn't rudeness . . .'

He snorted at that.

'It isn't! I have to be more forceful to get my stories. It isn't easy for a woman in my profession.'

He stopped and stared at her pointedly. 'And just which profession is that?'

Satisfied with her open-mouthed shock, he smiled cruelly and pushed on. Until he heard a sob come out of her that stopped him dead. *Bloody hellfire.*

He wanted to kick himself. He should just press on. Let her cry it out. But he couldn't. Not with that sound of weeping behind him. With a great gusted sigh, he turned and slowly approached. 'I . . . I'm sorry. That was uncalled for.'

To be fair, she was no wagtail. She kept herself in the height of fashion in a tight-fitting gown of angled plaid, cinched tight at the waist with a dark sash, with a split coat that showed the lacy blouse beneath, and those distinctively large, puffed shoulders above. Her hat was similar to his, only smaller and made of straw, with a spray of dark feathers above it. He didn't know what wages a reporter earned, but it must have been a decent sum for the variety of couture he had seen her wear. She had always looked far more respectable than him.

'I have to make a living for myself, you know,' she said between gulps of air. 'I don't *want* to seem unfeminine, but if I'm not forceful I can't do my job. Can't you see that?'

Tim lifted his hand and tentatively patted her shoulder. 'There, there.'

'Can't you help me the least little bit, Mister Badger?'

'Wait. Didn't you threaten me that last time we met? Didn't you say you've got enough to have me put away in the Fleet for good?'

She dabbed at her nose with a kerchief. 'I never said any such thing.'

'Yes, you did! "I have enough on you to send you to Fleet, my man,"' he said in his best falsetto imitation of her crisp speech. '"I've had my eye on you for a long while, Tim Badger." That's what you said to me, word for word.'

She patted her hair, wiped at her cheeks, and stuffed her kerchief into the little handbag hanging at her elbow. 'I had to say that. Because I know you're a criminal. I wanted you to understand that I know who you are and I am not afraid of you.'

'But I'm *not* a criminal! You saw for yourself how Mister Sherlock Holmes attends to me. He's my old guv. He wouldn't care a fig about me if I were a criminal, like *you* say.'

'Well. That's neither here nor there. *My* sources say—'

'Hang your sources.'

'Weren't you just leaving gaol because you were housebreaking?'

That woman could stop him dead with the mere stab of that tongue. He girded himself and said, more quietly, because he'd noticed people were starting to stare, 'That was a . . . a misunderstanding. I was investigating.'

'And what have you found out?'

'I'm not going to share that with you.'

She wasn't crying anymore. Good. Now he was free to go. He turned away and marched up the lane, looking for a cart selling pasties and maybe one selling bottles of ginger beer. He spotted one and hurried across the street toward it, when he noticed that fool woman was still hot on his heels.

'Mister Badger!'

'Look, Miss Littleton, I . . .'

'Meet me at Campbell's Cookshop. It's on—'

'I know where it is.'

'I'll await you there for tea and a bun. I'll buy. Then we can talk like civilized beings.'

He almost naysaid her. A woman buying for *him*! But when he took a moment to think about it, he decided that it was she who was being troublesome and *should* buy. 'Very well.' This finally dismissed her and he turned to the task of bringing the poor man Brent some food.

He bought four meat pies and several bottles of ginger beer and, with arms full, returned to the room below the bootblack. Brent was grateful and offered his thanks.

When Tim got out to the street again, he looked around, remembering Ellsie Littleton. She was a fair lass indeed, and he wouldn't mind a girl like her to take to the music hall or to stroll with in the park. Except that she was always trying to catch him at something so she could write about him in the paper. Maybe he could convince her to write something good for a change. A little free notoriety. That couldn't hurt. If he could manage to be polite and smile a bit, maybe she'd be inclined to do so. He could try, he reckoned. And get some tea and a bun out of it as well.

Campbell's Cookshop was a small establishment on Hart Street near Covent Garden. It wasn't an area Badger was used to being in, and at first he felt a bit uncomfortable. But as he passed a shop-front and caught a glimpse of himself in the window, he had to admit that he cut a decent figure, if he did say so himself. He looked like any other gent on the street. And no one was looking at him cock-eyed, as they used to do when he had on a tatty coat, worn trousers too short for him, and a flat cap.

He stood a little taller as he pushed through the door, feeling a bit more as if he belonged, and wended his way to the small table where Ellsie Littleton with her pert hat and fancy figure sat.

He stood at the front of the table until she looked up. 'Miss Littleton,' he said, and removed his hat, setting it on the far edge of the table, and settled into the seat opposite her.

'Mister Badger.' She surreptitiously looked him over, spotting the gleam of his pocket watch, the smooth lines of his waistcoat, the cut of his coat without any patches. 'I see that – whatever it is you are doing – it seems to sit well with you these days.'

He scowled. 'I thought we were done with insults. Or am I merely wasting my time here?' He made as if to rise, but she motioned him back down.

'I meant it as a compliment. Dear me. I admit, I know little about you other than what I observe . . . and your police file.'

'I have a file?' This had never occurred to him. Or that just anyone could access it.

The tea arrived. The server – a woman in a starched apron with matching starched cuffs – unburdened her tray of teapot, cups, saucers, sugar bowl, milk jug, and small plates with perfect round buns on them.

The warm, yeasty aroma of the buns made his mouth water. He hadn't realized he was hungry, but he politely waited for Miss Littleton to splash in a bit of milk, then offered him sugar – of which he took two lumps – before she poured tea into each cup.

'Please, Mister Badger. Don't stand on ceremony. Tuck in. I wonder if I may ask you a few questions while you do.'

Ordinarily, he would have dug in, slurping the tea and gorging himself on the bun. But as he glanced around at the other genteel patrons, he hesitated. Instead, he slowly took up his teacup as if it were a fragile thing and gently sipped, before replacing it in the saucer. He tore a piece from the bun and fed himself, its heavenly flavor melting as he chewed. He decided that the wealthier citizens of London had it good, better than him, with their clean cookshops and their swept pavements, and he'd enjoy it for all it was worth in the brief time allotted him. He tried to pace himself with the bun, though, hoping Miss Littleton would order more, and he barely managed to avoid making sounds of delight when he popped another chunk of bun into his mouth. 'What do you want to know?' he said, after swallowing.

Daintily, she took up her cup, drank, and set it down again. She hadn't yet touched her bun. 'If you aren't a criminal, as you claim, then what is it you do? What has formed your life in London that belies your police file?'

He ate the last of his bun and drank his tea. He took up his serviette and nearly wiped his mouth before remembering his earlier lesson with Mister Holmes when he had *dabbed* at his mouth instead. 'Well then, when I was a lad in Shadwell . . . I was a handful, and no mistaking. Mum . . . well. She went off with a bargeman when I was about . . . oh, eleven, I think. Had to make my own way.'

'That's awful! Did you have no relatives to take you in?'

'Nah. My dad fell in with some bad men, and one night he just never came home.'

'Why didn't you take yourself to one of the orphanages in town? Surely that would have been better – with warm meals and a dry place to sleep.'

'And marching to their drum and doing factory work? No, thanks.'

'Surely you didn't believe—'

'This is what I know from other boys on the street, Miss Littleton. Some of them orphanages were little better than workhouses. And some were worse. Lending boys out to farms and factories as slave labor while the *owners* made the wage. Believe me, I was better off on the streets with me gang. I mean . . . *my* gang.' He fiddled with his serviette, not meeting her eye. 'We looked after each other, the older for the little ones. You felt like a family. That is, if you got in with a good gang. Of course, we had to steal. That's how we ate.' His thoughts clouded with memories.

When he looked up at her again, she wore a shock of sympathy and . . . tenderness? He pulled at his tie. 'So . . . whatever you may have heard about "Parliament reforms" or some such rubbish, it's still bad for tykes like I used to be. Little wonder I got a police file . . . if that is indeed the truth.'

She stared down into her teacup as she drank. 'I didn't lie, Mister Badger. But . . . now I might understand the situation a little better. It wasn't for greedy gain that you stole. It was to survive.'

'Anyone else would do the same. Oh, I'm sure there are some who would seek out an orphanage if it occurred to them, but not many. Why don't you write about that?'

'Perhaps I shall.' She lifted the plate with the bun. 'Do partake of this one, Mister Badger. I'm not very hungry.'

He closed his fingers over it and set it down on his plate. 'Don't mind if I do. I mean . . . thank you.' He bit into it.

'And what of your association with Sherlock Holmes? How did you come to be in his employ?'

He smiled around his cup as he drank. 'Well now. That was fourteen years ago when I was twelve. I was picking this old duffer's pocket and I thought that he was none the wiser, until his fingers clutched around my wrist like steel. I thought I was for it, then. Clapped in prison the rest of my life. But when I looked up at the man, he didn't seem to have revenge in his heart. He was smiling. Amused.'

'And that was Mister Holmes.'

'Aye. He seemed proud of my accomplishment. Even said, "I never felt a thing, lad." That made me proud too. And then he told me what he wanted of me, and it seemed a simple thing to earn some coin. Just to spy on particular gentlemen in different parts of the city. Report to Mister Holmes where they went and who they were with. There was a whole gang of us after a time. He called us his "Baker Street Irregulars." A funny name, that. Well, as I got older, he started to share some of the tricks of the trade, so to speak. Taught me a bit how to observe, how to deduct.'

A faint smile pursed her lips. 'I see.'

'He trusted me. Thought I was a smart lad.'

'Then why did he stop using you?'

Tim sighed as he sipped his tea. 'Grew out of it. Too old to be an invisible street urchin. At eighteen, I was getting to be a liability, so he said. I didn't take offense. He never said the job was forever. But by then, I'd learned a thing or two.'

'That is very interesting, Mister Badger.' She scrambled at her bag and pulled out a notebook and took some time scribbling in it. 'And now, about this murder. And why *you* chose to investigate for the man that the Metropolitan Police force thinks is the guilty party.'

He almost opened his mouth, full of bun, to talk, but suddenly remembered the manners he had been trying hard to learn, something even Watson tried to drill into his thick head. Watson had far better manners than he had, after all.

He chewed, held up a finger, swallowed, took a sip of tea, and then leaned toward her. 'I have an instinct for this sort of thing. Mister Holmes saw the same in me when I was a lad and worked for him. I'm sharp, is what it is, miss. I can see through a man's soul. You have to be good at it to live on the streets and survive. You have to be able to carve away the face they show to the world and get down to the dark, sticky insides, so to speak.'

'That's good. That's awfully good.' She wrote quickly with a bobbing pencil. '"Carve away the face . . ."' She smiled. 'Frightfully good. Go on.'

Once Tim got going, he lost any pretense to the toff role he had tried to cultivate. 'So me instinct tells me that Brent is a victim of circumstances. He ain't responsible. And he's an easy target. I mean, nine times out of ten, it's the bloke you first think that did it. But there is that one who's just easy to blame. And rozzers don't want to do the hard work to find out who *really* might have done it if they've got a fish on the line already. See what I mean?'

'"Fish on the line." Yes.'

'Take anyone what works in a house, whether it's a town house or a manor house in the country; any servant anywhere. Just because the master or missus has money and an education, they immediately assume their servants are dumb as dirt. Or worse, children. You see it all the time. We're talked down to, called stupid or clumsy. Punished like a child. Never thanked. Never given the simple courtesy you'd give your blee— Er, *blooming* horse. They never give a thought to who we are, or that we've got thoughts in our own heads. So we're the easiest to blame crime on.' He forgot to dab at his mouth and wiped it with his serviette instead. 'Or . . . that a lady of manners could ever have something with a bloke like me . . . fr'instance.'

She busily wrote and abruptly stopped and looked up with widened eyes.

Tim grinned and sat back in his chair, adjusting the tableware. 'Just so,' he said under his breath.

She blinked with reddening cheeks as she lowered her eyes back to her notebook. 'I . . . I don't think all people who have servants treat them like that.'

'Yes, they do. Do you have a maid, Miss Littleton?'

She set her notebook down with an impatient huff. 'As it happens, I do. She's been with me for years and years.'

'And what do you know about her?'

'What do you mean?'

'Like you'd know about a friend. Her likes, her dislikes. Her favorite food. Her favorite song. What color she likes to wear on her day off. What she does on them days.'

Miss Littleton was poised to answer, her rosy mouth open . . . but she said nothing. Her brows angled into a frown.

'You don't know, do you?'

She raised her chin primly. 'But we aren't friends, Mister Badger. I'm her employer and she is my employee. How much should I know?'

'She knows all about you. *Your* likes and dislikes. The color of your . . .' He smirked. 'Clothing.'

Her neck flushed this time, and he tried to stifle a grin.

'That's her job,' she said prissily.

'And how often do you thank her? Give her gifts? She's the closest person you've got in your life, never mind your relatives. When did you treat her like a girl, not an *employee*, as you say?'

She said nothing.

'And if some little thing goes missing, who's the first one you're going to blame?'

Those rosy lips pressed tightly together.

He raised his palms as if to say 'that is that,' before folding them together over his stomach.

She carefully laid her serviette on the table. Still not looking him in the face, she gathered her notebook. 'There . . . may be something to what you say, Mister Badger.'

This time he said nothing. He wanted her to stew on it. It was the first time he'd ever spoken the truth to someone of her class, and he was just as curious at her reaction as she seemed to be with her own.

And then, like lightning, her porcelain face completely changed, as if someone had lit a lamp behind it, making it glow. 'And that's an interesting angle to write about. How we all assume it is the lowliest of us who commit the crimes. How society treats its underclasses. Yes! Give me a reason to champion Thomas Brent, Mister Badger, and I can assure you that my stories will sway the public's hearts.'

'Oh. Er . . . that would be most helpful, but, er, I'm not quite ready to share details as of yet. I tell you what, Miss Littleton. Here is my card with my new lodgings. You can contact me there. Or . . . perhaps I can have *your* address . . .' He proffered his card and she looked at it, hopefully considering his last comment . . .

When her fingers closed on the card, those bright eyes rose again. 'I'm not in the habit of giving strange gentlemen my address. After all, as you say, I don't know *your* likes and dislikes, *your* favorite foods, *your* favorite song.'

He smiled and nodded. 'Fair enough.' He rose from the table and gave her a bow. 'Perhaps I'll give you a chance to know those things. Or . . .' He squinted and studied her. 'You asked me what is it I do. I detect. I deduct.'

Her face was almost comical in its twist of enquiry. He thought about his words and tapped into his memory. The guv used to say, '*I don't guess. I deduce.*'

'Oh. I mean, I *deduce*.'

'And what, pray, would that entail?'

He vowed to wipe that smug smirk off her face. 'Your address, miss.'

'How could you possibly deduce where I live?'

'By your hat.'

Her hands leapt to the little straw hat perched on her abundant crown of hair. 'My hat?'

He concentrated hard, observing every inch of her. He had to get this right. His pride was at stake. And so was his future.

'Yes. Because I happen to know that that particular hat is only sold at a haberdasher's on Oxford Street, St John Potter proprietor. I've seen it in the window. Why should you go any further than your own back garden? I reckon you reside close to Grosvenor Square, by your accent. *And* by the look of your boots, I'd say east of it.'

'My shoes?'

'There's construction there, with a bit of red clay running all through it, and I fancy that you take a shortcut through there to catch a cab or omnibus to your newspaper. Your boots have red clay on them.'

She stuck out a foot from under the table and looked at it. 'Good heavens.'

'And by the clay, the hat, and the general look of you, I'd say you live somewhere on . . . Brook Street, Mayfair.'

She gasped, cheeks reddening. 'That's an extraordinary guess.'

'I don't guess, Miss Littleton. I deduce. That's what I do. And Thomas Brent is innocent. I plan to prove it.' He tapped his hat into place upon his head. 'Thank you for the tea.' He turned to leave, then paused. 'And as it happens, my favorite song – currently – is "The Man Who Broke the Bank at Monte Carlo."' He inclined his head toward her notebook. 'You can write that down.'

Whistling it, he strolled through the cookshop toward the entrance, and, feeling a flush of intuition, glanced back over his shoulder. She was still looking at him. *She is the jammiest bit of jam*, he mused, and passed through the door.

Once outside, he adjusted his hat and buttoned his coat. The look on her face was most satisfactory. He'd have to look up Miss Ellsie Moira Littleton to see where exactly she lived. He wondered if he had been right about Grosvenor. He wondered if she lived with her daddy dear or a matron aunt. There were no boarding houses in that area, so it had to be with a relative. *Look at me, deducing all over the place*, he chuckled.

But he was just reckoning he had to put aside any thoughts of the lovely Miss Littleton and hurry to meet with Watson at the solicitor's when something thudded into the doorjamb beside him.

At first, he thought something had dislodged from the entry: a lamp, a placard. But it wasn't anything like that. He stared at the object. Couldn't quite believe what he was looking at, until his brain caught up with his eyes and his blood ran cold.

A dagger. A strange sort of dagger. Stuck in the jamb and still quivering after someone had evidently thrown it at him.

The same height as his heart.

# TEN

## Watson

Ben returned to 49b Dean Street, happy to see his crate of chemistry equipment waiting for him in the outer room of his bedchamber. He wasted no time setting it up, doffing his coat and hat and slipping his apron over his head. He set to, studying his books and papers with the two envelopes of dirt before him.

He opened his battered, translated copies of *Justus Liebigs Annalen der Chemie*, Fallou's *First Principles of Soil Science*, and Holmes's monographs on soil analysis, and commenced comparing notes.

He made certain he separated the dried mud found on the sill from the sample removed from the garden. After taking the time to carefully mix small samples in a test tube with various chemicals, he concluded – and wrote it down in a little book just as the chemist did – that they were from two separate sources. There was more clay and iron in the sample from the sill than in the garden sample.

He stared at the test tube in his hand and pondered it. The only problem with knowing that the soil was from elsewhere was to determine where that elsewhere was. And so far, he didn't have any way to do that. He didn't have collections of soil from all over London like Mister Holmes did, but now he was bound and determined to do just that himself. He carefully sifted the samples into little bottles that he stoppered with cork, wrote scrupulously in small letters what each sample was from, and set them on a shelf. He smiled to himself, admiring them, and proud that he – Ben Watson – had begun the scientific collection as a sort of reference that Mister Holmes had undertaken. It could certainly come in handy in future cases.

But what could he make of it now? That the murderer either came in through the window or made his way out of it. One conclusion. But another began to occur to him. Maybe someone washed the windows days before. Of course, that was likely Jenny herself. Yet he couldn't see her *standing* on the sill to do so, when so many others simply sat on the sill and used a mop. But also, why would there be different soil on her boots than from the garden?

No, someone *stood* on that sill. More's the pity that there were no boot marks to compare and trace. But muddy soil – with clay and iron in it – was deposited on that sill very close to the time Quinn was murdered, or the industrious maid would surely have cleaned it off by now. And by the look of that room, she was likely too timid to go back in there. At least for now.

The clock chimed in the sitting room and he stood. Nothing for it but to clean himself up and meet Badger to tell him the news.

He paced along Tottenham Court Road, wondering if Badger was ever going to arrive. When he finally spied his familiar figure striding down the pavement, he perked up. But the man wore a peculiar expression that meant something was wrong.

Without realizing it, Ben walked toward him and met him on the street in front of a clerk's office. 'What's the matter, Tim?'

Badger screwed up his mouth, bit his bottom lip, then screwed his mouth again, brows popping up then down. 'I'll tell you later. Let's see to this solicitor first.'

Oh, he didn't like that. Ben never liked it when Badger held back from him. He almost grabbed his arm and demanded he tell him now. But he couldn't force Tim to do anything he didn't want to do. That was a fact etched in stone.

Instead, Ben led the way to the office of Miles Smith, Esquire. A clerk with half-moon glasses sitting atop his balding head was seated at a desk, neat piles of papers sitting around him under a green glass lamp. He looked up, looked down at his writings, and quickly looked up again, as if he wasn't sure he'd seen what he thought he saw. Ben stepped forward first, presenting his card. 'Messieurs Watson and Badger to see Mister Smith. On police business.'

Badger's eyes were on him, Ben could tell, even as *he* kept his gaze on the clerk.

The clerk studied the card. 'On what police business?'

'The murder of Horace Quinn.'

Instead of chucking them out and threatening to call a constable, the clerk merely raised his brows, pushed himself from the desk, and retreated behind a closed door. Ben felt a warmth radiating from his chest at the satisfaction of it all.

Badger nudged him and, in a whisper, asked, 'What was that "messers" thing you said?'

'It means the both of us. In French. Instead of misters. Frenchified. It's got more gravitas that way.'

'What's "gravytas"?'

'Shush. I hear him coming back.'

They both straightened as if posing for a photograph when the clerk returned. 'Mister Smith will see you now. Come this way.'

When the clerk turned his back to lead them to the door, Ben gave Badger a wink.

At a grander desk and in a leather chair sat Mister Smith, with brown hair parted in the middle and a stylish mustache curling up at the ends under a square nose. He was in his forties or thereabouts. 'Come in, gentlemen,' he said, glance lingering on Ben, who stopped any questions on Smith's part by stepping forward to offer his hand. There was the smallest of hesitations from Smith, but Ben was well

used to it. Badger extended his hand as well and, once all the propri-
eties had been observed, they both sat in chairs before the desk.
'May I offer you sherry?'

Ben sensed Badger was about to assent, so he interrupted. 'No,
thank you, sir. We are here to discuss your former client, Horace
Quinn.'

'Private detectives, eh? Well, well. I won't ask who *your* client is.
And Mister Quinn is only my client until the will is read and executed.
But until then, I'm afraid there is little I can legally tell you.'

'Not even who the heir is?' piped Badger.

'Very much not that in particular. The reading of the will follows
the funeral. I'm certain you will find it interesting. You both should
attend.'

'We will, thank you,' said Ben.

'Then come to the Quinn household at two o'clock tomorrow
afternoon.'

Disappointing but not entirely unexpected. Ben glanced at Badger
who, for once, seemed to have little to say. Ben, on the other hand,
canted forward in his seat. 'Mister Smith, you were also the solicitor
for Quinn's business partner, Stephen Latimer. Is that not true?'

'Indeed.'

'What could it be that Mister Quinn wanted from his deceased
partner that he couldn't ask it of you? After all, that was the purpose
of the séance, where he was ultimately murdered.'

'It is strange, isn't it?' He reached for a box at the corner of his
desk, opened the lid, and offered it to them. 'Cigar?'

'No, thank you,' said Badger, wrinkling his nose only slightly.

Smith took one and proceeded to clip the end and light it. He
puffed thoughtfully.

Ben inhaled its aroma. Ah. A *Romeo y Julieta*, by its mild smoke.
Now he wished he had taken him up on the offer. He watched as
the ash formed at the tip of the cigar, and remembered poring over
Holmes's various monographs about tobacco ash, never dreaming
he'd actually ever meet the man, let alone be his . . . what? Protégé?

If he had been born a white man, Ben might have become a
chemist himself. He had to make do with the few years he spent as
a chemist's assistant, though the chemist never considered him an
apprentice as much as Ben had considered himself so. After all, he
went above and beyond what the chemist had hired him for. He had

read the man's books, poked around in the bottles and recipes in the scripts, experimented with various tinctures. Which was also why he was sacked. Though he had acquired enough information that he probably could have opened his own shop. If he'd had the money.

Abruptly, he called himself back from his ponderings when he realized Smith was talking.

'. . . such a thing as a séance. Mister Latimer was a poor business partner, at least in terms of finances. He died in penury as it was. Wouldn't take my advice on investments. Well . . .'

'Did he die of natural causes?' asked Badger.

'Yes. It looked as if he hadn't eaten in days. He was in very poor health. Couldn't seem to afford the coal to keep his room warm. It was dreadful.'

'A man like that,' said Ben, clucking his tongue. 'And he couldn't ask for help from his own friend.'

'As I heard it . . .' Smith puffed again. 'He *did* ask Quinn. And Quinn refused.'

They all sat in silence, Badger in his thoughts, Ben in his, and Smith puffing on his cigar, tipping a perfect cylinder of gray ash onto a small, silver dish. Ben watched it and thought what a miserable old bastard Quinn was, and maybe he deserved getting a knife in his chest.

'So,' said Badger, a thoughtful look on his face, 'Mister Quinn had no expectation to inherit anything from Latimer.'

'No, indeed. He knew Latimer's situation. The sale of the house will certainly go to creditors. I can't imagine what it was he expected to receive. All of Latimer's papers were water-damaged, I'm afraid. Quinn had gone through them, as I understand it, and the rest went up the flue with the other rubbish. It was a very sad affair.'

Badger shook his head. 'Then this doesn't make sense at all. He was so desperate to find something that his business partner had, that he sat in a séance. You don't have any idea, Mister Smith, what that could possibly be?'

'As I said.' He puffed on the cigar, the smoke making Badger green, while Ben inhaled it blissfully. 'I cannot fathom it.'

'Well,' said Ben, rising. Badger followed suit, standing as far away from the cigar as was polite. 'I suppose there's little more to discuss.'

'Not until the reading of the will. At the Quinn residence.'

'We shall see you there. Thank you for your time.'

Smith shook Ben's hand without hesitation this time. 'Thank you, gentlemen. And, if you don't mind, I shall keep this card. It's possible I might in future have work for such men as you.'

Badger grinned. 'A pleasure, sir. You keep that handy.'

Smith returned the smile and they both left to stand on the pavement in front of the solicitor's office. 'How d'you like that, Ben? Just by talking to the man, we might have made another client.'

'See what a decent suit of clothes can do for a man. But here, Tim. What's amiss?'

Slowly, Badger opened his coat and showed . . . something . . . protruding from a pocket within. It looked like a . . . knife handle?

'What's that?'

'Something someone threw at me just as I left a cookshop. Something stuck in the doorjamb.'

Ben grabbed his arm. 'They *threw* a knife at you? What had you done?'

'Nothin'! I was on my own, minding my own business. This is a warning, that.'

'Did you see him?'

Badger's cheeks ruddied. 'Nah. I was so shocked, I forgot to look around. But the street was busy. They likely blended in.'

'I want to take a more thorough look at that.'

'By all means,' said Badger, and off they went back to their lodgings in Soho.


# ELEVEN
## Badger


Watson laid the strange knife on the table in his workroom while Tim leaned over it. 'What do you reckon, Ben? I never seen a knife like that.'

The blade was curved outward on both sides, giving it the appearance of a spade, and only the blade's point was sharp, not its rough edges. The whole of it was at least ten inches long.

'I have.' Watson picked up the blade by the handle, turned toward the wall, and heaved it. It went end over end so fast that it was a mere blur, but when it struck the wall, it was embedded perfectly in the center of a flower design on the wallpaper.

Tim's face paled to a stark white. 'Ben! Were you once an assassin too?' he squeaked.

'Gawd, Tim! Of course not. I worked for a funfair. This knife is part of a knife-throwing act.'

Tim approached the knife and studied it, still embedded in the wall. He didn't seem to want to touch it. 'Why would . . . I mean who would . . . Blimey! I'm flummoxed.'

'Who from a funfair or circus would throw a knife at you as a warning, you mean?'

'Well . . . yes. Does this make sense to you?'

Watson shook his head and walked to the knife. He wrapped his fingers around the handle and yanked it free, tossing it into the air, letting it spin, and catching it when the handle came round again.

'Ben,' said Tim thoughtfully. 'What was the murder weapon again?'

'I think the papers said it was a letter opener.'

'But what if it wasn't? What if it was like this, only the coppers didn't know what it was?'

'Say.' Watson tossed the knife in the air again and caught it smoothly. 'That's something, eh? Quinn was facing the window, wasn't he? But how are we going to . . .?'

'I know who's in charge of the case. Inspector Stanley Hopkins. Let's go talk to him.'

'How about a little refreshment first?' Watson walked through to the sitting room and took up the bell on the mantel.

Tim hated the idea of ringing a bell to bring a servant. It was like someone snapping their fingers like you would for a dog. But, in the end, Watson must have decided to do it, since Mrs Kelly had told him to.

Tim didn't suppose – like Watson looked like *he* did – that it would actually work, but then they heard footsteps approaching, and suddenly the door was flung open. A pretty maid with a blunt nose and ginger hair piled up on her head stepped through. She wasn't shy as some maids were. Her chin was raised and she looked them both over as if they were hanging by their feet in the butcher's stall. She wore a black frock with a white apron and a white cap. 'Gentlemen? I'm Murphy. What will you be wanting?'

But it was Watson who looked gobsmacked. He slowly dragged his hat from his head and walked forward. 'What's your Christian name, miss?'

She frowned. 'Well, it isn't "miss."' The Irish was strong in her accent. '"Murphy" is good enough for the likes of you.'

'Ah, but . . . it ain't right calling a pretty lass like you by her surname. Come on.'

She straightened. 'I prefer you call me "Murphy." A little distance between employer and employee is fitting.'

Tim laughed. 'You're a snob, Miss Murphy!'

'It's just "Murphy," sir.'

'We'll get it out of you eventually . . .'

With a sigh, she seemed to see the uselessness of putting them off. 'It's Katie. Katie Murphy. But I won't be answering to anything but "Murphy," so you might as well get all that out of your heads now. So. What will you be wanting?'

Amused, Tim deferred to Watson. The little spitfire would have her way, no mistaking. She and Mrs Kelly would be more like matrons in a prison than servants. That sat a bit better with Tim, since he wasn't particularly comfortable with having servants of his own.

'Thank you for that,' said Watson in his most conciliatory of tones, but then seemed at a loss for words.

Tim stepped in to help. 'Well . . . Murphy. If you please, we'd like a little tea and some grub. It's hungry work we're doing. Some sandwiches? Meat and cheese would do.'

'Very good, then.' She didn't curtsey as some maids did. She merely whirled on her heel. But when she reached the door and turned to close it, she did glance once at Watson, which seemed to make his day.

Tim patted his back. 'What's this? Falling for the servants, are we?'

'Haven't you got eyes, mate? She's gorgeous.'

'She's pretty, I'll give you that. But not my type at all. Could you listen to that brogue the rest of your life?'

Watson nodded dreamily. 'I think I could.'

Tim laughed heartily. 'Let's settle in. In a few moments, you'll see her once more and moon over her all over again.'

It wasn't long till Murphy returned with a tray and set it on the sideboard. 'The post and afternoon paper as well, Mister Badger, Mister Watson. Anything else?'

Watson didn't speak, couldn't seem to, and so Badger rescued him. 'That will be all for now, Murphy. Thanks.'

She nodded and flounced away. Tim glanced at his friend and could see it all on his face: Katie Murphy would be making his bed, smoothing out his very sheets; touching his clothes; emptying his—

'Blimey,' Watson whispered, scandalized.

'Best not to think about it,' said Tim, pouring the tea and grabbing a sandwich made of two thick slices of bread, with a slab of meat and a decent slice of cheese within, and some spicy mustard and butter spread between them. 'Now that's a proper sandwich,' he said around the wad in his mouth as he sat at the table. 'I hope there's a joint or sausage for dinner.'

Watson drank his tea, ate his sandwich, and opened the letter. 'It's from the agency where Thomas Brent was hired from. I wrote to them earlier today.' He read silently as Tim ate. 'All seems in good order. Nothing out of the ordinary.' Then he took up the newspaper, flattened it, and read . . . then suddenly stilled. 'Oi, Tim. What have you done today?'

'What do you mean?' His mouth was full of bread as he slurped his tea.

Watson took a breath, snapped the paper to square it up, and read aloud. '*Consulting Detective's Criminal Past*, says the headline,' he told Tim. '*By Ellsie Moira Littleton.*'

Tim stilled. From the look on Watson's face, this wasn't good.

'*Timothy Badger, self-proclaimed private detective,*' Watson read, '*would have you believe he is on the hunt for clues for his most recent client, the murderer-on-the-run Thomas Brent, whom Scotland Yard would like to apprehend regarding the horrific murder of Horace Quinn of Bloomsbury. But he cannot seem to manage to shed his own criminal past. "When I was a lad in Shadwell . . ."* said Badger, *"I was a handful." His own mother "ran off with a bargeman" never to be heard from again.*' Watson lowered the paper. 'Oh, Lord. It gets worse from there.'

Tim felt the blood drain from his heart. His whole body felt loose, like wet string. He reached over and snatched the paper from Watson, tearing through the story.

"'*I was better off on the streets with me gang*,'" he read aloud. "'*We looked after each other, the older for the little ones. You felt like a family. That is, if you got in with a good gang*," said Badger, with a proud tilt to his head.'

He stared at the tight, dense ink imprinted on the paper. 'She . . . she . . . twisted my words! I look like a . . . like a . . . Bloody hellfire!'

'When was you talking to her?'

'I . . . oh God!' He dropped his face in his hands, letting the paper fall to his feet. 'She's ruined us.' But just as quickly, he snapped his head up, face hot and full of blood. 'I'll strangle her!'

'Look, if we get famous like your Mister Holmes, it's expected that we meet with those of the journalistic class what don't like us. Because we'll be naysaying them when they shout from the headlines that one man is guilty that we say ain't done it. That's their job, mate. And we're stepping all over it. They'll twist your words every time.'

'But we was having tea, just chatting . . .'

'She's a reporter. Everything is fair game unless you tell her it isn't. And even then, well. There's no honor amongst the thieves of print.'

'I'll never speak to that she-devil again.'

'Now, now. You can't be going off like that. We just may *have* to talk to her from time to time. Best we are careful with our words.'

'I trusted her,' he rasped.

'Well, there's your trouble right there. Never trust a woman.'

'I thought . . . I thought she'd write something good, something to give us some notoriety.'

'Well . . . they know us now. Badger and Watson of Dean Street. Says right there.'

'Bloody—'

'I daresay your Mister Holmes has read that already.'

Tim shot to his feet. 'Oh, gawd!'

'Tim, there's nothin' for it. It's done. Lesson learned, eh?'

Deflating, he sat. 'Lesson learned.'

'Let's get to your Scotland Yard inspector and talk to him. Go about our business as usual.'

'How can I face him now? How can I face any of them?'

'Like any affronted gentleman. With aplomb. Like you don't care.' He took on the air of the upper class as if he was performing like a *lion comique*. 'It's just a grubby reporter what got it all wrong about you . . . as *usual*,' he said in a patronizing accent. He gathered himself. 'Look, Tim. Whatcha think I have to do all the time when they call me "blackie" or worse? When they snub me, when they tell me to clear off when they just look at me, don't even know my name or my business. You think black sods like me don't live with it every day?'

Tim felt his face fall, his shoulders. It dragged him deep into his chair. 'Oh, Ben. I forgot.'

'Because you never think of me as one thing or the other, that's why. That's because we've known each other for a while – seems like forever. But it ain't the same for others. My infamy comes with my skin color everywhere I go. I don't need to be in the blooming newspaper for that.'

'I'm sorry.'

Watson shrugged and moved to the desk. He pulled out an envelope with a penny lilac stamp on it, and opened a drawer, carefully taking a sheet of paper out and laying it on the desk. He dipped his pen in the inkwell. 'You don't need to apologize to me. I'm just saying you need to thicken it up. They'll call you names. There will be a time our new clothes and our calling card won't amount to a fig, and we'll be tossed out on our arses. We gotta be ready for it.'

Tim nodded. 'We're *gonna* be ready for it. Cripes, Ben. You're the wisest man I ever met.'

'Nah, I'm just smarter than you, that's all.'

Tim noticed the twinkle in his eye as he said it, and then Watson set to writing. Maybe he was jesting, but Tim knew it to be true. 'Awright. I'm done crying in my beer. We've got to get to Scotland Yard before dusk. Let's go.'

Tim saw Watson leave the letter with Mrs Kelly with instructions to post it.

'What's that?'

'Never you mind. Let's catch that 'bus!'

The green omnibus pulled up. All the seats both inside and on the knifeboard bench on top were crammed with commuters, so they ended up holding onto the outside. They jumped off before the stop at Charing Cross and, after straightening their coats, marched down the lane to Victoria Embankment, down to Whitehall Place, and up the steps to the entrance of Scotland Yard.

A long desk (which Tim had been dragged past many a time) sat foremost in the center of a great arched room, with hexagonal-tiled floors and pillars, which separated offices with frosted-glass windows surrounded by dark wood. Benches and chairs lined the wall opposing the desk. Globe gas lamps hung above.

Tim stood before the sergeant at the front desk and leaned on it, waiting for the man to look up. He didn't, being busy carefully writing and dipping his pen. His large mustache was curled up at the ends with wax, and his dark brows were more prominent than his small eyes. 'How may I help you?' he said, still working on his papers.

'You may direct me,' said Tim in his toffiest accent yet, 'to the office of Inspector Stanley Hopkins.' He made certain to puff out the 'aitch'.

Without looking up, the sergeant thumbed behind him to his left. 'Third door on the left. Name's on the door.'

'Thank you, my good man,' he said, and motioned for Watson to follow, when the sergeant finally looked up.

'Hear now! What are you playing at, Badger?'

'I am not playing at anything, Sergeant. I'm here to see 'em.'

'No, you don't. You sit right there until I'm good and ready to send you in.'

'Why? You were willing to simply let us pass before.'

'Because I know you. You're up to no good.'

'I'm not. Here. My card.'

'What's this?' he muttered, taking the proffered card. 'Badger and Watson, private blooming detectives? What rubbish is this?'

'It ain't rubbish. It's our profession. Sponsored by the Great Man himself, the one and only Mister Sherlock Holmes.'

'Pull the other one. Clear off.'

'I want to see Inspector Hopkins. It's me right as a citizen.'

'I'm giving you one chance, me lad. Do I have to count it out? One . . .'

Watson nudged him and Tim changed tack. He sidled up to the desk again. 'Look, guv. I've got me business to attend to. A real paying job. If you don't let me to it, I could end up destitute. End up in a workhouse. Just because *you* couldn't trust me. I mean . . . look at us! Do we look like the vagrants and thieves we used to be?'

The sergeant stood and leaned far over the desk, scouring the two of them with one eye squinted hard. Gradually he sat back. 'Well . . . you do *look* different.'

'Course we do. Gainfully employed is what we are. Now. How's about you let us go see the guv, eh?'

The sergeant jabbed an index finger at him. 'If you are lying to me, Badger . . .'

'Not a bit of it.' Tim edged forward in the direction of the inspector's office. 'And I'll mention how you were personally helpful to us, won't I, Ben?'

Watson said nothing. Just kept his lidded eyes on the sergeant as Tim slid by him.

They made their way past the doors, not looking over their shoulder but nevertheless feeling the eyes of the sergeant burning into their backs, and found the door with the inspector's name on it. Tim knocked and they heard the muffled, 'Come.'

'Good afternoon, Inspector Hopkins.'

The sandy-haired inspector frowned. 'Badger. What do you want?'

'Inspector,' said Tim, posturing with his hand on his lapel. 'This is my colleague, Benjamin Watson. We are here in the capacity of private detectives. Show him the card, Watson.'

'What?' Hopkins said with a laugh.

Watson, with all dignity, presented the card to the inspector, who studied it like it was something from the bin. 'What the blooming hell is this?'

'You are certainly acquainted with my mentor, Mister Sherlock Holmes . . .'

'Is this about you being hauled to gaol? Just last night, wasn't it?'

'Nothing whatsoever. We are here investigating the murder of Horace Quinn, late of Bloomsbury.'

Hopkins sat back and stared, mouth agape. 'Of all the utter gall . . .'

'Now, now. We're colleagues now, Inspector. I shall be happy to give you all the respect you are due, if you can extend the same to us.'

'Blasted cheek,' he muttered. He pulled his chair forward. 'All right. I'll play your little game. You know I can check on this with Mister Holmes.'

Tim noticed the telephone device on his desk and gestured toward it. 'I enjoin you to make a telephone call to him this moment.'

'Very well, my man. I'll call your bluff and do that right now.'

Tim had seen many of these same contraptions – a box with a crank on the side and a device with a listening end and a speaking end lying on a cradle on top, all brass and black metal – but he had never used one himself. He wondered about talking through wires and how useful they would be in the end. But Hopkins picked up the speaking and hearing device and cranked the side of the box with a trill of a bell.

'Hello, hello!' he said, rather loudly, into it. 'Connect me to 221 Baker Street. Yes, that's right.' He waited with the hearing end pressed to his ear. It wasn't long until Tim and Watson could hear a voice seeping through. 'Mrs Hudson? This is Inspector Hopkins. Hopkins! Yes, ma'am. Sorry to trouble you, but could you bring Mister Holmes to the line? . . . Yes, I know he doesn't like these instruments . . . Yes, but if you could tell him it's me . . . Well, do your best.' He waited, glancing at the two of them doubtfully, until he heard a voice on the instrument. 'Mister Holmes? Yes, sir, *again* so soon. I know you don't like the . . . Yes, sir, I appreciate your talking to me. I'll be quick. I have before me two gents who claim to be your protégés . . .' Hopkins listened. 'Yes. Yes. But sir . . . Yes. Very well then, Mister Holmes. Sorry to have troubled you.' He took the device away from his head and set it carefully into the cradle once more. He stroked his mustache, buttoned his coat, and raised his face. 'Well! It seems that Mister Holmes *does* vouch for the two of you . . . much to my surprise. He also admonished me to help you; said that you use his methods and therefore I should put my trust in you. And so, chaps. What's it to be?'

Tim smiled his satisfaction at Watson. Maybe a telephone device *was* a good thing, after all.

'Inspector, as I have told you, we are investigating the Quinn murder. We have uncovered many interesting facts, but we are uncertain about one thing. The murder weapon. It has been reported in the newspapers that it was a . . . a . . .'

'Letter opener,' put in Watson, who seemed to have found his voice at last.

Hopkins looked from one to the other. 'Sounds like you want to see it.'

Watson held his lapel, probably to keep his hand from shaking. 'That would be most accommodating, Inspector.'

'Good heavens,' he rasped under his breath. He threw his hands up in despair. 'Why not? It's here.' He reached down to a drawer in his desk and drew out a large paper envelope. He untied the string that enclosed it and dumped the contents with a clatter onto the blotter on his desk.

Tim and Watson rose at the same time to study the thing. 'Shall *you* tell him?' Tim asked Watson.

Now it was Watson's turn to wear that same satisfied grin. 'Inspector, that is no letter knife.'

He shrugged. 'Well . . . we assumed so, because it wasn't a knife one would use in the kitchen . . .'

'And not in the kitchen neither,' said Tim. He withdrew a similar blade from his coat, only bigger than the murder weapon, and laid it beside it. 'It's a throwing knife, like what you'd see in a circus or funfair.'

Hopkins had finally lost his skeptical expression. He came around the desk and stared at the two weapons. 'I'll be blowed,' he whispered.

# TWELVE
## Watson

'We are endeavoring to discover the culprit in the case,' said Ben, eyeing Hopkins. Friend of Sherlock Holmes he might be, but as a rule, he didn't trust rozzers. Not that he'd ever involved himself in criminal activity. That is, *before* he met Badger. It was just that . . . well. Constables always gave him trouble.

Hopkins examined the new knife carefully before sitting back in his chair. 'Gents, am I given to understand that you are not considering Thomas Brent as the culprit.'

'He's our client,' said Badger, *un*helpfully.

Hopkins closed his eyes. 'You are aware that Scotland Yard would like a word or two with Mister Brent.'

*Thanks, Tim*, Ben thought with a sigh. 'We are, sir. But we don't think he's guilty. And in light of this new evidence, it doesn't seem likely at all.'

'Has he ever worked for a funfair?'

Ben and Badger exchanged glances.

'Well . . .' Badger released a huff. 'I . . . never asked him.'

'So you *don't* know that he doesn't know how to use this knife?' The inspector shook his head. 'Gents, it's best you leave this to the police. Now why don't you tell us where he is, then?'

'That would hardly help our business,' Badger insisted.

'Well let me just tell you exactly what won't help your business, lads. You withholding vital information from the police. I have a mind to lock up the two of you. That can't help your business at all.'

Ben showed a calm face, though his heart was beating madly. 'That wouldn't sit well with Mister Holmes.'

'I'm bally well not interested in what Mister Holmes thinks. This is *my* murder investigation.'

'And so far,' said Badger, 'you've got it wrong.'

Hopkins reached over his desk and aimed a finger at him. 'Now look, you . . .'

'Please,' said Ben to them both. 'Why can't we work together? Exchange information. Like Mister Holmes would do for you?'

Hopkins stared at him for several seconds before he burst out laughing. 'Like Mister Holmes would do? Yes, just like that, I reckon.'

'Awright,' said Ben slowly. 'Like *we're* going to do. Look, we've done the legwork. We've interviewed those involved. Most of them, anyway. Why can't you share with us the notes *you've* got?'

Hopkins had a surprised look on his face. 'You must be mad.'

'Er . . . not *that* mad.'

Badger opened his hands. 'Look, Inspector. What have you got to lose?'

Hopkins glanced from one to the other, and sat back in his creaking chair, steepling his fingers. 'I tell you what, gents, I'll make a bargain with you. I'll share what information I have, you share yours with me; and, in a week, if you haven't come up with another criminal in the case, you let me know where Brent is. One week, mind.'

Ben let out a slow breath and made eye-contact with Badger. The latter imperceptibly nodded. Ben put out his hand to Hopkins. 'You got a deal.'

Hopkins shook on it. 'Very well.' He reached down to that bottom drawer and pulled out a file box, opened it, and laid out very few scraps of paper. 'This is all there is. And it all leads to Brent.'

A library table stood under the window, and Ben dragged the box and loose papers to it, laying them out. He and Badger bent over them, reading as quickly as they might under the wan light slanting in from the tall window and soot-smudged glass.

Ben pointed a finger at a line in some handwritten note. 'This is wrong. I got it from the maid. Let me sketch out where everyone was sitting.' He took out his notebook from an inside coat pocket and dabbed the point of his pencil against his tongue. He carefully drew a circle representing the table, and then four walls surrounding it, marking the window, the fireplace and the passage door. He wrote the names in each of their places and showed it to Hopkins.

'I'll have to ask who got this wrong in the first place,' Hopkins muttered. 'But here. Brent is still next to Quinn.'

'But it's awkward, innit?' said Badger. He mimed a backhanded stabbing. 'And he got him right in the heart. You've got to have practice at that.'

'But it can be done,' said Hopkins.

Badger conceded, his head bobbing. 'Well . . .'

'But look here,' said Ben, his finger on the drawing. 'Here's the window, opposite Quinn. Anyone could have thrown it.'

'Through a first-floor window? He'd have to be fifteen feet tall.'

Ben was not put off. 'He could have been on the ledge. I found dried mud on the sill.'

Hopkins squinted at him. The man seemed to use that expression when he was skeptical. Ben went on. 'I checked the window m'self.

The ledge on the outside was wide enough to stand on comfortably. The murderer could have come through the nursery window and stepped onto the séance room sill and thrown it from there. Then, he could get back through the nursery window, quick-like, and run away.'

Hopkins's fingers fiddled as they knitted together. Ben could tell that he wasn't best pleased to receive information he hadn't previously had. 'This is a bit distressing,' he said, confirming Ben's thoughts. 'If you're right, then—'

'Then Brent isn't guilty,' said Badger eagerly.

Hopkins calmed him with a hand. 'Let's slow down, shall we?'

'Right, Inspector,' said Ben, giving Badger the eye to stop talking. God only knew if it would work. 'I analyzed a sample of the dried mud and compared it with the soil in their garden. They didn't match.'

'Oi, Ben,' whispered Badger.

He ignored him and ploughed on. 'So, that means the person standing on the sill wasn't from the household.'

'Or it could just be a . . .' Hopkins paused, putting a finger to his mustache and smoothing it.

'Coincidence?' said Ben.

'You really analyzed it?' said Badger, a bit breathlessly.

'Yes, Tim. Apprenticed with a chemist, didn't I?'

Hopkins aimed a squint at Ben. 'You apprenticed with a chemist?'

'Yes. I do know a thing or two about chemistry. And I have texts and monographs from scientists, and even Mister Holmes himself, in order to draw my conclusions. As you will see, Inspector, we perform our due diligence.'

Hopkins slowly nodded. 'So I do see.'

'As Mister Holmes always said,' said Badger, 'we never guess. We deduct. Er . . . *deduce*!'

Hopkins rose and carefully walked around his desk. He strode to the window and looked down on the spread-out papers – far too few of them, in Ben's estimation – and scanned them. He raised his head to the window and stared out thoughtfully, unbuttoning his coat again and fitting his hands into the pockets in his waistcoat. 'Then tell me, lads. Who do you think did it?' He turned back to them. 'If you were to "deduce" it?'

Badger looked at Ben, and Ben gave him wide-eyed befuddlement.

'Well, Inspector,' said Badger, stepping in, 'we haven't worked that out yet. But we haven't yet talked to that medium, which might throw more light on it all.'

'Yes, the medium. We haven't been able to track her down.'

'Have you talked to the Gypsies . . . or even them Nomades, Travellers out at the edge of the city?'

'Can't find them when we need to.'

'That's because you're all dressed like rozzers. Me and Watson can find them.'

'Very well, gents. I suggest you do just that. And do me the courtesy of keeping me informed. You've got a week, remember.'

Ben tipped his hat and they both turned to go.

'And Badger . . .'

They both looked back at Hopkins when they were halfway out the door.

'Stop talking to reporters. That won't do your business any good either.'

Badger's face purpled. Ben gathered him up to hurry him out the door before he could blurt out anything else.

He realized too late he'd left the knife behind.


# THIRTEEN
## Badger


Tim felt his hot blood churning through his veins. He let his anger at Ellsie Littleton subside. Anger was not a useful tool. And, in the end, she and her pesky stories didn't amount to a fig in his estimation.

Instead, he turned his attention and his vigor to the larger picture. The game was afoot! Just like the old guv used to say.

'We'll find the Gypsies, eh?' he told Watson.

'I don't see no other way around it.'

Tim had seen their caravans on some empty land near Battersea. If they were still there, he and Ben had a long walk ahead of them.

As they made swift strides in that direction – down wide avenues and taking shortcuts through alleys and courtyards – they talked. Watson seemed apprehensive to meet with these Gypsies and Tim reassured him.

'I spent some time with Travellers m'self when I was a lad. They were right welcoming to me. I reckon it was because I had a deft hand as a pickpocket and could be useful to them. But I wasn't no Nomade. For one, I ain't Irish. And for another, I didn't fancy going from place to place like they liked to do. Sometimes they met up with Romany proper.'

'I thought they were one and the same.'

'Nah. The London Nomades – or Travellers as they will call themselves sometimes – got the idea from the Romany folk. Irish, mostly. Got themselves the same sort of caravans and the like, but they didn't speak no foreign tongue. They mostly don't like to mingle and, truth to tell, I thought some of them Romany folk were a bit frightening. They were dead serious and didn't like to fraternize with the likes of me. It was mutual, I can tell you.'

They neared Chelsea Bridge when Tim noticed that, while he had been talking away, Watson had fallen behind.

'Oi, Ben! What's amiss? Whatcha looking at?'

Watson had stopped dead and was looking up with a strange expression at a shopfront. It was a miscellany shop, full of this and that. Old things, broken things, second-hand things, with a dirty window and a sooty sign. Watson said nothing and hadn't moved an inch. With a sigh of frustration, Tim plodded back toward him. 'What are you doing?'

Watson lifted a hand and pointed to the weathered sign, paint peeling and white lettering chipped away.

'What?' Tim looked. 'What am I supposed to be seeing here, Ben?'

'Look at the name, ya daft sod. It says "Atic's Jumble and Curiosities."'

'So?'

Watson turned to him with an exasperated expression. 'Atic? A-T-I-C? Remember?'

'Oh.' Tim's arms fell loose to his sides as he, too, stared up at the sign. 'What do you suppose that means?'

'It means we'd best go in.'

'Do you truly think it has aught to do with us?'

'Don't know until we look around.' Watson led the way in. A little bell tinkled from above the door as he stepped through.

Tim followed Ben into the dusky interior. Wooden chairs were stacked to the ceiling; bureaus and chests of drawers were lined up and facing each other in regimented rows; picture frames – some with paintings and some empty – hung from the rafters; all manner of ceramicware – from vases to candle-holders to porcelain shepherdesses, all dusty – sat in rows on side tables; strange sculptures made of unknown materials stood by themselves, while a wooden figurehead from the front of a ship, with her chipped-painted face, looked out serenely past all the jumble. There was taxidermy of all sorts, too, from the occasional deer's head, to two angry pheasants squaring up to one another, to what appeared to be a badger in a tweed jacket and waistcoat complete with miniature watch fob, all displayed in smudged glass cabinets. The place smelled stale, like an unused room, and the light seemed to get dimmer the farther in they got.

'Do you suppose there's anyone here?' asked Tim in a hushed tone. The cramped space seemed to close in on him.

'Halloo!' cried Watson suddenly. Tim grabbed his arm and shushed him. Watson merely gave him a withering look.

'Gentlemen!'

They both startled into each other.

An old man, wearing an embroidered smoking cap with a faded tassel, shuffled into a portion of sunshine that had pierced the gloom. He wore a patched ankle-length smoking jacket with wide quilted cuffs, and tattered slippers on his feet. His grizzled gray mustache and muttonchops added to the appearance of a cotton-headed codger who had stumbled dazedly out of his own parlor to wander about.

'Gentlemen,' he said again, now peering and squinting at them with some enquiry in his faded blue eyes. 'How may I help you?'

Tim glanced mutely at Watson. He hadn't a clue what they were doing there.

Watson, on the other hand, seemed to fall easily into the inspector role. 'Good afternoon,' he said with a slight bow. 'Am I addressing Mister Atic?'

'Why, yes,' the old man sputtered. He rubbed his papery hands together and came closer, continuing to look them over. 'Randolph Atic, proprietor.' He bowed.

'Ah. Our pleasure, sir,' Watson went on in an agreeable manner.

'We were passing by and noticed your shop. What an . . . er . . . interesting collection.'

The man's eyes suddenly shone with light. 'Then you are a connoisseur of the unusual, too. There's quality here.' He ran his hand tenderly down a carved chair leg hanging just at head-height. 'Oh yes. A great deal of the artist's touch.'

'I can well see that,' said Watson, even as Tim wrinkled his nose at it. 'I wonder, Mister Atic, where it is you acquire such . . . er . . . bounty?'

It clicked suddenly in Tim's mind and he smiled at his clever friend. 'Yes, Mister Atic. Do you, by chance, get the goods for your shop from, say, estate sales?' He gave Watson a wink.

'Oh yes, from a variety of resources. Sometimes the owners contact me, asking if I wish to buy some of their gems, as it were. And sometimes I am made aware of the death in a family from a newspaper obituary and, realizing that debts must be paid, I offer to purchase some of their goods to help them to that end.'

'That's most charitable of you,' said Watson, hand to heart.

'Oh yes, I do consider it a service to the community.'

*While turning a profit or two for y'rself*, thought Tim.

Watson gave the man his sincerest smile. 'Do you recall, sir, if you recently acquired . . . erm, offered your charity to a man named Stephen Latimer? I believe he was in reduced circumstances and looking to repay some debt. He died a fortnight ago, so it could be his solicitor contacted you for the estate?'

'Latimer, Latimer.' Atic rubbed his chin and shuffled to a counter that Tim only just realized was there, under a mountain of rolled rugs, ancient pillows and stacked leather volumes. Moving behind the counter, the old man pushed some of the materials aside with a puff of dust and opened what looked to be a ledger. He ran his finger down the scrawled names penned between neat lines on a penciled graph, going back several weeks. 'No, I don't appear to have done any business with a man named Latimer.'

'Or Miles Smith, the solicitor? At this address?' Watson gave him Latimer's home address.

Again, the finger slid down the ledger and the man shook his head. 'No, sir. I did not. A pity. I hate to miss an opportunity.'

'Hmm,' said Watson, flicking a glance at Tim. 'Have you heard of a Horace Quinn of Bloomsbury?'

'Horace Quinn? No, gentlemen, I'm afraid that name awakens no memory. And I have a memory as solid as an iron safe.' He tapped his temple, and the gray hair protruding out from under the smoking cap.

Tim bit his lip and aimed an enquiring glance at Watson, who was looking back at him with an equal amount of confusion. 'Well then,' said Watson slowly. 'I think we've taken up too much of your time already. Thank you.'

He tapped Tim's arm to go.

'Wait, gentlemen. Is there nothing here that tickles your fancy? Perhaps a deer head? I don't know of any gentlemen who wouldn't like such a thing to grace their smoking room or library.'

Tim and Watson cast their eyes upward to the sorry-looking glass-eyed deer, appearing somewhat befuddled itself with its uneven ears and cock-eyed stare.

They both shook their heads at the same time. 'No, thank you, sir,' said Tim. 'I'm off me venison these days. Good day to you.'

The older man slumped in disappointment. 'Oh. Well. Good day to you, gentlemen.'

Tim led the way out and was rather glad to get outside to the fresh air again. 'I see why you wanted to ask him, Ben. But it was just a coincidence, wasn't it?'

Watson had that stubborn look about him that Tim had become used to.

'Forget it, Ben. We've got some Nomades to talk to.'

They reached the outskirts of Battersea by three o'clock, and hunted through the streets for open land. Three men had gathered around an iron brazier. Two old codgers hunched over it, hands in fingerless gloves and talking close to each other, trying to keep warm. One had an unlit and bent cigar hanging from his lips, with a ragged beard and a long dark coat, frayed at the hem. His companion wore a dented topper that he must have retrieved from a bin. His mustache was bushy and covered nearly his whole lower face and mouth. He was chewing something, probably tobacco, and telling his companion a joke. One of his sleeves was pinned up to his shoulder, empty of its arm. The third man looked up to his companions from time to time, chuckling at their conversation. He appeared to be an old sailor with a wooden leg, carving a piece of wood and tossing some of the scraps into the flames. He glanced up at Tim and Watson once as they passed, before turning back to his whittling and puffing on his pipe. His nose and cheeks were red, bespeaking many hours in a gin shop. His coat collar was positioned up to his ears, and his captain's hat was pushed back away from his forehead. A strange tattoo nearly covered the back of his carving hand.

Watson approached the group at Tim's urging. 'Pardon, gentlemen . . .'

The three of them looked up. Badger could see their eyes as they drew closer. The two companions had bloodshot eyes. They were still in their drink, he reckoned. The sailor, at least, seemed clear-eyed for the moment.

'Eh?' said the old seaman, loudly, as the near-deaf were wont to do.

'We was wondering,' said Watson, 'if you'd seen any Travellers or Gypsies hereabouts.'

The pipe rolled to the other side of his mouth, its smoke tumbling over the bowl. He glanced at his companions. 'What's it to you?'

'It's tuppence if you know, old-timer,' put in Tim.

The other two seemed to awaken at the idea of coins. The first one licked his lips, toothless behind them. The other scratched his head and swayed a bit from the exertion. But the clear-eyed seaman gestured with the knife while he kept his eyes on his work. 'Past the park. There's open land there. With their troublesome caravans.'

Tim stepped forward and offered the man tuppence with a touch of his hat brim. 'Much obliged.'

The gnarled fingers took the coins with nary a word, stuffed them into the peacoat pocket – much to the disappointment of the other two men – and he went back to his carving as if nothing had stopped him.

Tim worried for the seaman for only a moment. His companions were too much in their cups to pose a threat, and the seaman had a knife. He nodded for Watson to proceed onward.

Soon the streets opened out to the ruins of demolished buildings and some expanses of flat land grown over with weeds and grass. Typical caravans – wagons with a stepladder for a front stoop, arched roofs with chimney stacks protruding from the top – sat in a loose circle, no more than six of them. Shaggy horses browsed in the tall grass, wildflowers disappearing between their square teeth and whiskery muzzles.

Pit fires raised more smoke than glow, but metal kettles and pots sat on hobs beside them, along with men in ragged clothing and women with men's weathered hats with their brims stretched and flattened, heavy scarfs wound round their necks, with their layered skirts cinched by wide leather belts.

Some men stood a few yards away, engrossed in some sort of contest and cheering from time to time, exchanging money.

All of them seemed to have dirty faces. Funny that Tim would notice that nowadays, and – stranger still – with a bit of disdain. He shook the expression from his face, put on an amiable smile, and approached them with a friendly wave.

'Afternoon, all,' he said.

The men stopped their contest. The women near their cooking pots stood. The other men, by the fires, rose and bit down harder on their pipes and cheroots.

No one said a word.

Watson smiled too, though Tim could tell it had not reached his eyes.

Tim swallowed but tried not to show his nervousness. Maybe they didn't speak English. 'Salutations, good people. My name's Tim Badger. This here's my associate, Ben Watson. We're looking for a woman who does séances.'

Honesty was best, he reckoned, but it had yielded him nothing this time. He cleared his throat and started again, doffing his hat to the ladies. 'Pardon me, ladies. But do you or your female friends do a bit of séancing and fortune telling on the side?'

'Don't talk to our women,' said a burly man with an Irish accent, moving forward. So, Travellers after all, not Gypsies. His sleeves were rolled up his hairy forearms. He wore an open waistcoat revealing his braces, and a threadbare and dirty white shirt with no collar in sight. His misshapen hat was pulled low over a face tanned to leather like a sailor's. He sported a dark beard that had seen neither razor nor scissors in many a week.

'Beg pardon,' said Tim, still smiling and addressing himself to the man, and touching his hat brim politely for good measure. 'We're looking for—'

'I heard you. Clear off.'

Tim's gaze slid toward the men with their contest, took it in, and made a decision. 'Tell you what, lads. If me partner here can best your gents in whatever contest they're doing, will you answer our questions?'

Watson spun toward Tim with an almost imperceptible but urgent shake of his head.

All the men exchanged glances, spreading lips in feral smiles of yellowed teeth. 'Aye,' said the burly man. 'It seems only fair to put a copper or two toward it as well. Seeing that you're so sure of yourself.'

'Oh, of course.' He reached into his pocket for his purse, took out a few coins, and held them up.

The men laughed and opened their arms in welcoming gestures. Watson leaned toward Tim with a scowl. 'What the ruddy hell, Tim?' he rasped.

'Don't worry, Ben. I've got your back.'

'More like you've slid a knife into it.'

'Funny you should mention knives.'

Around the corner of a broken wall was a board set up against it. A chalked circle was scrawled on that . . . on which several throwing knives stuck fast.

Watson's breathing suddenly changed. Badger patted him on the back. 'Awright?'

Watson nodded his head in resignation. 'Awright,' he said quietly. 'You rogue.'

The Nomade men pulled all the throwing knives – very much like the one that killed Quinn and that nearly hit Tim – from the board, and stood about five generous paces from it. They toyed with their knives, rubbing their thumbs over the handles. Tim could see that the edges weren't sharp. It was the point alone that mattered on these blades.

'I go first,' said the burly man. Someone had etched a line in the dirt and he took a few steps behind it. He held the knife by its wooden handle, but instead of looking at the target etched in chalk on the wooden board, he stared at Watson, a feral smile on his face, teeth clenched on a matchstick. Abruptly, he took a wide step forward, whipped his head toward the target, and heaved the knife, arm extended. The knife seemed to simply disappear from his grip . . . and stuck fast within the chalked circle on the board.

He handed Watson one of the three left from his other hand.

Watson hefted it, studied the target, and glanced at the other men surrounding him. Tim looked too, and noticed that the whole camp had gathered. He wiped the perspiration from his upper lip. *I hope he don't miss.* In a whisper, he said, 'Keep an eye on it, Ben. You can do it.'

Watson gripped the handle, placing his fingers carefully. He stood near where the first thrower had positioned himself, took an additional step to the side, and licked his lips. He paused a moment to breathe . . . before he stepped forward and, with body extended – and the knife horizontal to the ground – he chucked the blade hard.

It stuck fast, closer to the center.

The men couldn't help themselves and cheered his expertise. But now the burly man scowled and grabbed one of the two knives left in his opposing hand and positioned himself.

He took an extra moment before he hurled the knife forth.

It bounced off the wood with a clang and fell to the ground. The men groaned.

Watson stepped into position again when the man handed him the last knife.

He sucked on his teeth, focused on the target, and took a step forward. He raised the knife to throw when a scream split the air.

Everyone turned.

Ellsie Littleton, her hat pulled askew from her suddenly unkempt hair, her bag this way, her notebook that way, struggled in the grip of several Nomade women, against an arm slung tight around her neck and growing tighter . . .

# FOURTEEN
## Badger

Tim leapt forward and skidded to a stop in a cloud of dust before the women. He grabbed the one who had the arm around Miss Littleton's neck – as her face was turning red then purple – and yanked till he had thrown the Nomade to the ground.

He felt hands on his shoulders pulling him back, and by God's grace ducked in time to escape the blow from the man's fist.

But not the kick to his shin by a woman.

He went down just as he spotted Watson leaping into the fray. Fists swung. Watson caught one on the jaw, but it never slowed him. Watson was a beefy fellow himself, and when *his* fists landed, there was no mistaking it. Men toppled before him, even as blood streamed from his own nose and covered his beard.

Tim rolled away from the woman who tried to bite him, and popped up from the ground, only to dodge another fist coming his way. He ducked under the man's arm, landed a punch to his gut, and moved on to the next.

But he knew he had to get back to Miss Littleton, for she was not taking herself out of the fray as any sensible person would have. Glancing over his shoulder, he saw she was in full combat with one of the women over her notebook, of all things. Her purse – not surprisingly – was already lost and stolen away.

Out of breath, Tim stood off to one side, bent over his knees to inhale sharply, and straightened again as he put two fingers to his lips and shrilled a long note as loud as a train whistle.

The struggling slowed and finally stopped.

'Oi!' he announced. 'All you men and women. Just put a stop to it. You women have got no call to attack Miss Littleton. True, she's a nosey parker and one hell of an annoying person, but that's no excuse for throwing a punch. And whoever's got it, give her back her purse. *With* all its contents. Or I'll call a copper. And believe me, I have no use for rozzers any more than you do, but I'll do it.'

There was some shuffling, some muttering, with even some curses that Tim could just make out, but a man did break off from the crowd and stomped over to one of the caravans. Inside they heard him arguing with a strident woman, before they all heard a slap and he came stomping back out with Ellsie Littleton's embroidered bag clutched in his hand. He shoved it at her and she gratefully took it.

'Right then,' said Tim. He measured Watson and his injuries, but the man waved him off, wiping his beard with his kerchief. 'Miss

Littleton can be on her way knowing full well now why she shouldn't follow us no more, and then we can get down to business.'

'I have no intention of being on my way!' the troublesome woman said with a huff. She vainly tried to push her hat back into place, but since her hair had come out of its pins, the crown of those auburn tresses kept sliding to the side.

'Dammit,' he rasped. The men seemed to grasp the fact that she and he knew one another, and there were low mutterings, laughter, and a few elbows being edged his way. He scowled and plodded toward her. He got in close . . . close enough to inhale a whiff of her rose perfume . . . and rasped in her ear, 'If you know what's good for you, you'll clear off now.'

'I have a story to write.'

'You were following us.'

'And like the grand detectives you make yourself out to be, you never noticed me.'

That certainly galled the most. What could he say to that? 'That was . . . an oversight. But now that you see how dangerous it is, I beg you to leave.'

'I utterly refuse. I must get my story.'

'You are the most damnable woman—'

'Tim,' said the gentle tones of his colleague over his shoulder. 'Don't bother with that. I'll wager she won't even dare to mention in her precious story how you just saved her life.'

'I had it well in hand!' she cried.

Tim drew back, arms folded tight over his chest. 'You need to leave. Now.'

She raised her pert but dirt-smudged nose. 'Make me.'

He had never hit a woman in his life and had no intention of doing so now. But it was awfully tempting.

Instead, he stepped away and deliberately turned his back on her. 'Gentlemen, we'll need to conduct our business over there' – and he pointed to a flat area, far from the caravans but littered with refuse, dented pots and broken furniture.

When Miss Littleton tried to follow, he cast over his shoulder, 'Ladies, I'm sure you can do your best to discourage Miss Littleton from following the men?'

The Nomade women offered toothy smiles, and glared at her fine dress, hair and askew hat. She made a move toward the men, but the women surrounded her, mindful not to touch, but Tim was certain that – as soon as he got a decent distance away – they'd move in on her and she'd learn her lesson at last.

He strode with the men toward the open field, but the burly man stopped them. 'Wait. You didn't win the contest. So why should we talk to you?'

Watson sighed long and hard. He searched on the ground for the discarded knife, found it sinking into the mud, and pulled it out, wiping the mud off it.

He looked back at the target and, without positioning himself or looking again, heaved it.

It hit the target dead center.

He clapped the mud from his hands and proceeded toward the field, with the Nomade men trailing submissively behind him.

Tim asked again if there was a woman in their midst who did fortune telling and séances.

The burly man, apparently leader of the rest of them, hitched up his trousers and scratched lazily at his neck. 'Why would you be wanting to know?'

'Look here, gents,' said Tim, taking out another calling card. And now he understood how useful they were. 'Me and Watson here are private detectives. And we're investigating a murder . . .'

'You're rozzers!' cried one of the men.

'No, we ain't!' Watson yelled over their shouted grumblings.

'Hold!' Tim shouted. 'We're not. But we do work *with* the police from time to time to help solve cases. We're trying to prove a man's innocence.'

They quieted, shuffled their feet, hands pushed sullenly in pockets.

'Well?' said Tim. '*Do* you or *don't* you?'

It wasn't the burly man who finally spoke up, but a wiry fellow with a head that looked far too heavy for his scrawny neck. 'Josie. Josie Williams. She's here.'

Tim moved toward the man, his hands on his hips. 'Well, then. Bring us to her.'

The scrawny fellow raised his eyes to the burly man, who shrugged. Having been given permission at last, he made his long, bow-legged strides back to where the women had begun to harass that stubborn reporter again.

He lifted his arm and pointed to a woman hanging back from the rest of the crowd. Her arms were clamped over her chest and her hair was like a bird's nest protruding out from beneath the misshapen brim of her man's felt hat. 'That's Josie Williams!' he said.

She took one look at the men staring at her . . . and bolted.

'For the love of . . .' Tim swore, and fled after her.

She was nimble over the piles of bricks, the discarded beams and broken walls of their temporary home on the vacant lands of Battersea. She didn't hesitate to jump from pile to pile, her filthy skirts billowing out around her like a bumbershoot, slowing her fall.

Tim was having a time of it just keeping her in his view. She disappeared behind walls and piles of debris, until he had lost her completely, seemingly into thin air. He skidded to a stop and searched about for her but, like a rabbit weaving and darting through the countryside, she was as slick as any creature in their own domain.

Watson puffed up beside him, wheezing to catch his breath. 'Did you lose her?'

'Damme. I surely did.'

'That was a useless exercise.'

'We'll catch up with her yet.'

'Yes, but not today.'

'You're right.' Tim swiped his hat from his head and slapped it with a grunt of frustration across his thigh.

'Come on,' said Watson. 'We've earned our keep back on Dean Street.'

Tim brightened at that prospect. A nice, warm place to think and sleep. And eat! Dinner would be waiting for them. *Who could have imagined it!*

Though, he couldn't help but feel he'd let Mister Holmes down.

Watson's reassuring presence and his strong grip covered his shoulder. 'We got her name and we'll talk to her yet. Let's go.'

Tim acceded to it and trudged back to the men. 'She's a slick one,' said Tim, red-faced and apologetic.

The men grumbled their agreement.

As they waved their farewells and picked their way over the muddy land, Tim heard the tramping of stumbling footfalls behind him. It could only mean one thing.

'Clear off, Littleton,' he groused.

'Who is Josie Williams? Why did you want to talk to her?'

He took a breath to yell some choice words back at her when Watson's hand was back on his shoulder.

'Miss Littleton,' said Watson politely, not turning to face her, 'we've had a busy day. We will leave you now and I trust there will be no more disparaging articles in the *Chronicle* this evening. You will remember that we could have left you to your fate, but that my colleague Tim here is of the chivalrous sort. Even though you would paint him the leacher you believe him to be, he saved you, no mistaking.' He stopped and turned to her. And they could both see that her left sleeve was torn at the seam and that there was a smudge of dirt on her cheek. 'If you wish to be the reporter you think yourself to be, then you should tread more carefully. Think beyond the single story and remember that not only can you help us in our course, but you will be helping your own. It isn't unlikely that we can help *you* in the future. Think on that.'

He turned on his heel, patted Tim on the arm, and trudged away with him over the mud and finally to the cobblestoned streets.

'I'm not gonna help her,' grumbled Tim.

'Oh, yes you will. Maybe sooner than you think. She has the potential to be a good ally, writing decent articles about you and me if we give her some scraps now and then. And who knows what we can get outta her?'

Tim flashed on an image of her creamy skin, her delectable lips. He shook his head free of it. Not her. Not in a hundred years.

They made it back to Dean Street and trod up the steps. When they entered their lodgings, the fire was laid, the room was warm, and it smelled clean and fresh. Tim sighed in contentment. He removed his hat and found they had a hat rack by the door, which they both made use of.

Tim flopped into a wing chair while Watson grabbed the letters left for them on the mantel and then eased into the other chair. They both rested their booted feet on the fireplace fenders, feeling the warmth on the soles of their shoes.

'Why don't you ring for the missus?' said Tim.

'Ring for her yourself,' he said, shuffling through the letters before choosing one to tear open.

Tim didn't have the strength to argue, and so dragged himself up from the comfortable position he had thought to stay in the rest of the night, and took up the bell from the mantel. He remained by the hearth until Mrs Kelly arrived. He noticed Watson got to his feet as well. Servants they may have now, but knowing they were not *their* betters, he and Watson both seemed to feel that they needed to be deferential in these foreign surroundings.

'Good evening, Mrs Kelly,' said Tim with an embarrassed smile. Would he ever get used to this?

'Good evening, gentlemen. Is it dinner you'd be wanting?'

'Oh yes, please.'

'I've got good, hearty soup to begin, some nice fish in a butter sauce, hot woodcock along with some potatoes and onions with watercress, and some boiled cabbage. A plum compote for afters, and then cheese to finish.'

Both Badger and Watson stilled, mouths sagging open.

'For . . . the *t-two* of us?' said Watson softly.

'Is it not enough?' she said, cocking her head.

'Oh no, no,' they both said in unison. 'That will be more than adequate,' Watson added.

She gave a satisfied nod. 'Murphy shall bring it in presently.' She gestured toward the small round table near the window, already set with silverware, plates, and different-sized glass goblets.

After they watched her leave, Tim got in close to Watson. 'Ben, what have we got ourselves into?'

'I don't know.'

With a snatched glance at the table, Tim rubbed his chin worriedly. 'Ben, there's more than one glass set at each place. What are we supposed to do?'

Watson bit his lip. 'The . . . the maid won't stay and watch us, will she?'

'I hope to goodness that she will not.'

'We can tell her to leave, eh?' Ben kept staring at the table. 'She's the maid, after all.'

'But what if she don't want to?'

Watson scrubbed his hands and then looked down at them. Tim looked too. They'd both been in a fight, and there was mud and blood under his fingernails.

'Tim, we gotta wash our hands. We can't sit there with them nice linens looking like this.'

In a panic, Tim ran to his room. He splashed water from the jug into the basin on the washstand and dunked in his hands. The water bloomed with brown from mud and God-knew-what-else. He tried the soap cake sitting on a dish, foamed it up in his hands, and scrubbed, getting all the dirt and mud from every crevice. He caught his reflection in the mirror stand beside the basin, and decided his face could use a wash-up too. When he was satisfied, he took the basin to the window and chucked out the dirty water, never noticing the cry of surprise from a man on the pavement below. He dried his wet hands and face on the towel hanging from the washstand and clumsily folded it to stuff it back where he'd got it.

Straightening his waistcoat and brushing his lapels, he returned to the main room just as Watson was doing the same. Ben looked up at him, stricken. 'Where should we wait?' he asked. 'Back by the fire, or . . .'

'Look, Ben, you've been an apprentice. And you must have eaten with your guv'nors. And they must have had servants. What did *they* do?'

'Well . . .' He bit his lip in thought. 'Sometimes they would be reading the evening papers by the fire and wait for dinner to be announced. And sometimes they'd sit themselves at the table and we'd wait there.'

'That ain't helpful!'

'Let's just . . . let's sit at the table as if it's what we do all the time, eh? Look. There's the paper. Let's each grab some of it and . . . you know. Look casual.'

'Look casual,' Tim muttered. 'Yes, casual.' He took some pages from the paper that Watson offered him and they both sat stiffly in their chairs, their faces in the paper. Tim couldn't read any of the words. He simply couldn't while he nervously waited.

He almost dropped it when Murphy came in unceremoniously. 'Good evening, gentlemen,' she said, carrying her big tray.

Watson rose and looked as if he would help her with it. But then he seemed to catch himself and slowly sank to his seat again, the newspaper discarded in a tent at his feet.

She set the tray down on a sideboard, removed the lid of the soup tureen and, with all dignity, walked it first to Watson and allowed him to ladle the steaming soup into the bowl set on the larger plate in front of him. She did the same for Tim and returned the tureen to the sideboard. She took up a decanter of wine and showed it to the two of them. 'Shall I pour the wine?'

Watson, still apparently distracted by the delicious aroma emanating from their bowls, said nothing. Tim, frightened he'd have to drink it while she watched, offered his hand graciously (even as it trembled). 'Murphy, you go ahead and pour, if it's fitting.'

'Very well.' She poured some of the golden contents into the smaller glasses at their places.

'Will there be anything else, gentlemen?'

'No, thank you, Murphy,' said Tim, more confidently than he felt. 'That will be all.'

Much to his relief, she turned – the little ribbons on her white cap flouncing behind her – and left.

They both sagged in their places.

'Blimey,' muttered Watson, before he picked up his spoon and dug into the soup.

Tim had to admit, the food was excellent, more than the two of them had consumed in quite some time. Each course seemed to have a different wine, but he kept longing for a pint of beer instead. Still, the wine tasted good, not like any wine he'd ever drunk before, certainly. He reckoned Mister Holmes instructed Mrs Kelly and Murphy to cook as if they were cooking for him and his own Watson. But it seemed an awful waste. All that wine for two men, and bottles snatched away before they even finished them. But as the dinner went on, he figured out that different wines were supposed to go with different foods. He didn't know what they were, but for some reason, fancier folk ate this way. *Give me a good ginger beer or bitter any day*, he mused.

Finally, they were poured a port with the cheese (some of which he politely refused because it had *mold* running all through it!) and they were alone at last.

Watson sat back in his chair and unbuttoned his waistcoat. 'Blimey. I never ate so much in me life!'

'Me neither. Do you suppose we're to do this every day?'

'I don't know. My old guv'nors ate a lot too, but nothing as fancy.'

'I reckon it's what Mister Holmes is used to.'

'You're right there. I suppose we'll have to muddle through, then.' Watson smiled and patted his stomach. He pulled a cheroot from his pocket, grabbed the table lamp, and lit it from the heat from the top of the glass chimney. Tim winced as the smoke billowed toward him. Watson, oblivious, took up the glass of port, studied it and sipped. His brows rose. 'This isn't bad.'

Tim took a sip. Sweet, with the taste of raisins. 'I like it too. But I'm thinking we should tell them women not to give us such fancy fare. I was hankering for a beer m'self.'

'Yes, you should tell them.'

Tim sputtered, taking his serviette and wiping down his waist-coat. 'Me? I thought *you* would.'

'Why should I? You brought it up.'

'Ah, Ben.'

'Awright, awright. Tomorrow. After breakfast.' He puffed on his cheroot for a few moments. 'So . . . are we any closer to exonerating Brent?'

Tim downed his port in its silly little glass and set it aside so he wouldn't break it. Strangely, even after all that wine, he didn't feel drunk. Must be the heavy food that soaked it up. 'I don't know, Ben. I still don't feel it was him. And that mud on the windowsill.'

'And the cold spot in the room.'

Tim squinted. 'What cold spot?'

'Didn't I tell you about that?' And then suddenly Watson looked embarrassed.

'No, you didn't.'

'Oh. Well. All that talk of ghosts . . . I didn't want to say. I mean . . . it wasn't ghosts.'

Tim edged forward. 'But what if it was?'

'Don't be daft. Course it wasn't.'

'Awright,' Tim said, sitting back again. 'We'll need to take a second look at that room. I've never been in it, after all.'

Watson yawned. 'Blimey, it's been a long day. I think I'll turn in.'

Tim yawned in turn. 'It was. Yes, turning in sounds good.'

They both rose and then stared at the detritus on their dining table, glanced at the hearth, and both silently wondered what they were supposed to do about it all.

'It's the maid's job,' blurted Watson, and then he seemed abashed.

'That's right. Wouldn't want to step on any toes, right? G'night, Ben.'

'G'night, Tim.'

They each retreated to their own rooms. Vaguely, as Tim readied for bed – brushing his teeth from a canister of tooth powder sitting on the washstand with his old bone toothbrush, then stripping off his clothes down to his chemise and drawers – he heard the soft sounds of Murphy cleaning up the main room, poking the fire, and the lights dimming from under his door as she snuffed out the lamps. So that answered *that* question.

He climbed into the bed – oh! The softest damned thing he'd ever laid down upon. White-painted cast-iron bed. Not fancy, but serviceable. But when he drew the quilted coverlet over him . . . the rapturous feeling of being wrapped in a cloud! He sank down, barely able to rise again to douse the lamp. He settled into the comforting warmth, praising the day that Mister Holmes first pulled him from the streets. 'And thank *you*, good Lord Almighty, for putting the notion into his head.' He closed his eyes, and with food in his belly, and a pleasant buzz of the wines and port making his lids drowsy, it wasn't long until he drifted to sleep.

He didn't know what roused him. But it was still dark. And after a disorienting moment when he had forgot where he was, he *felt* the movement rather than heard it.

His wilder instincts kicked in, and his arms shot out from under the warm comfort of the coverlet to grab the hands reaching for him. He gripped the wrists, one of which sported a knife, and twisted. The distinctly feminine sounds of a cry almost startled him enough to let her go, but his primitive instincts prevailed. The knife dropped and he leapt from the bed and tackled her to the floor.

He must have yelled, for it had brought Watson – dressed in a saggy union suit – running. Slamming open the door, he held a lamp aloft, the light casting down on the two of them scrabbling on the floor.

'Well, well, well,' said Watson, still making no move to help a frustrated Badger with the biting, scratching woman. 'Josie Williams. Again.'

# FIFTEEN
## Watson

'We owe you no courtesy,' said Ben. 'You were, after all, trying to kill my friend and colleague.'

Badger held a chair thrust into her, chair legs surrounding her torso and pinning her to the wall, like a lion tamer keeping her from attacking. She spat at their feet.

'Steady!' cried Badger. 'That's a decent rug, that.'

'Never mind,' hissed Ben. What the hell were they going to do with her? And it was the middle of the night. Best to ask the questions they had intended to ask yesterday, he reckoned.

'Josie Williams.' He looked her over. At first, back in Battersea, he had thought she was young. Her body was slim and shapely enough, but this close to her – and under the scrutiny of the lamp's light – he could well see the careworn creases at her eyes, the deep grooves on either side of her mouth, a bit of gray in her dark hair, the beginnings of a wrinkled neck. Her face was nut-brown like the rest of her Nomade brethren, though how much of that was sun and how much dirt was difficult to tell. 'Were you the medium at Horace Quinn's séance the night he was killed?'

'I don't know what you're talking about.' He had expected her to have some sort of Gypsy accent, but instead she sounded Irish. So, she was a Traveller pretending to be a Romany for the séance.

'We know it was you,' he lied, 'so you might as well make a clean breast of it.'

She raised her chin and glared defiantly, saying not a word.

Watson took another tack. 'Why were you trying to kill my friend?'

She turned her face away, lips tight together.

'I done nothin' to you,' said Badger, rather sullenly, Ben thought.

With hands at his hips, Ben stared at her a good long time before he leaned right into her. 'You sat directly in front of Horace Quinn at the séance. You were the only one to have a throwing knife just like you brung here to kill Badger with.' And he shook it at her as he made the accusation. 'So only *you* knew how to chuck it at him, and then you escaped by the window. The evidence is stacked against you. And if you don't confess, the police will haul in Thomas Brent for the murder, and hang an innocent man.'

She jerked her head toward him, wearing the most horrified expression he'd ever seen. Before he could make another remark, they all froze at the sound of urgent pounding on their door.

'This is the police! Open up!'

Ben's first thought was to make a run for it. But he had to pull that back. He'd never had the police after *him*. The holy hell of a noise they'd all made in the struggle must have alerted Mrs Kelly, and *she* had likely gone in search of a constable.

They all broke at once from their immobility. Ben grabbed an overcoat and threw it on over his union suit. Badger scrambled across his bed to wrap himself in the coverlet. But when he'd let the chair go that had been caging Josie Williams, she broke for the window, cast up the sash, and leapt out of it.

Ben ran to the window and looked out, afraid he'd find the broken body of the woman sprawled on the dark pavement, but she was a nimble thing, even at her age, and was nowhere to be seen.

He swore under his breath and marched to the main room and to the door, unlocked it, and cast it open. 'Gentlemen,' he said.

Detective Inspector Hopkins barged in first, looking like he'd just tumbled out of his own bed, with beard-shadowed cheeks and mussed hair under his bowler. Mrs Kelly, knowing Holmes as she did, must have called Hopkins herself. The constable who accompanied him looked smart, as the copper on the beat would, all silver buttons glinting in the lamplight, mustache curved down over his mouth, and custodian helm strap tight under his bottom lip.

Behind them was Mrs Kelly, holding her dressing gown closed tight at her neck, and a sleeping cap barely containing the rags tied round her curls. The woman's face was stark and wary but not frightened. Mister Holmes appeared to have chosen her well, for she had done what was required without hysterics, and he was entirely grateful for that.

Though Ben had strategically placed himself before Badger's bedroom, Hopkins rushed past him anyway, made a quick sweep, and returned to the main room with an exasperated expression. 'What goes on here, Watson? Badger?'

'Oh, just a little break-in,' said Badger casually. He had draped the coverlet over himself like some Roman emperor.

Hopkins took that in as well. He pushed his bowler up his fore-head. 'Your landlady said there had been a fight.' He glanced at Ben, no doubt noting the swelling to his nose from the earlier altercation with the Travellers.

'There had been,' said Ben, turning away from the oil lamp Mrs Kelly had brought into the room and the constable's lamp shining in his face. 'But the suspect got away.'

'Is this to do with your murder case?'

'It's all to do with it,' said Badger grandly, like he was in some music hall. He seemed to find it amusing, even though he was the one who had been threatened. Sometimes Watson just didn't know what was in his friend's empty head.

Hopkins wasn't amused. 'Well, isn't that just fine. Got me out of bed just to face you two in the middle of the blooming night.' He dragged his hat off his head and slapped it against his thigh.

'We had it well in hand,' said Ben apologetically to Mrs Kelly. But by her expression, he thought he had better add, 'And we thank you, Mrs Kelly, for such smart and quick action on your part.'

She made a curt nod. 'Mister Holmes advised me to keep an eagle eye on the two of you. Looks like it's needed.'

'And that you did. False alarm, Inspector.'

Hopkins waited, bleary eyes still steady on Ben. But with nothing more forthcoming from them, he gave up, popped his hat back on his disheveled hair, and blew a gust of air past his fluttering mustache.

'You've got six more days, chaps. Just six. And no more of your midnight shenanigans. Let's go, Constable,' he said wearily.

'Thanks for stopping by, Inspector!' said Badger brightly. Ben elbowed him hard and he doubled over. There was no need to antagonize the blighter. He was on their side. At least for the time being.

Mrs Kelly was the last to leave, and gave them a scathing and suspicious glare before taking her lamp and closing the door after her.

Ben listened at the door to their tromping down the stairs, and Mrs Kelly closing and locking her own door, before he turned on

Badger in the darkness. 'Why d'you have to treat the man that way? He's giving us a chance.'

'In the end he's just a copper like all the rest of them. Do you really think he's gonna give us a chance?'

'He said he would, and I believe him. Otherwise, he could have hauled *us* away for disturbing the peace. When are you gonna be a man, Badger?'

'Aw now, Ben. There's no call for that.' He yawned suddenly and elaborately. 'I was got out of me bed with the cold hand of death at me throat. Grant me a little consideration. My blood was up.'

Ben couldn't blame him, he supposed. It must have been a shock. Badger was just coming down from it. 'Awright. I reckon so. Did she get away?'

'Yes, right out the window.'

'Window . . .' Ben began to ponder and sat on the arm of the upholstered chair in the sitting room.

'Blimey, you're thinking again. I know that face. We have her for the murder, don't we?'

'Yes, we do . . .'

Badger threw back his head and trudged to stand before him. He trailed his coverlet like a regal train. 'I know that look, Ben. What? What the bloomin' hell is it now?'

'I've been thinking. She sat across from Quinn.'

'Right! The perfect place to throw a knife at him.'

'But that's just the thing. You see, you have to stand a decent distance from your target if you're throwing a knife. It has to tumble end over end to stick the target. It provides momentum. If the target is too close, the handle will hit first.'

'So she was lucky.'

'You don't walk into that kind of situation and hope for luck. You make damn sure you can do the deed, eh? Think about it.'

'I don't want to think about it. I want to go back to bed.'

Ben was adamant. 'But it don't make any sense. She couldn't have done it.'

'But . . . but what about the mud on the windowsill? That could have been her. You said the soil sample wasn't from the household.'

That stopped Ben and he stilled in thought. 'I . . . I don't know. And why would she *want* to kill him? We haven't established that.'

'She didn't like him. He sounded like a right bastard to me.'

'But why?'

Badger flopped into the chair and laid his head back against it. 'You're right. I'm not using the guv'nor's methods, am I?'

'"When you know why, then you know who". Isn't that what you said Mister Holmes always told you?'

Badger rubbed his face and nodded.

Ben went on. 'She had to have come to the Quinn household with murder in mind. So what's it to her? What did Quinn do that she became his judge and executioner?'

'Probably cheated her as well as he cheated everyone else in that household.'

'Could be. Looks like we've got to do some digging about this Josie Williams.'

'Can we do it in the morning?' he said with a yawn. 'I'm knackered.'

'Awright. Get to bed, you.'

Badger didn't reply as he trudged to his room. Ben remained in the sitting room for a long while, staring at the dying coals in the grate.

In the morning, Ben sagged in his chair from lack of sleep, even with the drapes pulled back to their widest position as a weak sun tried to brighten the main room. Badger, however, despite the life-threatening peril he had found himself in last night, was as chipper as a schoolboy. He dug into their breakfast of crispy bacon, scrambled eggs, kippers, toast and porridge.

Ben drank his coffee like a mechanical soldier, toyed with his toast, and spooned some porridge into his mouth. The porridge was unexpectedly good, with a bit of butter, sugar and . . . was that nutmeg?

He looked again at the letter that had arrived this morning from *The Daily Chronicle*, and tucked it away in his coat pocket.

'You look thoughtful, Ben,' said Badger.

Ben set down his cup and rubbed his eyes. 'Stayed up late to think.'

His companion seemed to sober at that pronouncement. 'Yes, I've been thinking too.'

'Have you? A wonder you could, while your jaw was flapping with all that food.'

'Can you blame me?' He gestured toward the sideboard. 'We'll be fat in no time.'

'I reckon.'

'Anyways,' said Badger, buttering a slice of crunchy toast, 'I been thinking about what you said. That this Josie Williams couldn't have thrown the knife that close to him. But if you will remember, when the lights went out, she was nowhere to be found. Could be she jumped up, stabbed old Quinn, and hopped it out the window. That would account for the mud on the sill.'

Ben cocked his head and crunched down on his crustless toast, savoring the taste of the bread and butter. The bacon suddenly smelled good to him. He rose from his place with plate in hand, opened the covered dish with the rashers and grasped several strips. While he stood there, he reasoned that he might as well get some eggs too, filled the plate high, and sat down again. He picked up a rasher with his fingers and chewed it down.

'There's something to that,' he said with mouth full. 'But I'd still like to know why.'

'That would make the case, wouldn't it?' agreed Badger. 'We've got to get her dead to rights.'

'But the other question is, should we tell Hopkins?'

Badger never paused to think or stop eating. 'No,' he said around a wad of food in his mouth. 'Definitely no. What if he comes up with some excuse that she didn't do it? And we know she did. He'd want to nab Brent and he'd make us tell him where he is.'

'I agree. No to Hopkins. For the moment at least.'

They ate in silence for a time until, with a last splash of coffee, Ben felt satisfied. He pulled the serviette from his collar, wiped his lips, and pushed away from the table. 'We've got to find Josie. But we also have to get back to the Quinn house so you can look at the séance room.'

'And blimey, Ben, we've got the reading of the will today as well.'

'Crikey, I almost forgot that. Right. You go to the house and give it a look round, and I'll find Josie. Meet you back at Quinn's at two o'clock sharp.'

With coats fastened and hats firmly on their heads, they each set off in different directions.

\*     \*     \*

Ben stuffed his hands in his pockets and kept the collar of his coat up around his ears as the spring rain pelted him. He watched with longing as carriages and hansoms clattered by him on the cobblestones. Ah well. Maybe someday if he and Badger could get a few more clients, they'd be able to afford such luxuries. But if he couldn't locate that minx Josie Williams, they'd be in a right state. How would they profit if their first high-profile client was hauled to gaol and hanged?

'Not well,' he muttered to the wind.

He thought of catching a 'bus but decided against it. He was close enough to the open lots of Battersea, and was relieved to see that the Travellers' caravans were still there. The piles of bricks remained in evidence, but now they were gleaming from the rain showers. A rusty crane with a long beam hanging from its rope, and swaying with the windy rain, hovered over the narrow passageway like the lintel to the gates of Hell. He wondered how safe it was passing under it, when a couple of rough-bearded men sauntered forward with truncheons in their hands.

'Morning, gents,' said Ben, as pleasantly as he could with the sudden appearance of a stone in his gut. He touched the brim of his hat for good measure. 'You remember me from yesterday, yes? The man what could throw a knife?'

They didn't seem inclined to retreat, but they weren't coming at him either. He took some small comfort from that.

'It's just that . . . well. Josie Williams paid us a visit last night with the intention of skewering my colleague. And we can't have that. Unfortunately, she got away before we could talk to her proper. Would either of you know where she's got to? Back to your camp maybe?'

They continued staring at him so long he began to wonder if they spoke the Queen's English. He shuffled his feet, looking down at his shoes. All that nice leather covered in mud. 'Look, lads . . .'

'We don't talk to no black devils,' said the one on his right.

Ben sighed. He looked heavenward for only a moment. 'Would it help to offer some brass?'

The men exchanged glances.

'But the question is,' Ben went on, almost to himself, 'would you answer after I gave it over? You see . . .' He began walking in a circle, eyes gauging how far away the caravans were. 'I've had this trouble before. Some jacks like yourselves tell me you don't trust me due to the triviality of my skin color. And then I offer to pay and you take my coins and then laugh in me face and *still* don't tell me, only you're richer with *my* coins in your pockets.' He shook his head at the tragedy of it. 'It ain't right. And so. I've learned not to pay out my hard-earned coin to no wastrel bogtrotters.'

That stopped their smirks and smiles. They raised their chins . . . and their clubs . . . and approached. 'What did you say?' said the one on the right.

'Now you see how hurtful it is,' said Ben, backing away. 'I wouldn't have said a thing, except that I really need to talk to her. And . . .' Swifter than they could spot, he reached into his inside coat pocket and drew his Webley Bull Dog with the checked walnut handle, cocked and aimed it, seemingly all in one smooth motion.

They stopped their approach and stilled.

'I apologize for the "bogtrotter" remark. I was looking to rouse you and I did. And I hope you'll apologize for the "black devil" comment as well when you get a moment.' He took aim in turn to each man's face. 'But as you can see, I mean business. I need to talk to Josie Williams and she needs to come with me now or I swear I'll swarm this place with rozzers.'

'She ain't here,' said the one on the right.

'I don't suppose you could drop your club on the ground? Good lad. And you, fella.' He aimed at the one on the left. He soon dropped his club. 'Is that right? Is she not in your camp? She murdered a man, you know.'

'We don't know nothin' about her,' said the one on the left in a light Irish brogue. 'She came to us 'bout three years ago. Came from a different Traveller camp, so she said. Does some fortune telling. Maybe a séance or two for the punters.'

'That's all very well, but I still need to talk to her.'

'Let Collin decide,' said the other.

'I'd love to. Which one is Collin?'

'Me,' said the burly man from yesterday, coming from around a broken wall. 'You two,' he said to the men, and thumbed behind him back to the caravans and the smoky fire. 'Get on.'

They looked at Ben and his revolver, glanced at their abandoned clubs, and made the right decision by leaving them where they lay and making a hasty retreat.

'Greetings, Collin,' said Ben with a smile. He uncocked the revolver and stuffed it back in his coat pocket. 'Won't need this, will I?'

'We'll see.'

Ben was careful to maintain his distance but be close enough to seem polite. 'Maybe you heard I was looking for Josie Williams. Again.'

'Heard tell she paid you a visit last night. Stupid woman.'

'Not too smart, no. She killed a man.'

He shrugged. 'I have no knowledge of that one way or the other. It's nothing to me. Nothing to them,' he said, jerking his head to where the two men retreated. 'We took her in and that's that.'

'But she tried to kill my partner, which says to me she killed that man in Bloomsbury. *During* the séance she was holding for him.'

He shrugged again. 'She does what she likes. We aren't responsible.'

'I get you.' Watson kept a sharp eye on the doings behind Collin. Like feet gathering behind the wagon. He shot a quick glance over his own shoulder, just to make certain no one was ambushing him back there . . . Damn. It surely looked like they were. Two men creeping around the haphazard piles of bricks. His eyes roved, quickly assessing.

'Well, Collin. It looks like you gents don't want to talk to me no more. I don't like going where I'm not wanted, so maybe I'll just take m'leave.' The Bull Dog was in his hand again, like a magician's trick. Collin raised his empty palms. But Ben had the feeling his throwing knives were stuffed down the waist of his trousers, within easy reach.

So there was Collin before him, two men behind, and more men gathering and waiting to pounce.

And just *one* Ben Watson with only five bullets. He didn't like the odds.

He straight-armed his gun, cocked it. Collin hesitated, crouching down. Ben smiled and suddenly jerked his arm high. He fired.

Collin ducked at what he expected was a bullet to his chest, and he laughed when he realized he was all right. He took a step forward and the men at the caravans came running. Ben took a step to the side so he could see the men coming from behind him.

And that's when the beam finally fell.

The bullet had pierced the rope but not severed it immediately. But with the weight of the beam, and the rope now a thread, it couldn't hold it any longer. Down it came. Collin barely got out of the way, but some of his men weren't as lucky.

The Travellers behind Ben stopped dead at the shocking carnage, and he took advantage of that by bolting to the side. By the time they collected themselves, he was already on the main street, and running hard. He looked back only a few times as he ducked down alleys, courtyards, and all manner of shortcuts, until he was convinced no one was following him.

# SIXTEEN
## Badger

Tim glanced at the funeral coach beside the curb, its black horses still as death, seemingly conscious of their solemn duty. The black-draped glass sides of the coach showed it was currently empty and the coachmen were nowhere to be seen. He supposed they were in there now, boxing Quinn up in his coffin and preparing to transport him to his funeral.

*The funeral!* he thought. One of them should probably attend the funeral to see who came. And of course, that would be him.

Tim swallowed. Death, in all its forms, was an uncomfortable business. He knew he read too much penny-fiction as it was, but the ones he liked the best always seemed to be a tale of horror around corpses and graveyards.

The real thing, however, gave him the willies.

He straightened his waistcoat, stepped up to the shiny black door with its black funeral wreath, and rang the bell. Mrs Martin answered, recognized him, and frowned. 'Mister Badger,' she said stiffly.

'Ah, Mrs Martin. A good morn to you. If you don't mind, I need to see the room where poor Mister Quinn was killed. I won't be a bother.'

'It is a bother, Mister Badger. It is inconvenient when police assistants come clamoring about when there are already men in the house at their unpleasant business.' She had no need to nod to the funeral coach directly behind him.

He realized that he hadn't doffed his hat, and so he took it off now and pressed it to his chest. 'I can appreciate that, Mrs Martin. But I shall be quiet as a mouse, in no need of tea or any other fuss. I know you've a funeral today.'

'Yes.' She took a moment to show on her face and posture her disdain for the entire affair before she stepped aside to let him through.

He nodded to her, put his hat back on, and hurried inside to the stairs, but paused at the foot of them with his hand on the newel post. The undertakers were carrying the coffin through the parlor doorway. He doffed his hat again and pressed it to his chest.

The funeral men were all long-faced in their black finery, toppers shiny and wrapped with large black bows. They didn't change their glance from their forward progression to even flick a lash at him, but instead marched in slow solemnity across the foyer to the front door, which Mrs Martin had left open. She watched with detachment as her employer made his final passage over his own threshold.

Tim hurried up the stairs, shivering at the sight of the coffin. He was able to leave its image behind as he poked his head into the upstairs rooms one at a time.

Watson had said there was a strange feeling in the room, something that gave him a shiver . . . and he was right. As Tim passed over the threshold, he felt that shiver rise up the back of his neck. 'Blimey,' he whispered, looking around. Could it be the presence of an unholy ghost?

'It's them stories I read,' he muttered. But Watson had felt it, too, so he had said. And Watson was as logical and scientific a fellow as he had ever met, beside Mister Holmes himself.

'Then take this logically, like Mister Holmes would,' he admonished.

He looked at the round table in the center of the room and pictured in his mind how the people in the room had been situated. The medium – Josie Williams – had her back to the window; Brent, to her right, in front of the fireplace. Quinn sitting opposite Josie, his back to the door. Mrs Martin next to Quinn on his right, and Jenny Wilson, the maid, to the right of Martin and to the left of Josie Williams.

He moved around the table and sat at the chair Josie would have sat in and looked at the chair that Mister Quinn had died in. And dammit. Watson was right. It was far too close. He had just assumed that throwing a knife was a straightforward affair. But it never would have stuck him at this short distance if it had to spin end over end. Then how? How had she done it? He looked behind him at the window. Even if she had stood in the window, it wouldn't have been enough distance, because the window was only another mere foot away.

Could she have rushed him in the dark? How could she be sure to get Quinn and not someone else?

He ran his hand along the table and couldn't help but look at the lamp hanging above it, with its amber crystals hanging down, its shade now dark.

Someone was coming up the stairs and he stood on alert . . . but it was only Watson and he was grateful to see him. But wait.

'Weren't you supposed to be apprehending Josie Williams?'

'The men at the Traveller camp had other ideas.'

'Oh. Not as cooperative as the day before, eh?'

'Not at all. It was a good thing I had my revolver with me.'

'Gor, Ben. Truly?'

'Yes.' He wiped his hand across his forehead. 'It was a slim thing for a time.'

'I'm glad you're awright.'

Watson strode to the window and looked out of it. 'I see Quinn is on his way.'

'I saw them carrying the coffin.' He shivered. 'Look here, Ben. I got that shivery thing you felt in this room too. Have you got a cheroot with you?'

'What? Why? You hate them.'

'It's just that I got an idea, is all. Light up that foul thing.'

Watson narrowed his eyes at him before he withdrew a cheroot from his inside coat pocket. He lit the thin cigar and Tim stepped back, trying not to inhale the smoke unfurling around it. Tim strode to the hearth and made sure the flue was closed. He went around to the window and made certain it was shut. Then he closed the door to the room.

'Now, keep smoking and puffing,' he said, 'and walk all around the walls of the room. Close to them. Blow the smoke at them.'

Watson's eyes changed from annoyance to a gleam as he figured out what Tim was at. He took slow, measured strides against the walls, inhaled deeply, and blew the smoke at the plate rails, the wallpaper, the moldings, until he got around the room to the side opposite the fireplace . . . and stopped.

They both saw it. Tim crept closer just to watch. The smoke seemed to suck through a wallpaper seam. Watson deliberately blew smoke at it again, and once more the seam, like some strange magic trick, sucked the smoke inside itself.

Blowing more smoke, a horizontal seam above the vertical one also sucked in smoke, and, following the path of the fumes, it made a perfect rectangle.

Tim pushed on it. When it made a soft click and popped open, a whispered, 'Blimey,' passed his lips. He barely believed it would prove to be true. Warily, he walked through the secret doorway to the next room . . . which had been the nursery.

The cheroot hung flaccidly from Watson's lips as he gawped. 'I missed that entirely.'

'There's always a logical explanation, ain't there?' And now he honestly believed it to be true.

'Not a ghost, then.' Watson looked relieved.

'So this is the passage between the nursery and the nanny's room. Makes sense.'

'Does it? What's this?' Watson knelt and ran his hand up the side of the jamb. 'Look at this, Tim.'

Tim knelt beside him and looked where Watson pointed. The wallpaper had torn at the edge, but it wasn't an old tear. It was recent. The wallpaper paste had yellowed at the other edges, but not this tear. It was whiter.

Badger rose again. 'I think we need to ask if Mrs Martin or Jenny Wilson knew of this passage.'

'Surely they did.'

'Not if there was no Mrs Quinn or baby about.'

'Right.' Watson stood and looked about the room. He approached the hearth and carefully tamped the end of the cheroot on the stone, putting it out before stuffing it back into his coat pocket.

'We'd best go to it now,' said Tim.

They went together down the steps, found the bell rope in the now empty parlor, and pulled it. Tim wanted to go directly to the kitchen but Watson shook his head, saying with that gesture that it wasn't proper for them to do so. Tim thought about Mister Holmes and supposed that was probably true. Servants came to *them*, didn't they? It was going to be difficult remembering that.

When Mrs Martin entered the room, she looked none too pleased at being summoned. She grasped her hands together in front of her so tightly that the fingers whitened.

'Can you get Jenny Wilson, too, Mrs Martin?' said Tim.

She pruned her mouth, yanked on the bell rope again, and waited. It wasn't long till Jenny Wilson came up the back stairs looking perplexed.

'We have a question to ask the two of you,' said Tim. 'Were either of you aware of the hidden door between the nursery and the nanny's room?'

For a moment Martin lost her stiff expression, and her eyes widened. 'A hidden door?'

Jenny Wilson gasped. 'I ain't never heard of such a thing. Have you, Mrs Martin?'

The housekeeper had composed herself again. 'I have not.'

'So it's unlikely either of you used that passage lately,' said Watson.

Martin bristled. 'Extremely unlikely, since neither of us were aware of its existence.'

'That's funny, innit?' said Tim, casually. 'You working here all these years and not aware—'

'As I have told Mister Watson before, I started working in this household a month after Mrs Quinn had died. No one has occupied the nursery, nor the nanny's quarters, in all that time since. And the housemaid has been instructed not to clear these two unused rooms but for a quick dusting every fortnight. There is no point in the wasted effort.'

Watson grabbed his lapels in thought. 'Was it Mister Quinn who suggested the séance be in one of these unused rooms?'

'Yes, it was.'

He nodded. 'Well then,' said Watson. Tim nudged him. 'What?'

'I'm thinking it would be proper of us to go to the funeral,' he whispered.

Watson faced the women again. 'Er . . . might you know which graveyard they've taken Mister Quinn to?'

'Paddington Cemetery,' she said.

'Blimey,' said Tim. 'That's Kilburn, innit?'

Watson nodded, thanked the housekeeper and maid, and led the way out the door.

Tim stood on the pavement before the closed door and looked up at the building. 'A hidden passage recently used,' he mulled. 'What does that mean?'

'It means someone used it.'

'Oh, well spotted, Ben. Any other obvious things you'd like to point out?'

'Eh? Sorry, I was thinking.' He, too, looked back up at the walls of the Quinn residence. 'I'm afraid what it might mean is someone else got into the room and killed Quinn.'

'I was afraid you'd say that.'

'It's scientific, Tim. Having a theory is one thing. But if new evidence comes along, you have to form a new theory.'

'Or . . .' he said hopefully, '. . . it's just a false lead?'

Watson gave him that familiar stare that said he meant business.

'Awright.' He looked at his pocket watch. 'How are we gonna get to Kilburn in time for this bloomin' funeral?'

'We're going to have to spend some of Mister Holmes's cash and get a cab.'

Tim sobered. 'I've never been in a cab.'

'I have. A few times for the chemist I worked for when a delivery was important. We'll have to hail one and take it back here to get to the reading of the will.'

'Blimey,' breathed Tim.

Watson stepped off the end of the curb and began waving his arm. The hansom cabs clattered on past him.

'Maybe you're aren't doing it right,' said Tim.

But Watson's face was shrouded in fury. 'Maybe my skin ain't doing it right.'

'What?'

'Tim . . .' He seemed to swallow what he was going to say, took a breath, and patted Tim's shoulder instead. 'I think maybe you'd better hail it.'

'What? Why?'

Watson shoved him to the curb. 'Just do it, Tim.'

Tim shook his head at the vagaries of his partner's directives and stuck out his arm, adding a piercing whistle to the proceedings. The next hansom cab pulled up.

'Where to, guv?'

'Paddington Cemetery,' said Watson, shouldering his way in first.

Tim gave the driver a smile. 'What the man said,' and climbed in.

With traffic as it was, it took them a good three-quarters of an hour to arrive, and it had already begun. They told the cabby to wait and hurried to the chapel.

Tim blinked at the nearly empty interior. He could understand the housekeeper and the maid staying behind. Who would pay for their cab? And further, they had to prepare refreshments for the reading of the will. Servants were always busy with something, he reckoned.

They found a seat in the back, and Tim was trying to remember the last time he'd set foot in a church. It had been longer than a year. Maybe longer than two. And it had probably been a funeral, too, come to think of it. A chap he knew from the old parish. Got himself knifed in the gut trying to rob someone. The people he knew . . .

He glanced at Watson, the most dignified friend he'd ever had. Loyal. Honest. He'd never rob anyone. Watson was definitely a better class of person than those fellows he grew up with in Shadwell. He had no doubt in his mind, from the moment he met him, how they'd work together. And hadn't it all proved true? Eventually. There was no call for those cabbies to turn their nose up at him because of his skin color, for it hadn't taken him long to figure out why Ben had been cross. That made no sense. He looked as proper as Tim did in his new clothes.

Tim counted no more than a handful of men in the chapel. Businessmen perhaps? But then he heard a step at the door.

He elbowed Watson and when *he* looked, a scowl bloomed on his face.

Ellsie bloomin' Littleton.

# SEVENTEEN
## Watson

She had the audacity to sit next to Badger, even shoving him over to make room for her in the pew. She gave him a smile and a polite nod before looking straight ahead.

Ben sighed. He could feel Badger tense beside him. Could she have followed them? No. More likely, she'd found out about the funeral. It was probably published in her newspaper. She'd simply made her way here.

Ben barely heard the vicar as he droned on. His thoughts were on the hidden door and who could have gone through it and why. Josie Williams might have been a neat package all tied up with string, but it seemed to be untangling fast. She couldn't have killed Quinn by throwing a knife. She wasn't the one on the sill. Someone else came through that hidden door . . . He kept spinning it through his mind until he noticed everyone rising.

Six men came forward – half of those in attendance – and carried the coffin from the chapel toward the cemetery.

Once it passed them, Littleton hurried to follow it, but Badger grabbed her arm. 'Just where do you think you're going? And, by the way, I'm not talking to you. Not after that rot you wrote.'

'Unhand me, sir.'

He released her and pushed past her. Ben soon followed, but there she was, walking right behind them outside on the footpath, when she suddenly asked, 'Who is Josie Williams?'

Badger jerked to a halt and Ben nearly ran into him.

Badger twisted around and shook a finger in her face. 'Stop following us. And I am not talking to you.'

'Don't be absurd. You're talking to me right now.'

'I am *not* talking to you.'

Ben pushed Badger along and got in between them. 'I think he really means it,' he said to her.

'Then what about you? Benjamin Watson, isn't it? You've had quite the colorful career.'

Now it was Ben's turn to stop. 'Tim, you go on ahead. I'm going to have a word with Miss Littleton.'

'She'll twist everything you say, Ben.'

'I know. Go on.' He urged him forward.

Badger kept looking back with a scowl until he rounded a clump of beeches and disappeared with the funeral party.

Watson squared up to her. 'You've got no call to write about me. Not my past, my current work, or anything I do in the future. You're poison, is what you are. You're dangerous. And your reporting is irresponsible. Someone could get hurt just because you want a story. If you can't write a civil word, we're done with you.' He gave her a final nod and turned on his heel. Her look of shock was quite satisfying, he had to admit.

He walked quickly to catch up with Badger, who was still stiff with anger. Ben leaned into his friend and said out of the side of his mouth, 'Don't worry about her.'

But Badger glanced over his shoulder and must have spotted her. Ben couldn't help himself and turned to look as well. She was there, hiding in the shade of a stand of trees.

The vicar continued on, sprinkling the grave with holy water, reading some passages of scripture, and finally nodded for the gravediggers to lower the coffin into the ground.

The scant gathering soon dispersed. No one lingered to talk with any other. Ben scoured each face, their dress, their personalities, and wondered if he should ask who they were but also feeling it was inappropriate, given the circumstances. He wondered how Holmes would handle such a situation.

When they had all gone, Ben tapped Badger on the arm and they both soon trudged back to the gate . . . where Ellsie Littleton was waiting for them.

'Look, gentlemen. I apologize for anything I've written. Mister Badger, I thought you had disclosed a very touching portrait of your childhood. I wanted my readers to understand you, and possibly forgive your criminal enterprises.'

He turned to Ben, fuming. 'Did she just say "criminal enterprises"?'

Ben held him back. 'Don't blow up, Tim.'

'You've got a blooming nerve!' he yelled around him.

'There's no need for foul language, Mister Badger.'

'Oh? You want to hear some foul language?'

'Tim!'

Badger pressed his lips tightly together. *Not talking to you*, he seemed to be saying with his mouth shut up tight and an index finger in the air.

'Mister Badger, I am truly sorry if I misinterpreted your statements. I'd like to make it up to you. Let me help you. Won't you tell me who Josie Williams is and why she is important to the murder? My articles could exonerate Thomas Brent.'

Ben shouldered Badger behind him. 'I'll handle this, Tim. Miss Littleton, you misrepresented my colleague here. My solicitor said as much to your editor.'

'Ben,' said Badger, grabbing his arm. 'You wrote to her editor?'

'Our *solicitor* did,' he explained, winking where she couldn't see. It was a letter written on a solicitor's *letterhead*, after all, a few sheets of letterhead he had nicked some years ago and placed in his files. And a good thing, too. 'As a matter of fact, we received quite a lengthy apology from your editor today, Miss Littleton.' He patted the letter in his inside coat pocket. 'And he promised to print a retraction.'

She bristled. 'Yes, my editor has already spoken to me on this point. And . . . well. I am here primarily to formally apologize to you, Mister Badger.'

Badger put a hand to his ear expectantly. 'Funny. I don't hear nothin'. Nothin' that says "I'm sorry, Tim, for treating you like a street rogue."'

She screwed up her rosy lips. Now that he was standing close to her, Ben could well see for himself what Badger had been so attracted to. But a woman was only as attractive as her character, he decided. His thoughts drifted unbidden to their maid, Katie Murphy . . .

'I apologize, Mister Badger. And to you as well, Mister Watson. And Mister Badger, I do understand that you spoke to me of personal things, and that . . . well . . . I might have construed them differently. That perhaps I *might* have an imperfect vision where criminals are concerned, seeing them at every turn . . . where they are not.'

It seemed to Ben that she was parroting what her editor might have said to her. *Good*, he thought. Hopefully, it would finally sink home.

She sagged under her cloak, looking down at her muddy boots. 'So I am sorry. Sincerely.' When she looked up again, she seemed to use her lashes and her large eyes to their full intensity, staring at Badger.

Ben rolled his eyes. Did she really think that would work? But when he glanced at his friend, he saw that he *had* softened. *Crikey!*

'Well . . . right,' said Badger. 'Just so you know. We're doing our best as honest citizens, righting the wrongs on these seamy and dangerous streets of London.'

*Straight out of a penny dreadful.* Ben sighed.

'I worked for Mister Sherlock Holmes in my youth and learned his methods,' Badger went on. 'And Watson here has a bit of learning in the sciences. We . . . complement each other. That's how we do it.'

Her face seemed to glow with the beautiful radiance of satisfaction. *Oh, Tim. You're hooked good and proper, aren't you. And she bally well knows it.*

Badger was gazing at her with a very familiar soppy look as he sidled closer. 'And like I said. If you're fair to us, I see no reason why we can't share our cases with you. But only *after* we've solved them. And there's no use in asking who this person or that person is because you'll compromise our case if you go and print it. So just take your little notebook away with you until we're done. I'll send you a note when it's all wrapped up in string.'

'But can't we—'

Ben cut her off by raising his pocket watch. 'We have to be off, Tim. Remember?'

'Oh, yes.' He touched the brim of his hat. 'Good day, Miss Littleton. Be good.'

'But Mister Badger . . . why don't you meet me tonight for the music hall? And then a late-night supper? I'd truly like to make it up to you.'

'*Tim*,' warned Ben out of the side of his mouth.

'It would be a pleasure, Miss Littleton. Only I'll be taking *you*. How would it look, me receiving enticements from a reporter?'

She wore the face of a demure, blinking up at him through her lashes again. 'Of course, Mister Badger. Then shall we meet at the Canterbury Theatre on Westminster Bridge Road?'

He tipped his hat to her. 'Shall we say quarter past seven?'

'I'll be there.'

'Till then, Miss Littleton.'

Ben all but shoved Badger toward the curb, where the cabby – remarkably – had waited.

Once in the cab and on their way back to Bloomsbury, Ben smacked him on the shoulder. Badger had been looking much too pleased with himself.

'Oi! Whatcha do that for?'

'Are you a simpleton or what? She's playing you false, Tim.'

'Or am *I* playing *her*?' he said with a wink.

Ben had no need to answer when he gave Badger the *look*. His colleague squirmed.

'Look, Ben . . .'

'No, *you* look. You're much too quick to forgive her, just because she has a pretty face. I've warned you about her. About talking to her, and now you're going to see her.'

'I'm not *seeing* her. We're catching a music hall and having a bite to eat.'

'And she was willing to pay. What does that tell you?'

'That she don't want me to slip away? Aw, come on, Ben. I'll not let her dupe me again.'

Ben put his hands up. 'I surrender. I've tried. God knows, I've tried.'

'Honestly, Ben. She's a bit of awright. You said so yourself.'

'That don't make her trustworthy.'

Badger propped himself in the corner of the cab, not as sullenly as he might have done. It looked to Ben as if he were thinking for once. *Imagine that!* he mused. It was confirmed, when Badger piped up with, 'So what did you make of that lot at the funeral?'

Ben relaxed. When they were down to business and not arguing (over a woman as usual), they were both in their element. 'Just looking at their clothes. I gauged them to be in a similar class, possibly neighbors, though more likely business associates.'

'I noticed a few of them had rough edges to the cuffs of their sleeves. A shine to their trouser knees.'

'Very good, Tim. Yes, like they were in similar straits as poor dead Latimer.'

'I wondered about that. Were all Quinn's acquaintances badly done? But if *he'd* done them, they wouldn't have shown up to his funeral, except to spit on his grave.'

'And none of them did.'

'Conclusion: all of a similar class. No one stood out to me. And thinking about it, I don't believe they knew each other.'

Ben scrubbed at his bearded chin. 'You're right. None of them spoke to each other, greeted one another, even after it was done. They all moved their separate ways.'

'Business, for certain, then. I wonder if we'll see any of them at the reading.'

'What a sad thing. To go to the Great Beyond and no one really caring.' Ben shivered. 'I don't want to go out like that.'

'Don't worry, mate. I'll make sure I'm crying nice and loud at your funeral.'

'What makes you think I'm going first? I'll wager it will be you. And all them women weeping and wailing, except for the one that done *you* in.'

Badger smiled. 'Aw, you paint a nice picture there.'

It was almost two by the time they pulled up to Quinn's Bloomsbury residence. They gave the cabby extra for waiting for them at the cemetery, and they climbed up to the wide porch together.

Mrs Martin was there to let them in, narrowing her eyes just that much at them. They were led to the parlor, where all trace of Quinn's laying out and the dead flowers had been removed. Tea things were set out on a sideboard, with a tiered plate of cakes. The chairs were arranged to face the solitary desk, and Mister Smith, the solicitor, was already seated, pulling papers from his satchel and laying an envelope on top of what looked like deeds and stock certificates.

Smith recognized the two of them and gave them a solemn nod.

Jenny Wilson hovered in the doorway, and Mrs Martin stood at the parlor entrance. Badger looked at his watch and compared it to the clock on the mantel, which suddenly struck two with a soft chime.

Mrs Martin came into the room and sat in one of the chairs and, after a moment of hesitation, so did Jenny Wilson.

No one else had entered the house.

Smith cleared his throat, gave a last look at the clock showing a minute past two, and took in the few in the room. 'Am I given to understand that Thomas Brent will not be in attendance?'

Badger put a hand up and nodded solemnly.

Smith cleared his throat. 'Then let us begin the reading of the will.' He tore open the envelope, tipped out the folded pages, and spread them before him. He retrieved a pair of gold wire-rimmed spectacles from his waistcoat pocket and placed them carefully on the bridge of his nose, winding the curved earpieces around his ears. He cleared his throat again and read,

'*I, Horace Lionel Quinn, being of sound mind and body, do hereby declare this to be my last will and testament.*

'*I give and bequeath the following:*

'*To Mrs Amelia Martin, I leave the sum of £50 for her faithful service.*'

She made a sniff at that. Ben watched her face. Yes, the annuity Quinn had promised her and then revoked was likely far more than that paltry amount for twenty years' service.

The solicitor went on. '*To Mister Thomas Brent, I leave the sum of £40 for his service as my valet and footman.*'

Smith lowered the paper for a moment and removed his glasses as he addressed the room. 'Of course, if it is determined that Thomas Brent was guilty of the murder of Horace Quinn' – and here the maid Jenny Wilson squeaked – 'then Thomas Brent will not by law be allowed to benefit from any payment from the deceased's will. But . . . be that as it may.' He placed his glasses with care back over his ears and nose.

'*To Miss Jenny Wilson, maid, I leave the sum of £15.*'

Jenny Wilson sniffed but, unlike the housekeeper, it was with a muffled sob.

'*And finally, the bulk of my estate – the house on Gower Street, Bloomsbury, in the parish of St Giles-in-the-Fields, London, all stocks remaining, the furniture in the Bloomsbury house, and papers therein or under the care of my solicitor – to be bequeathed . . . to my son and heir, wherever he may be found. I live in the hope of Christ that he will be alive to recover it. I hereby require of my executor, Miles Smith, Esq., to discover his whereabouts.*'

No one spoke. No one moved . . . except for Smith, shuffling the papers together, folding the will again and laying it atop the deeds and stocks. 'So, as you can see,' he said to the assembled, 'there is – somewhere – a son and heir.'

'But . . . but . . .' said Badger, gesturing to Ben and himself, '. . . Mister Smith, we was given to understand that some twenty or so years ago a child was born to Mister Quinn, but . . . it died soon after the mother in childbirth.'

Smith pulled off his glasses and pinched his fingers into his eyes. 'Yes, Mister Badger. Everyone was given to understand that. And I believe I may be the only one left alive who still knows the *real* story . . .'

# EIGHTEEN
## Badger

Mister Smith settled in and passed his gaze over the house-keeper sitting stiffly and the maid with a handkerchief pressed to her face. Tim glanced at them, too. But they had joined the household *after* Mrs Quinn had already died. Mrs Martin had told him that the baby had died or, at least, this was what *she* was told.

Smith made another nervous glance at the housekeeper and maid when Tim stood. 'Mister Smith, might this most delicate of tales be conveyed to the men alone? After all, Mrs Martin and Miss Jenny have no need to hear this. And, perhaps, you might wish to hire us to find the, er, client?'

'Quite right,' said Smith, relieved at the decision.

Mrs Martin stood, looking upset for the first time since Tim had met her, and made for the other door, collecting the maid at her elbow and pushing her along as they exited out of the servants' door.

Tim and Watson took seats closer to Smith. 'It was why I wanted you gentlemen to come to the reading. It is a very disturbing portrait of a family.'

'Go on,' said Watson, sitting on the edge of his chair.

'Well,' said Smith. 'Mister Quinn was . . . a man of passions. He . . . well. He was not a faithful man to his wife. When he was a much

younger man, about twenty years ago, he . . .' Smith shook his head
in distaste. 'Some men are no gentlemen, it is sad to say. He had an
affair with his housekeeper, Mary Brennan. She fell pregnant. He told
me in the strictest confidence that he kept her on all through her
pregnancy. You see, his wife could give him no children. And so the
deception began. As Mary grew with the child, she was secreted away
in one of the rooms upstairs that was to be the nanny's room. Mrs
Quinn – only God Almighty knows why – agreed to be part of the
deception. She was to pretend as if she were the one with child and
took early to her bed. The maids attended to her sparingly on Quinn's
orders, while Mary was confined to her own room. Such a foul thing
to take place in such a wealthy and respectable parish!' He stared at
his spectacles, twisting the frame between his fingers. 'Ah, well. When
it was Mary's time, a doctor with his nurse came to the house. The
child was born. A boy. He was brought to Mrs Quinn with the strictest
order of secrecy from the doctor and the nurse. For all the maids
knew, Mrs Quinn had given birth, for they were under strict orders
to remain downstairs during the ordeal. Mary Brennan was cared for
by the nurse in a rushed fashion. She was to stay on as the boy's
nanny. But, in a manner most foul, Quinn told me that he had decided
to rescind this offer and wanted her to leave his employ. He feared
that she would make demands as time went on, and he wanted no
aspect of illegitimacy to taint his son. He told her she was sacked
and to leave immediately. I cautioned against this action but he would
not be moved.'

He stared at his glasses in his hand again and set them aside.

'But that night,' he went on, 'Quinn said that Mary Brennan had
come back into the house, had killed Mrs Quinn by suffocation with
a pillow, and stolen the baby away.'

'No!' gasped Badger.

'Indeed. It was . . . unbelievable. A terrible, terrible event. There
was some intervention, though not by the police. He told the police
that his wife had died from childbed fever, and that the child had
succumbed as well. No one questioned it. He hired men to search
quietly, secretly for Mary Brennan and the child, but they were
unsuccessful.'

Watson blew out a breath. 'And no one has heard a peep from
them since?'

'Not a one, sir.'

'So it isn't actually known if the boy is still alive?' asked Tim.

'That is true.'

'And if he isn't?' asked Watson. 'Who inherits then?'

'There is a codicil to the will. If the boy cannot be found or is proved to be dead, then the bulk of Mister Quinn's estates goes to the Royal Hospital Chelsea for the relief of old soldier pensioners.'

Tim flicked a glance to the lances and military paraphernalia on the walls of the parlor. 'I see.'

Watson looked too and rubbed his beard. 'And you say that some blokes already investigated this Mary Brennan?'

'Yes,' said Smith, 'but that was some twenty years ago.'

'I don't suppose you know the names of them blokes?' said Tim.

'I'm afraid I do not.'

Watson fiddled with his pocket watch. 'Mrs Martin told us that there was a cousin of some kind. In Dartmouth?'

'I contacted him, but let it be known that he was not mentioned in the will. Such was the only thing I was legally allowed to convey. Under those circumstances, he declined to make an appearance. He will not inherit in any case.'

'What about the name of the child?' asked Tim.

Smith looked down at his papers. 'I believe the child was named Edward.'

He looked to Watson before asking, 'Are there any papers on Mary Brennan? Any references from any registries?'

'Only this one letter from a registry in Marylebone: Mrs Hunt's Servants' Registry Office, Duke Street.' He handed it to Tim, who read it while Watson leaned close and read it over his shoulder.

*Mary Brennan has been a good and honest servant in the household of the Stuarts of Holburn for five years. In that time, she rose in her situation from housemaid to parlormaid and thence to lady's maid. Had the situation presented itself, she would have risen to housekeeper, but the post was filled. She wished to better herself and therefore sought the position of housekeeper with our registry and found a position at the Quinn residence on Gower Street, Bloomsbury, 24 September 1875.*

Tim looked at Watson. 'Well, that's a start. May we keep this?'

Smith gestured in the affirmative.

'And so,' said Watson. 'Shall we discuss our fee?'

*   *   *

Flush with real money this time, not the few pence Thomas Brent had managed to forage from his threadbare pockets, they stood on the pavement on Gower Street, looking back at the sad little door of the Quinn residence. Smith had told them that the housekeeper and maid would be kept on until such time as the solicitor decided that he could not further pay them from the stocks and ready cash. The house might be boarded up, awaiting either the heir – should he be alive – or the sale where the money would go to Chelsea Hospital.

'Have you ever heard of such a thing, Tim?'

Tim gazed at his friend with his somber expression. 'That Quinn, eh? A piece of work he was. He was good at promising things and then cheating poor sods out of their reward. But sending a mother on her way and keeping the child? That's as low as can be.'

'Legal, though. He was the father.' Watson seemed to muse on it a moment. 'Do you think he's alive? The son?'

'Dunno. I suppose we could look for an Edward Brennan. But where would we begin?'

Watson glanced back at the house. 'My guess is to check the coppers first. He might have grown to be a man who got himself into trouble.'

'Oi. You don't suppose it's me, do you? Born on the wrong side of the blanket, a young lad in trouble with the law . . .'

'Except that you're twenty-three not twenty, ain't you? And your mother would have something to say about all that. Don't you suppose your Mister Holmes would have known if you was an heir?'

'Well, dash it all. Looks like I'm always just that behind. Then it's the Yard for us.'

'Wait. We still have to find Quinn's murderer, don't we?'

'Ben, isn't it obvious? It's Edward Brennan, ain't it?'

'Kill his own father?'

'He don't remember him as a father. All he knows is that he done his mother wrong. And if the old codger is dead, he stands to inherit.'

Watson stared up at the house, thinking. 'Wait for him to show up?'

'It's a possibility. Oh! I've got another idea. If we get nothing from the Yard, let's put an advert in the paper.' He spread his hands out, as if smoothing out a bill he pasted on a wall. '*Looking for lost heir to an estate, Edward Brennan.* That will get some attention, eh?'

A light dawned on Watson's face. 'Tim, that's not a bad idea. My intelligence must finally be rubbing off onto you.'

'Very funny. Let's get to the Yard.'

It was nearly teatime when they reached the Embankment. Now that they had money in their pockets, they were reluctant to spend it on cabbies and so they had walked. But Tim could see that this wouldn't last. Getting about in a cab, well. It was expeditious. And there was nothing like the respect you got when you climbed out of one. But of course, Watson was right about his skinflint ways. They couldn't go throwing their coins about willy-nilly when they'd earned so few. The omnibus was good enough for their like, or their own feet. At least for the moment.

They got inside to the front desk where the same sergeant sat, looking down at them with suspicion. 'I suppose you think you're going to see Inspector Hopkins again.'

'If you don't mind,' said Tim, tipping his hat to the uniformed man. 'We know the way.'

He strutted past the desk, waiting for the hammer to fall . . . but the sergeant seemed to have bigger fish to fry when several bobbies rumbled in, shoving some men before the desk, fisting the miscreants' coat collars like scruffs.

He knocked on Hopkins's door and stuck his head through as he opened it. 'Ah, Inspector. Good to see you again.'

Hopkins's mustache frowned. 'What are *you* doing here?'

'We have new information to impart, just like you told us to.' He sat in one of the chairs before Hopkins's desk and a more timid Watson slid into the other, even as the inspector glowered down at them. 'Mister Quinn turned out to be a rather unlikable gentleman.' And then he related all that Smith had told them.

Hopkins sat with mouth agape for a moment before he pressed his lips into an 'O' and whistled. 'By Jove,' he whispered.

'Thought you'd find that interesting. So we was wondering if this Edward Brennan couldn't be responsible for Quinn's murder. And we was also wondering if maybe he'd gotten into trouble before, being raised under troubling circumstances.'

Hopkins's face changed to one of recognition. 'And he might

have a police record? You might just have something there. Edward Brennan, did you say?'

'Yes. And he'd be about twenty years old. Mother's name Mary Brennan. Might even have the cheek to go by Edward Quinn.'

The inspector wrote it down on a piece of paper with his pencil. 'Right. Thanks, lads.'

'We've been hired by Miles Smith, Esquire, to investigate the whereabouts of this Edward Brennan, as he will inherit a lot of money. That is, if he ain't guilty of murder. Or already dead.' Tim rose. Watson followed. 'Pleasure doing business with you, sir.'

'Yes, Badger, Watson. This might become as profitable an association as with your Mister Holmes.'

Tim offered a wide smile. 'That's a very nice thing to say.' He tipped his hat. 'I hope we will prove ourselves as valuable, Inspector. We'll be awaiting your message at our Dean Street flat.'

The three of them walked to the door, where Badger and Watson left him as the inspector hurried off to give the note to a clerk.

They walked back to Dean Street under a sudden shower and, after shaking off their damp topcoats and hanging them by the door, they made themselves comfortable in their sitting room, still feeling as if they were visiting.

'We still have to find that medium, Josie Williams,' said Watson, leaning back in his chair. 'She knows something. And was willing to kill for it.'

Tim blew out a breath. 'She was willing to kill *me*!' He pulled a finger around his collar nervously. But after a moment, he laughed. 'Oi, Ben, it would be funny if Josie Williams was really Mary Brennan.'

Watson laughed too. Until he stopped. 'Tim . . .'

'Nah. That's too far-fetched for even my penny-fiction.'

Watson sat up and leaned toward him. 'But think about it. If she *were* Mary Brennan, she'd have a mighty good reason to kill Quinn. And then it might have been her what went through that hidden door, knowing it was there.'

Tim stopped smiling. 'Ben. That gives me the shivers.'

'She disappeared right after Quinn was murdered. She'd know the secret way out of the room.'

'But why the mud on the sill?'

Watson's face fell. 'Damn that mud!'

'We're close though. I can feel it. The puzzle pieces are just a hand's span away.'

'That makes it all the more urgent we find her.' Watson sat back again.

'But she's on the run now. She could be anywhere. Certainly not back at the Travellers' camp. Unless . . . *she* thinks *we* think she won't go there no more, so she *does* go back there, just to fool us.'

'Now you're *talking* like your penny-fiction.'

He rested back against his chair and scratched his head. 'I gotta stop reading those things,' he muttered. 'But Ben, you know what we forgot? Why Quinn wanted to talk to Latimer in the first place. He wanted to find something.'

'And that medium told him it was in the A-T-I-C.'

'That again?'

'No, Tim, listen. That name's gotta mean something. It was there bold as brass on that sign. We need to go back there and search the place.'

'What if the old man don't want us to?'

'Then . . . then we resort to your old means.'

'Break in? Why Mister Watson!' he said, nose raised, hand on his lapel. 'You're asking me to commit a crime.'

Watson glanced around as if rozzers were hiding under the cushions. 'Keep it down, would you? It . . . may come to that. But it's all about investigating. There was a murder, after all.'

'I'm only joking with you. That'll be easy-breezy.'

They both nearly leapt out of their chairs when Murphy suddenly appeared in the room as if by devilry, and announced, 'There's a gentleman at the door.'

'Christ, Murphy,' said Tim, hand to breast. 'You scared me heart right out of me chest!'

'I will thank you not to take the Lord's name in vain in my presence, Mister Badger.'

'Oh . . . sorry.' Suddenly, he was back in the schoolroom.

'Very well. What shall I do about the gentleman?'

'Send him up,' said Watson.

She took another step into the room, her hands crossed over her apron. 'Well . . . it's like this, Mister Watson. The man is . . . not quite fit for drawing rooms.'

'But neither are we,' muttered Tim, 'and we're here.'

She cleared her throat and addressed him next. 'He's a little worse for wear, sir. From the streets. I don't think he would come up even if I told him to.'

'Oh, bl—' Tim shut his mouth again under her stern appraisal. He slowly rose from the chair. 'I-I mean . . . bloomin' . . . er . . . yes. I'll go down and see to it, shall I?'

'Very well, then,' she said, waiting for him. As soon as he began to move toward the door, she led the way down the stairs and to the foyer, whereupon she opened the street door on as disreputable a man as ever there was.

His long coat was pocked with holes. The dirty scarf wound round his neck was not something Badger would have touched, but it cupped the man's dark, scraggly beard and he didn't seem to mind. He had a patch over one eye with the floppy and misshapen brim of his hat hanging low, shadowing his face.

'I'm Tim Badger. What do you want?'

The man thumbed back at the painted sign by the door. 'I hear tell you're looking for Josie Williams, and there might be a few pence in it for me.'

He had a thick Irish accent and a slow way of speaking.

'Yes. Are you a . . . a Traveller?'

'Was. Still board with them from time to time.'

'I see. Well? Where is she?'

'Where's me brass?'

Badger dug into his pocket for his purse, opened it, and handed over the tuppence.

The man closed his fingers over it and smiled a blackened grin. 'Saw her over in a gin shop on Drury Lane. I think she dosses there.'

'Right. Well . . . thank you.'

The man began a labored stride away from the porch, limping over the pavement to the street. Something about him tickled at the edges of Tim's thoughts. Tim turned to go back inside and stopped. The eye patch. He'd seen it before. Leather with red stitching around it . . .

A wave of humiliation, anger and disappointment washed over him. He clutched his fists at his sides. 'Mister Holmes, there's no need for this,' he growled.

The limping man kept going.

'Mister Holmes!' he said louder. 'I know it's you, sir.'

The man stopped and looked back over a crooked shoulder. Then, like a magic act on the stage, he deliberately drew himself up, turned, and, remarkably, was limping no more.

His grin slowly grew on his face. 'Well done, Mister Badger,' he said in the cultivated voice of his old guv. 'It was the eye patch, wasn't it?' He pulled it up to his brow and then slid it higher to his forehead, blinking a perfectly good eye at Tim. 'I must extend my inventory of eye patches, I see.'

Badger rubbed his fists up and down the sides of his thighs, trembling with barely controlled rage. 'You had no call to try to deceive me, Mister Holmes,' he sputtered. 'We would have worked it out.'

'You mistake my intent, Mister Badger. I want you to succeed. As my protégés, it behooves the mentor to give the mentees all the advantages. I merely nudged you in the right direction.'

Then it dawned on Tim, and a whole new wave of humiliation washed over him. 'You were the old codger in the doorway directing me to where Thomas Brent was, weren't you?'

'Always know where your client is, Mister Badger. You should have asked that of Brent.'

Badger mentally kicked himself. Of course he well knew that! But he hadn't done it.

'And you were the old sea captain with the wooden leg by Battersea. A wooden leg, of all things! You planted yourself there to tell me where the Nomades were, didn't you? And now this fella . . .' He gestured brusquely at his disreputable figure. 'Why?'

Holmes pulled a cigarette from one of the inside pockets of his filthy coat and, with the flicking of his thumb, lit a match. Puffing contemplatively on it, he threw the match into the gutter before answering, holding the cigarette delicately betwixt his fingers in a manner completely incongruous to his uncivilized appearance. 'You were already headed for the Nomades in Battersea, so you needed little help there. And as for my current disguise, well. It was to help you with Josie Williams.'

Tim took a step down from the porch and approached him. 'Are we on the right track, Mister Holmes? Is it Josie Williams what done it?'

'It's *all* about Josie Williams. But I shan't tell you more.'

'Why not? Mister Holmes, we have to solve this quick before poor old Brent starves to death.'

'Your instincts are right, Badger. Trust in them. And I congratulate you on how you treat your fellow man.' He raised the coins with a smile, rubbing them together.

'Can't you give us more information, sir?'

'You're doing all right, Badger. Keep it up.'

'So this is all a test, then. You've already solved it and now Watson and me are just a pantomime for your entertainment.'

Holmes drew on the cigarette and let the smoke unfurl out of his nostrils. He didn't frown, but neither was he smiling anymore. His eyes, as always, took steely aim at Tim's face, even as the eyelids drooped. 'A test? Mister Badger, I have invested a considerable sum in you and your colleague. And, to that end, you must be up to the challenge of your situation. If you cannot achieve it on your own, then I cannot help you further. No one can.' He puffed on the cigarette again. His eyes darted here and there, taking in the street and the people on it, always aware of the goings-on around him. No one was near to them, and the bustle of traffic on the street masked their conversation. Tim was certain he'd planned it that way.

'There has been many a time I have called it a game,' said Holmes. 'Surely you recall it. But it is far from that. No one was meant to infer that it was merely a game to me, though due to my colleague Doctor Watson and his fanciful writings, he might have given the impression that I didn't take my work seriously. Nothing could be further from the truth. And you mustn't think it trivial what you do. Not any of it. You must be quick in your dealings, exact in your conclusions. You must never guess. You must always *know*. Is this a test? All of life is a test, Young Badger. This path you have set yourself upon is a test. The next one will also be a test. And the next. And the moment you feel it is easy or that you can take the simple road to achieve your ends, you must get out of the business of detecting.' He flipped his hand with the cigarette. The smoke followed it in a wispy circle around his words as if in emphasis. 'You must always remember that a life is at stake, whether you are rescuing someone from some devil's plan, or from the gallows when the police get it wrong. And they will. Frequently. Because I cannot always be there to set them right. *You* are now tasked with that. You and *your* Watson.' A flicker at the edge of his mouth was all the indication of his usual amusement with Ben's name.

'And so,' he went on, after another drag on the cigarette. The ash glowed for a moment. 'As you know, I do not have any children of my own, nor am I ever likely to have them . . .'

Tim moved incrementally closer. 'And . . . you think of me . . . as a son?'

Holmes looked down his considerable nose at him. 'Don't be absurd. Of course not. What I meant to say is this. Though you may not be my *progeny* you are most certainly my *legacy*. Remember your own history, your humanity. Always work toward the betterment of society, so that those who were raised as you were will not need to suffer the indignities of a hopeless life. You know as well as I do that the guilty are not necessarily those in poverty, though poverty feeds the engine of the criminal. More like, it's the greedy that are the guilty. It's the wronged who seek their revenge, not the pauper who takes the bread. For you, it will always mean doing the right thing, but that may not always necessarily mean doing the *legal* thing.'

'Yes, sir,' he mumbled. His disappointment at not being considered the Great Man's son nearly undid him. He was certain that this had been the case. But, with a heavy heart, he realized that there were probably more promising protégés than he. And if that were so, why was Tim chosen among all the inspectors and other Irregulars that had passed through Holmes's life?

In his mulishness, he almost missed the man's next words.

'Take the clues you are given,' Holmes went on. 'I'll wager you already know more than you think you do. You merely have to make sense of it. It is all laid out before you like a deck of cards. All of it. Do me proud, Badger. I'm counting on you.'

Before Badger could say anything to that, Holmes hurried into the street and darted past a hansom cab. Once the cab had passed, Holmes was nowhere to be seen.

'I know where you live!' Tim called obstinately to the empty street.

A scruffy dog with a muddy belly trotted by and turned to look at him, cocking its head, but it didn't stop and proceeded on.

Tim stood a long while, looking to the place Holmes should have been, longing to ask . . . *everything*. Was he doing it right? Was he asking enough questions? What did he mean that Tim already had all the answers? Why had Holmes thought Tim could do this in the first place? Why had *Tim*? Stubborn pride?

But the man had long since disappeared and was probably halfway home to Baker Street by now.

Sighing, he returned through the doorway and trudged up the stairs, one at a time, to their flat.

'Well? Who was it?' asked Watson, fiddling with his pocket watch.

Should he say? He was still hot with humiliation, but it wasn't good telling untruths to his partner. 'It was . . . it turns out it was . . . Mister Holmes. In disguise.'

Watson shot out of his chair. 'What? And I missed him?'

'By Heaven, Ben. He's been feeding me information all this time. In different disguises. And I fell for it . . . until now. God knows how many more times besides the three that I knew of that he's been doing this to us.'

'What did you say to him?'

'Oh, well. What did I say?' Embarrassed all over again, he shook his head. 'I said . . . enough. But he told me . . . he said . . . that he wanted us to succeed. And that he was merely nudging us in the right direction.'

'Good God Almighty.' Watson strode to the fireplace and stood before it. 'Is this a good thing . . . or not? I feel a little . . .'

'So do I,' he said softly. 'But . . . he told me that our instincts are good and that we should follow them.'

'Is that all he said?'

'No. He came to tell us that Josie Williams is at a gin shop on Drury Lane and that it's all about her.'

They stared at each other a long time, it seemed, each battling their own demons, trying to read the right answers in each other's faces.

But as for answers, there were none.

Finally, they both moved at the same time.

'To Drury Lane, then,' muttered Tim as they donned their hats.

# NINETEEN
## Watson

Ben felt for Badger. He could see how silent he'd become, how angry. Here he was, thinking he's a man and doing for himself, and then the guv – a man whom he'd come to think of as a father figure, a man he respected – was hovering over his shoulder all this time like he didn't trust him. It had to gall.

Still. Mister Holmes's interference meant that they had good lodgings, good food, and servants for the first time in their lives. An occasional push in the right direction wouldn't go amiss either, as far as Ben was concerned. But he knew how it hurt Badger's self-worth.

He wanted to say something but he didn't know what. They both kept silent as they walked.

Long shadows followed them through the streets of London, passing churches, pubs, cook shops, blocks of solemn-faced tenements, boarding houses and shops, until they arrived – fifteen minutes later – on Drury Lane. Watson knew of only one gin shop on the street, the Princess Beatrice Tavern, and quickly made his way to it. It was a brick structure of tall windows and gables. They could already hear the noise within, once they were only a few paces from the door. He began to wonder how he was going to keep Badger from the bar, since he knew he'd try to drown his sorrows in gin or bitter, but the man wore a different sort of determination on his face today that Ben hadn't seen before. Maybe he'd leave off for once.

When they got inside where it was warm and stuffy, they stood near the doorway, scanning the room. *Maybe we should have come disguised*, he thought with a warm, embarrassed flash to his chest. Surely she'd bolt the moment she saw them. They hadn't thought that through. That's what comes of emotions coming into it. He gathered himself. *Think*, he admonished himself. *What to do right now?*

He elbowed Badger and spoke quietly. 'If she sees us—'

'She'll run,' he answered. So at least Badger had thought of that too.

'Let's split up,' said Ben. 'Move stealthy-like along the edges and keep our hats down.'

Badger nodded and made his way left, leaving Ben to move right.

The place was bright with gaslight, shining on cheery faces, reddened noses and cheeks, toffs drinking next to tradesmen. A piano and a violin played off to the side, and there was the smell of bodies and sweat and spilled beer, the rustling of clothes, clinking of glasses, and the occasional uproar of laughter and backslapping before it died down again to a loud buzz of conversation.

The big-bellied gin barrels were lined in a row behind a sumptu-ously carved wooden bar, with dividers for a bit of privacy while tippling. Even the polished tin of the ceiling caught the light and made the inside all the merrier, drastically different from the dreary slums of Drury Lane outside the tavern's walls.

Ben pushed his hat down over his forehead and glanced up now and again from under the brim. 'Well, I'll be blowed . . .' There she was, tray in hand and dealing out glasses of gin and little cakes to the customers as they sat at their tables.

As stealthily as he could among the crowds, Ben kept one eye on her, and another on making his way in a wide circle toward her. He managed to get in behind her and, while she was busy pushing away the hands of a drunken customer in a boiled shirt and topper, Ben closed his hands on her arms. He got in close and hissed into her ear, 'Don't make trouble.'

She stiffened.

'We're going to walk out of here arm in arm, you get me? And then we're going to have a little talk about séances and throwing knives and you trying to kill me partner. Nod if you understand me.'

Slowly, she nodded.

'Right. Then let's go.'

He whistled a particular signal, which he knew would bring Badger running, and pushed his way – with his hands holding tightly to her – through the throng of people, mindful of her trying to kick him.

He got her outside and stood with her on the pavement, not letting up one inch.

'You're hurting my arm,' she said in a soft Irish intonation.

'I may very well be doing so. But you have a nasty habit of escaping. If you keep getting away, that innocent man will be done for murder.'

'He didn't do it.'

'Yes, that I know. Because *you* did.'

'No, I didn't.'

'I think you did. And there's no more use denying it. It's all about you,' he said, parroting Holmes's words.

Ben felt a presence behind him when the door to the gin shop opened – releasing the noise and music like a dam bursting – and then closed in the sounds once again.

'You got her!' said Badger.

'I did. Now. Take her to the Yard?'

'No!' she cried, trying to twist away.

'Here now!' warned Badger, coming around to face her. 'You tried to stab me in me sleep. I don't take kindly to that.'

'I wasn't going to kill you.'

'And how do I know that's the truth?'

'We need a quiet place to talk,' said Ben. Now she was trying in earnest to fight him off.

Badger curled his hand into a fist, showing her. 'If you don't still yourself, I'll have to punch you one. And I don't want to punch a woman.'

'I didn't kill Quinn.'

'Why were you there?' urged Badger. 'How did you get to that séance?'

She smiled, showing missing teeth at the side of her mouth. 'Ask Mary Brennan.'

'Are *you* not Mary Brennan?' hissed Ben.

She gave him a sharp look and then tried to wrench away from him.

'Stop fighting!' he shouted.

She pushed her face toward him. 'I'm Josie Williams. Have been a good long time.'

'That don't answer anything,' said Badger, still brandishing his fist.

'What goes on here?'

Ben swung Josie around toward the voice. A man with pushed-in features, like a prize fighter, scowled at them. He was in his shirtsleeves, and his waistcoat was open, revealing his braces and a stained shirt. The door was just swinging closed behind him, and he pulled his brimmed cap down over his forehead. 'I asked you lads what's going on here? Why are you holding this good woman?'

'We are private detectives,' said Badger, raising his chin. 'And this here "good" woman is a murderess. We're taking her to Scotland Yard.'

The man looked to the woman. 'Is that so, Josie?'

'I didn't do nothin', Alf. They're not who they say they are.'

The man took a step toward Badger, who held up his hands. 'Whoa there, man. Look. I got a calling card—'

'Stuff your calling card.'

Before Badger could reach into his coat pocket, the man was upon him, crumpling both lapels in his beefy fists.

Everyone stilled at the sound of a cocking revolver hammer. Even Josie stopped wriggling. Ben had the Bull Dog nearly pressed to the burly gentleman's temple.

'It's as my partner says,' said Ben. 'We are detectives and we are bringing this woman to the police. And I suggest you don't try to stop us.'

Josie jerked in Ben's one-handed grip and he suddenly cried out as a searing pain shot through his foot where she'd stomped good and hard on it with the heel of her boot. His fingers opened and she darted out of his grasp.

Badger dived for her but, as slippery as she was, she dodged him, ducked around Ben's reaching arm, and managed to twist around behind him, using the man in the doorway to block them from nabbing her again. Off she ran. Ben grabbed his sore foot. Badger lurched forward to give chase, when the man grabbed the scruff of his coat and yanked him back, throwing him to the ground.

'Look what you gone and done!' Badger cried to the man who was standing over him with bared fists. 'She's a fugitive from justice and you just let her escape!'

Alf's fists were still at the ready, but his face didn't seem so sure anymore.

Badger got to his feet and brushed at his trousers and coat. 'Blimey. And we worked hard finding her.'

'Are you . . . are you *really* detectives?' the man asked, his arms lowering.

Badger thrust his hand into his coat pocket and yanked out a card, shoving it into the man's face. 'See?'

The man labored over reading each word, but he finally lowered it. 'Oh. Sorry.'

'You should be! You awright there, Ben?'

The deep throbbing in his foot had subsided only slightly. 'Gor blimey,' he hissed, and fumbled the Webley back inside his coat. 'Just maimed for life.'

Badger waved his words away. 'You're fine.'

Ben gestured to his foot. 'I'm not. I'm maimed for life, I tell you.'

'What are we gonna do now?'

'Sorry, gents,' said the man in the doorway. 'I feel badly about not trusting you. It's just that . . . I know this lass. Can I buy you a gin to ease the pain?'

Ben thought about it, saw the eagerness on Badger's face, but ultimately decided against it. 'I thank you, mate, but we'd better not.'

'Aw, Ben . . .'

'How long have you known her?' said Ben, ignoring Badger.

The man rubbed at the back of his neck. 'Oh, a fair bit. Used to see her round the funfair. We both worked it back in the day. She did fortune telling. I did the high-striker.'

'Was her name always Josie Williams?'

He seemed perplexed at the question. 'Yes, as far as I can remember. That would be some twenty or so years I known her.'

'Did she have a kid with her?' asked Badger.

He shook his head. 'Not her.' He looked them over. 'Are you sure I can't buy you a drink?'

Ben sensed Badger was readying to go back inside with the tall stranger. 'Ahem. Aren't you forgetting you've got a date to fill tonight? And her without a chaperone.'

'Oh! I almost forgot.' He tipped his hat to the man. 'Sorry, mate. We can't stay. Here, you invalid. Let me get you home.' He took up one of Ben's arms and allowed him to lean on his shoulder.

'What a damned stupid thing to have happened,' Ben grumbled as they made their way slowly back to Dean Street. The roads grayed with the dying light. Funny how streets in the East End seemed to sport little color, and those on the West End seemed to sparkle with it. Even when the sunlight left it. The streetlights, winking on as the lamplighter did the job on his ladder, couldn't seem to offer the cheeriness of the better thoroughfares of London. Ben couldn't fathom why.

'I wonder if she'll scarper for good from there,' said Badger, interrupting his musings.

'Would *you* go back?'

'She might have to pick up a few things. But there's little hope of finding her there again.'

Ben sighed. 'Now what'll we do?'

'I suppose . . . I could ask Mister Holmes—'

'No, Tim. I can't stand the thought of it. Of you askin' him. You and me, we can do this. I'm sure we can. We've just got to employ his way.'

'I'm thinking,' muttered Badger. But Ben could clearly see how relieved he was.


'Don't stay out too late,' admonished Ben as Badger, all bristled up with a frock coat and tie, smiled at himself in the looking glass by the door.

'What are you, my nanny?'

Ben stiffened. That was just how he felt sometimes. 'Awright,' he said, waving him off and sitting himself a bit abruptly in his chair. He snatched up the evening paper and flicked it hard to straighten it. 'Why should I care? You're just going out with a she-devil, a slippery snake of a reporter. Nothin' to fear there, eh?'

'Ben, Ben.' He wagged his head and adjusted his tie. 'I'm onto her game now. I might try to feed her the wrong information, get her off our backs for a change. That's my smart thinking.'

'You and smart thinking? That'll be the day.'

'You gotta have more faith in me, old son. G'night, Ben. Don't wait up!' He pushed his hat down over the side of his face at a jaunty angle and sauntered out the door.

It wasn't that Ben had no faith in Badger. It was that he trusted Miss Littleton least of all. And they with a murder to wrap up sooner rather than later.

'Good luck, Tim,' he muttered, and commenced reading every

article in the small, tight text in *The Daily Chronicle*, scanning the pages for the name Ellsie Moira Littleton.

# TWENTY
## Badger

He checked his watch again as he stood outside the theatre. Raising it to his ear, he shook it, but it still had the sure, honest sound of steady ticking.

Five minutes past. What was five minutes? It was nothing. She had simply been delayed. She'd be there any minute. 'Any minute now,' he muttered, searching down the length of wet pavement and the line of people crowding under the eaves as the dusk mist slowly rose. It surprised him how much he had been looking forward to this.

He glanced up to the banners swagged over the front of the four-story tower and read again, 'The Royal Canterbury Theatre of Varieties.' The façade glittered with lights, and the fancy costumes of the people going in for a night of songs, comedy and frivolity.

Unexpectedly, he was jabbed with a moment of guilt that he shouldn't be taking the time off – and with some of Mister Holmes's money – for such trivialities, but he justified it to himself that he was setting Miss Littleton to rights about a few things. She needed to be more partial to them, and he knew of no better way than to let her know who the real Tim Badger was.

A hansom cab pulled up before him, and when the door opened, out stepped the lady herself.

She was arrayed in a lavender evening gown of some sort of satiny material that shimmered in the gas lamps outside the theatre, and that conformed amiably to a delectable figure. On her head perched a petite headdress made of the same fabric as her gown, with a jaunty ostrich feather atop it that fluttered with the odd breeze. She wore a simple, fur-trimmed cape over her shoulders and, when Tim stepped forward to take her hand, she offered it in its long opera gloves. The scent of roses formed a delicate cloud about her.

She joined him on the pavement and looked him over. He did feel a little underdressed, for he had no evening clothes himself, but he hoped that he wouldn't be out of place in the galleries. His collar was clean and white, and his coat fitted his trim form nicely.

'I am sorry I'm late.' She smiled and cocked her head just so. Her auburn hair gleamed red with the gaslight. She was an elegant woman when he thought about it, and he began to wonder about her and what made her want to be a reporter, and she from Mayfair, of all places. It wouldn't be that she *had* to work . . . was it?

He supposed that could all be part of their chit-chat.

'Think nothing of it,' he said magnanimously. 'Shall we?' He offered his arm and she laid her hand gently upon it. Instead of entering by the front doors, Tim tugged her the other way up Westminster Bridge Road to Upper Marsh.

'Where are we going?' she asked, looking back at the well-lit entry, and all the people queuing up to go in.

He gestured ahead. 'Oh, I thought I'd try something a bit different and sit in the gallery this time,' he lied. 'I hope that's all right with you. The entrance is just there.' He certainly couldn't expend £2/2d *each* for the ground-floor seating. He reckoned 6d each for the gallery would be good enough for a start.

He paid for the tickets and led her up the stairs, where they had a wide view of the lower hall, the seats below, and the balconies and boxes. He paid for programs and handed one to her. He clutched his as he looked out over all the finery and décor in wonderment. He'd not had the opportunity to come to the Canterbury before and he understood now why they called such structures 'palaces.'

Above, a large coved ceiling showed off the painters' art in panels that looked like Indian gods, gardens, snakes and such. But there was also its famous sliding roof, painted in a deep blue and picked out in gold stars like a night sky. Plasterwork in foliates sprang from columns along a ground floor filled with fauteuil seating, row on row . . . those two-pound seats, and cushy they looked, too. Three panels over the proscenium were painted with more artistic Indian subjects on a gold background, representing music, comedy and tragedy. Ornamental columns on each side of the proscenium were painted on both sides with elephants and Nubian riders, and all seemed to glitter in gold leaf and gold tiles. It was a modern wonder, to Badger's eyes.

He brought himself back to the business at hand and found their seats. From there, they could look out below to those seating themselves in the cushioned chairs on the ground floor, those across in the gallery, still more in the balcony, and the wealthiest folk in the ornamented boxes on either side of the proscenium. In between the balconies he could just make out the refreshment rooms on the first floor. Perhaps they could take their supper there.

He turned to her and smiled. 'I hope this meets with your expectations.'

She couldn't help but smile back at him excitedly. 'It does indeed. We have an excellent view of the whole place, don't you think?'

She took off her cape and set it on the back of her chair, revealing a décolletage of creamy skin and a long neck. Her shoulders, too, were bare in small sleeves; on the whole, she was completely enchanting.

He swallowed. Here he was expecting to dazzle her, and there she was . . . a woman, no longer just a stubborn reporter, dazzling *him*. He vowed to be wary.

Just then, the orchestra struck up their music and the gas dimmed. The enormous curtains on the stage were lit up with lime-light and Tim soon forgot his guilt and troubles. He glanced at the program at last and it was filled to the brim with entertainments. And just as he read her name, Marie Lloyd strolled onto the stage with her famous parasol amid thunderous applause. She was just as shapely in life as she was in her photographs – particularly in her scandalously short skirt, cut just below her knees. She began singing 'Oh, Mr Porter' and winking and nodding to make the words that much cheekier. The audience enjoyed themselves singing along. Tim sang too, and he was pleased to see that Miss Littleton knew the words and tune as well.

Lloyd next sang one of her old ones, 'The Boy I Love Is Up in the Gallery,' and she paid special attention to those on that level of the theatre. Men whistled loudly and waved, everyone sang along to that one as well, and Tim could swear that she looked directly at him more than once.

When she'd finished that song, she asked if the audience wanted more, and the loud affirmation in stomping feet, applause and cheers gave her all the encouragement she needed. She nodded to the orchestra leader and sang several more favorites, and a few new songs, and by the time she left the stage at last, she blew a kiss to the audience to wild acclaim.

A *lion comique* came next, a jaunty parody of the upper classes that Tim particularly enjoyed. Next was a ballet in stunning costumes that entranced. Then there followed more singers, and then an elegantly dancing duo.

Tim glanced often at Miss Littleton, but she was so completely engaged at the sight before her, eyes shining behind her lorgnette, lips parted in expectation, that she didn't notice his gaze. He quickly looked away back to the stage.

The time breezed by so that, when he looked at his watch at the intermission, he realized it was later than he thought. 'Miss Littleton, shall we get ourselves some refreshment? It would be nice to take a stroll about the place, stretch our pins a bit.'

'I do agree,' she said. He helped her carry her cape, and she strolled on, the soft swish of the fabric moving with her.

They took the stairs to the refreshment level and were seated by a waiter more elegantly dressed than Tim was, who offered menus of wine, beer and other enticements.

Looking at the prices, Tim apologized in his head to Mister Holmes before he allowed her to order for them. It was cooked oysters, cold meats, pickles and beer. He appreciated her choices, as did his coin purse.

As their beers were served and the waiter moved away from their table, Tim could finally face her, and quite an appetizing sight it was . . . if only she weren't so annoying most of the time.

He plunged in, hoping to keep her from her own prying questions. 'Why a reporter, Miss Littleton? It's not proper work for a woman, is it? And you from Mayfair and all.'

He could see her face go through a myriad of expressions. It seemed that her first instinct was to attack, but she thought better of it. She took a moment by sipping her beer and then setting it carefully down again. 'I wanted to see something of humanity. I wanted to understand it, understand what made a city as big as London tick like a clock, with all its gears and springs. And why crime and poverty was rampant in such a modern place.'

He nodded. 'I think you have the right of it there, miss. Those that grow up in poverty – like m'self – and I trust you won't print what we say here in confidence . . .' He gave her the eye. She demurred and nodded back. 'Well. There's little choice but for a life of crime. It's not like one wakes up in the morning and decides to be a criminal. It's that your kids have to eat. They're in rags. And you've got to do something about it.'

'Do you have any children, Mister Badger?'

He nearly spat out his beer. He choked instead, coughing. He held the serviette in his face and coughed into it until it subsided and he cleared his throat. 'No. I'm, er, not a married man, Miss Littleton.'

She gave him a secret smirk, hiding it in the rim of her glass before she gestured for him to continue.

'I just meant that no one sets out to be a criminal, as you say. There's generations of the poor in the city. How can they ever better themselves? Because it ain't just lack of education, but of opportunity. You can't get a job in a fancy shop when you don't have the money for better clothes. You can't clerk for no one unless you have a good hand and good grammar. Most of us just learned to read and write and little more than that. I mean, where's the opportunities? Where's the chances?'

'But you've bettered *your*self, Mister Badger. Surely anyone can if they—'

'Miss Littleton, I have a benefactor, someone who put me up in better lodgings and afforded me the chance to dress m'self proper. That means I eat proper too. The *tools*, Miss Littleton. I'll wager you never had to worry about having a roof over your head when it rained or snowed. Never worried about enough coal to heat yourself, or enough food to eat. The basics just to keep you alive.'

'But there are workhouses for the very poor—'

He hadn't meant to, but he tossed down his serviette a little more harshly than intended, making the glassware clink together. 'Have you ever been to one?' He shook his head. 'The problem with people like you is that you don't understand poverty. There's no such thing as "deserving" or "undeserving" poor. There's just poor. Awright, I admit, there are bad people on the streets, too. Cutthroats and pickpockets and murderers. There's no helping them. And there's those who drink a lot. But can you blame them? Waking up every day to the sameness of trying to get enough to eat and never getting enough.'

Just then the waiter arrived with their food and laid out the abundant plates from his tray. Badger looked over the platter of steaming oysters, the carefully carved strips of beef and pork, the dish of cornichons. He suddenly felt ashamed and sat back, touching nothing.

'Miss Littleton,' he said, not looking up from the tablecloth, 'I've had lots of jobs. And you can plainly see I'm no slow-witted man. But all of my guvs treated me as if I was a child, too stupid to do more than asked. Just because I was poor. Just because I was a servant. It's galling. It unmans you.' He sat a moment in silence before he mentally slapped himself. Meekly, he looked up. Surprisingly, she was gazing at him with concern, with eyes that seemed to have actually understood him. 'I'm sorry. I didn't mean to fly off at you like that. It's just that . . . well. Mister Holmes never treated me that way. He always talked to me proper, not *down* to me, if you get my meaning. He always seemed to have high hopes for me. That's all a man needs, really. And a leg up.'

Her hand was on his in comfort and he stared at it.

Her fingers had probably never callused from labor. Her nails never torn from hard work. They were beautiful hands, in fact. Pale, with shiny, slightly pinkish nails, the skin smooth. He took a moment to admire them. They were not like Jenny Wilson's or Katie Murphy's, sometimes red and raw. It was useless being angry at the fact that they weren't.

He slid his hand away out from under them. 'I got away from my original question,' he chuckled sheepishly. 'That was, why you became a reporter. You seem . . . genteel. You probably don't need to work, do you?' Slowly, he retrieved his serviette, tucked it back into his collar, and speared some slices of beef to put on his plate.

'That's not entirely true, Mister Badger.' She served herself oysters in their shells, some cornichons, and some slices of meat. She took up her fork and held it, but made no move to eat her fare. 'Though I do have an endowment from my parents, it isn't quite enough to live on.' She shook her head once and started again. 'Enough as I was used to, that is. Living where I live in their house, clothing myself as I do, attending the various functions necessary to keep myself in a class with my peers. I found I *did* need to supplement my income. I am no seamstress. I am inadequate to the task of being a shopgirl. Not a cook, nor a housekeeper. My options were few. So I decided to try my hand at journalism. It wasn't easy as a woman, getting such a job. But *The Daily Chronicle* was amused at the prospect. They thought at first that I would write "women's pieces" about fashion and household hints, but I quickly disabused them of that by writing uncompromising pieces about crime. Crime interests me, Mister Badger. Criminals interest me.'

'And that's what fascinates you about me, eh?'

She dabbed her lips with the serviette that she kept in her lap. 'At first, yes. I imagined you were trying to cheat your clients, that it was all a farce to you, some sort of confidence game. I thought that your claiming to have been employed by Sherlock Holmes was a lie. I have since been proved wrong.'

She admitted it! He suddenly got his appetite back and dug in, taking a swig of his beer, impaling a few oysters onto his fork, and shoving them into his mouth. They were smoky and sweet. 'Being a reporter has to be a bit like being a detective,' he said, cheek bulging with food. He swallowed it. 'You can't just assume things. You have to back it all with facts and some deductive reasoning. For instance, you assumed I was a criminal because I might have a file with the police, have spent some time in gaol even. That was all in the past. But if you had *looked* at the facts available, you would have seen – well, more recently at least – that there was a scheme to it all that had nothin' to do with *acts* of crime. It was me, looking for *clues* and *evidence*. As a matter of fact . . .' He wiped his mouth with the serviette and plucked it from his collar. 'Care to learn what it's really like investigating a crime?'

'You mean . . . now?'

'No time like the present.'

Her smile came slowly but, with eyes shining, she appeared to be up for the adventure.

They hastily finished their meal, gathered their things, and left the theatre. The night was chilly and Badger shivered at the curb to hail a cab. 'Pimlico Road,' he said to the cabby when he arrived. Littleton stared at him.

'Just where *are* you taking me, Mister Badger?'

He realized – through his penny-fiction reading – that she might have thought he was some kind of villain trying to sweep her away for cruel and salacious plans. He offered her a hand into the cab and scooted as far away from her as he could in the cramped space as it clattered along on the cobbled stones. Not that he wanted to be far away from her and her perfume. 'Miss

Littleton, my intentions are completely honorable. I swear. But if you're game – and I suspect that you are such a woman – you will see tonight what a detective's life is truly like.'

'This is not the direction of your lodgings.' She glanced out the window nervously.

'No. I'm not taking you to my lodgings. That wouldn't be proper.'

He said nothing more. He glanced at her in the dark of the cab occasionally as she continued to look out the window. He hadn't realized he was humming one of Marie Lloyd's tunes and he was suddenly amused by this adventure.

'You can stop here, cabby,' he said after they had arrived close to Chelsea Bridge. The streets fell quiet and, as the hansom left them, its clopping horse vanishing into the distance, their surroundings felt solitary and still.

'Why have you brought me here, Mister Badger? I demand to know.' She suddenly had a small pepperbox revolver in her hand and was aiming it at him.

'Blimey,' he said under his breath. He hadn't considered that she might still be wary of him. He approached her slowly, hands carefully reaching forth, and even as he spoke, his mind was not on his words but on clapping his hands on that gun. 'Please don't fear me, Miss Littleton. The thing of it is, it's a clue to the murder of Horace Quinn. And Watson and me were going to investigate it together, but I thought, since you're here, you might wish to do it with me. But it does entail a little housebreaking.'

'What?' She desperately looked about for a cab, but none were in the offing. But while she was occupied with that, he darted forward and – with one hand on the gun and stepping aside out of its way just in case – he snatched it from her hand.

'Mister Badger!'

'Now miss, you wouldn't want to be pointing a dangerous thing as that at a man what means you no harm. I'll return it to you . . . when you've listened to what I have to say.'

Her indignation returned, but at least it seemed to have wiped the fear from her eyes.

'Yes, you were talking about housebreaking. I should have known.'

'Don't worry. I've done it before.'

'And how often were you caught at it?'

He blinked, thinking. 'Well . . . truth to tell . . . a fair few times . . .' Her look was stern before she whirled on her heel and began walking back toward the heart of London. He scrambled to catch up with her. 'But this will be easy. It's one old man, and we won't be encountering him at all. Trust me.'

She hadn't slowed down. 'I can't believe you would bring me all the way out to Battersea and suggest I break the law. Is this some sort of retaliation for my story?'

'No! Not at all. I just thought you'd have the nerve to give it a go. But I see . . .' He caught up to her at last and kept his strides long. 'But I see I misjudged the situation. I'm sorry. I'll . . . find a cab for us . . . somewhere . . .' He looked down at the small derringer in his hand and reluctantly returned it to her. She snatched it up. He winced, expecting the worse, but she no longer seemed inclined to aim it at him again. Instead, she weighed it in her hand for a moment before returning it to her small purse.

Tim looked up and down several streets and could find nothing. Only the sounds of the nearby rail lines, putting the trains to bed for the night.

She slowed to a stop and, under the light of a street lamp, looked him over. 'You truly expected me to break into a house with you?'

'I thought you would. You seem . . . I'm sorry.'

She bit down on the tip of one finger of her long gloves and pulled the material, stretching it. She looked back toward where they had got out of the cab. And then she squared on him. 'You really thought I'd do that?'

'It wasn't no disparagement of your character, Miss Littleton. I just thought, blimey, here's a woman not afraid of getting a story, writing about crime, of all things. She'd be a helluva – er, a right . . . *daring* . . . lass to have on hand. That's all I thought.'

'Housebreaking?'

'Not a house, really. A shop. A jumble shop. We'd look around a bit, try to find out some information, and get out. Easy-breezy.'

'You must think I'm mad.'

But she didn't look mad. She didn't even look angry, he decided. She looked like she was actually considering it. He sidled closer. 'Wouldn't *that* be something to write about?'

'If I don't get arrested.' She didn't look as worried as she had earlier.

'You won't. I'll take the blame if the coppers show up. What do you say, eh?'

She only took a moment to nod her head with a smile. 'But I am keeping a close eye on you, Tim Badger.'

'See that you do,' he muttered, pushing his homburg into a jaunty angle.

He motioned for her to keep close to him and stay out of the lamplight. Once they found the shop, they skirted the perimeter, looking for windows, transoms, unlocked back doors, but everything seemed to be tightly barred.

He went around to the back again and, checking to make certain there was no one to see, he took his skeleton keys and lock picks from a wallet in his pocket.

'Are those what I think they are?' she said quietly.

'They are indeed.'

'That's fascinating.'

He turned to look back at her with her bright expression. Oh yes. She found criminals perhaps a little too interesting.

'Mind the street and keep watch,' he said. She did so, but as he bent over to work on the lock, her hand was pressed to his shoulder as a warm presence. It didn't please him to think how much he liked the feel of it. He flicked a glance up at her, but she was merely using his shoulder to steady herself as she strained to lean over and look one way down the alley and then the other.

He gathered himself and studied the lock. It looked to be a single lever lock, less complicated. His small skeleton keys would not suffice this time. Those were for small locks in drawers and such anyway. This required his lock picks: a large L-wrench and a smaller one. He first inserted the smaller wrench's L-shaped piece into the top of the keyhole, facing upward. With his finger giving it just a breath of tension, he could force the spring-loaded lever inside the lock to rise enough for the tab on the deadbolt to unlock from its slot on the lever, the part inside that was keeping the lock, well . . . locked. Maintaining the tension on the top wrench, all he had to do was insert the second, larger wrench in the bottom of the keyhole as if it were a key, L part facing downward. As he turned the bottom wrench slowly, he felt not only the lever rise further, but – acting as the key – it allowed the lever to do its job and pull back the bolt.

He sighed at the satisfying feel of the bolt sliding back out of the box and the striking plate in the doorframe as the door whispered open.

'You did it,' she hissed at his ear. 'You have *got* to show me how to do that!'

'I will. But now's the time to be quiet.' He put a finger to his lips and she nodded solemnly, the ostrich feather in her hat gently agreeing.

He returned his lock picks to his pocket, stuck his head in the door, and looked around. No sign of the old man. It was late enough that he would be in bed . . . wherever that was. He motioned for her to follow and she had the sense to close the door gently and quietly.

He moved around the shadowed items that loomed up in the darkness. He had thought it was bad enough with its close dustiness and murkiness in the daytime, but at night it was a cave of mysteries.

Suddenly, he smelled roses, and realized she was close beside him and whispering, 'What are we looking for?'

*A very good question*, he mused. What *were* they looking for? Some fool notion from Watson . . . although Ben was no fool at all. If his colleague thought there was something to this 'Atic', then there very well could be. Because Watson was right. It *couldn't* be a coincidence. What was it the medium – Josie Williams – had told to her séance audience around that table, pretending it was the dead Stephen Latimer talking? She had told him that whatever it is Quinn was looking for was in the A-T-I-C. And that's where they were now, in Atic's Jumble and Curiosities. What was so important to Quinn that needed to be found? And why here?

Something physical, then. Papers? It was logical to think so. That made more sense than an old chair or shepherdess figurine. But hadn't Thomas Brent broke into Latimer's house and brought back a strongbox? The papers in that hadn't seem to satisfy Quinn.

Atic had come upon them the other day like some old wizard, popping in out of nowhere, but he had to have come from his office, and God-knew-where that was in all these piles of rubbish. He thought back on that day; Atic had appeared to the right of the front door.

Tim rose on his toes and peered toward the front window. Even with a curtain before the panes of glass, the streetlights filtered through. At least they were headed in the right direction.

Littleton stuck close to him, but her long skirts caught, scraping a chair which sent a rug thumping to the floor. She lost her balance and started to fall. He whirled, grabbed her, and found himself nose to nose with her, his head filling with the scent of roses . . . and woman.

They both stilled, listening. Then . . . they stared at each other's eyes.

His arm wound round her, clutching the layers of dress, corset, woman. He couldn't help it. He couldn't look away. Her large, luminous eyes filled his sight. He had known they were brown but, in the darkness, they seemed like velvet depths of a deep unknown. He became aware that one of her hands curled over his shoulder and the other was trapped between them, flattened against his chest. Surely she could feel his heart thumping. Surely she could *hear* it.

For a long moment they merely held each other, much closer than they would have if they had been dancing. So close that if he leaned in a mere few inches, he could be kissing her. The thought heated his cheeks and his heart seemed to double its tattoo, yet still he did not move away.

Her breath quickened and her gaze finally lowered, perhaps looking at his lips as he was looking at hers, considering . . . Until she stepped back, righting herself.

'Thank you,' she whispered. 'My . . . my skirt got caught and . . .'

'Oh. Yes. I just . . .'

His fingers reluctantly released from the satiny dress, that slim waist, and they stood apart from one another.

It took another long moment for Tim's mushy brain to remember why they were there in the first place.

He cleared his throat, straightened his tie, though it didn't need any attention. He turned around and gathered himself. After a deep breath, he led the way once again through the labyrinth of objects and stacked furniture. He was more aware than ever of her presence behind him. *Steady, Badger,* he admonished himself. *Keep your head on the business at hand.* Squeezing through some of the narrower openings, they reached the office at last. It lay behind a long wall of multi-paned windows with a door with similar multi-paned windows on its upper half.

When Tim tried the door, he was surprised to find it unlocked.

The soft click made him wince, even though the building itself creaked . . . or was it the stacks of furnishings like a child's toys, vulnerable to the slightest breeze that might knock it all over like rows of dominoes?

He stood for a moment in the doorway and peered through the gloom, wondering for the hundredth time *what* he could be looking for and *where*?

'If you told me what you're after, maybe I could help,' she whispered.

'The thing of it is,' he said, equally as quiet. When he turned to her, her eyes were as enigmatic as before and glittering from the scant glow from a skylight. He saw excitement in them, for this sort of thing seemed like meat to her character. It made him wonder that much more about her and her situation. By her conversation, her parents were both gone, leaving her a small annuity that wouldn't go as far as they had planned for their . . . *only* . . . child? He found that he *wanted* to know more about her.

Suddenly, he realized he'd said nothing. It was her eyes that had enchanted him. Again. He made a valiant effort *not* to look at her lips. 'The . . . the thing of it is, Miss Littleton, during the séance in which Mister Quinn was killed, he had asked the medium to contact his dead business partner. And the dead man had told Quinn – through the medium—'

'Josie Williams,' she supplied.

*How the bloody hellfire had she . . .?* He took a breath. 'Er . . . well. Awright, so you know. Through what Josie Williams said, the evidence was in the Atic. Not the *attic* of a house but specifically the "A-T-I-C."'

'Atic's Jumble and Curiosities,' she murmured.

'So we think. So me and Watson was here the other day, looked about a bit, but there was nothing immediate to make sense to us. I thought it was just a coincidence, but even I had to admit later that it wasn't. So I think I'm going to look for some papers, maybe something from Stephen Latimer, his dead partner, that might show why Quinn was so desperate to find this information.' Even as he explained it to her, the idea of what it most likely was suddenly sprang to mind. But that, he would keep to himself.

He moved toward the wall where, out of the gloom, rose a walnut cabinet with eighteen drawers with tarnished brass cardholder handles. Each card was labeled with letters of the alphabet. Littleton quickly beat him there and grabbed the one with 'K–L' penned on it and pulled it out. She dug in and retrieved the stack of papers and looked about for a surface to put them upon.

'Over here,' he whispered, finding a desk and shoving the ledgers and books aside. He nearly shouted in fright when he encountered a stuffed squirrel, thinking it was a rat. Angrily, he pushed that aside as well.

She laid the papers down and started riffling through them. He read over her shoulder. 'I wish I had my police lamp with me,' he muttered. But perhaps her eyes were more acute and saw well enough in the dark.

She stopped when she got to the bottom of the pile. 'There's nothing here.'

'Atic said he'd had no dealings with Stephen Latimer, but I thought that maybe he just forgot.'

She flipped through them again. 'No,' she said, shoulders sagging. 'There's nothing here that has the name Latimer.'

He looked back at the drawers and the cabinet below them. He slid in front of it and, on his knees, opened the cabinets. They were stuffed full of ledgers, papers, rolled-up maps, and other sundries. But nothing there that had the name Latimer or Quinn on them.

He sat back and stared at it with a sour face. 'I was sure we'd find something.'

'Perhaps "Q" for Quinn?' she said.

This time Tim got to the 'Q–S' drawer first, rummaged through the stack, and sighed in frustration.

A match was struck and he was about to admonish the woman, when he glanced toward the over-brightness of match touching lamp wick. The bright glow subsided and left only the faint flickering in the glass globe.

But it wasn't Ellsie Littleton.

'And what is *this*?' asked an angry Randolph Atic, in dressing gown and night cap.

# TWENTY-ONE
## Badger

Tim slowly rose and straightened. Without thinking, he pushed Miss Littleton behind him. 'It's not like it seems, Mister Atic. I'm not robbing you.'

'Then I'd like to know just exactly what it is you *are* doing before I call for a constable.'

'Erm . . .' He looked down at his feet. How was he to get out of this one? He paused, took stock of himself, and lifted his face with a congenial smile. 'Mister Atic, do you remember me from the other day? Me and a black bloke were here and asked you a few questions about a Mister Horace Quinn and the late Stephen Latimer?'

His eyes squinted, studying him and he slowly nodded. 'Yes. Yes, I do. And you didn't buy anything.'

'That's because we was after information. Information you didn't seem to have. But now I see we asked the wrong questions.'

Atic shook his head and stepped back. And now Tim could see that not only did he have a lamp in one hand, but that he held up an elaborately carved and *bulky* cane in the other. Tim pushed the woman further behind him.

'And what has this to do with your breaking into my shop?'

'I . . . I apologize for this, Mister Atic. It was my hubris that made me do it. This young lady had nothing to do with this . . .'

'I am Miss Ellsie Moira Littleton, a reporter with *The Daily Chronicle*, and I'm afraid I urged on Mister Badger here to get me an exclusive. You must forgive us.'

'I mustn't do anything of the kind. Now. You just stand there while I fetch a constable—'

'Do you know Josie Williams?' Tim blurted. Atic kept moving. Tim's mind clicked in place like a lock. 'How about . . . Mary Brennan?'

Atic stopped in mid-turn. Clearly, he wanted to go on, but he seemed unable to. Finally, he turned back to them with a changed expression. A weariness seemed to come upon him and he sank to a chair, even though it had folded rugs and papers on it. He clutched the lamp in whitened fingers but the hand holding the cane fell to his side.

'That was a long time ago,' he said softly, voice strained.

Miss Littleton knelt beside him and Tim hadn't even noticed her moving. 'Is there somewhere we could make you a cup of tea?' She took the lamp from his quaking hand and looked to Tim.

'Er . . . ah . . . yes, Mister Atic. I didn't mean to cause you a shock. Can we help you to your . . . your . . .'

'Yes,' he said faintly. He allowed Littleton to take his arm and lift him. He turned back the way he had come through a dark doorway. The lamp lit the way to a long, narrow corridor with pictures hanging along both sides of it. It opened to a drawing room filled with swags of dusty fabric, ceramic odds and ends on little tables, a convex mirror in an oval frame above the fireplace, and thick, tasseled curtains. Near the hearth fender was a hob with a copper kettle, and a teapot next to it on a low stool.

'The tea is there,' said Atic, gesturing with a shaky finger to a tin on the mantel. He appeared to live in his drawing room, for there was also a pan and some pantry items on a bookshelf next to the fireplace, including a covered cheese dish, jars of marmalade, a butter dish attached to a toast rack, and stacks of cups and saucers.

Miss Littleton set about making tea while Tim placed the lamp on the mantel and gently lowered Atic into the upholstered chair that he seemed to have slept in.

'Who are you?' said Atic when he got his wits about him again.

Badger retrieved a card from his waistcoat. 'I'm Tim Badger, sir, and I am a private detective, as is my partner, the chap you saw me with the other day.'

Atic looked at the card. 'Private detective?'

'Yes, sir. My client is accused of a murder he did not commit, and we are searching for the evidence to free him from all possible charges.'

'Hmmm,' was all he said. He kept a tight grip of the card. 'What has this to do with Mary Brennan?'

Tim found a stool, pulled it over to Atic's chair, and sat. 'It was a long time ago, wasn't it, Mister Atic, that you knew Mary Brennan?'

'Yes. Yes, I knew her. She was a girl when she started house-keeping for me. She was all alone in the world, you see. She was a good girl. She . . . she helped me when I needed it. When my wife died. She stayed on until I couldn't pay her anymore, but I gave her an excellent reference.'

'But . . . that's not all it was, was it? You also knew her later when . . . when she was in trouble.'

His eyes glazed and he ran a hand down his face with its gray beard-stubble. 'How do you know about all this?' he asked between his fingers.

'I've been investigating, sir. It's all right to say.'

Miss Littleton suddenly came between them and handed Atic a cup and saucer. 'There you go now. Drink this. It will help you feel better.' She glanced sternly at Tim, daring him to stop her.

He waited till Atic raised the cup unsteadily to his lips and sipped the hot liquid. He swallowed and set the cup back into the saucer, and Miss Littleton set it down on a table beside him, taking the dusty objects off to make room for it.

'Mary Brennan?' Tim asked again. He could tell that Littleton was dying to ask him who *she* was, but he set his gaze on Atic and not on her dangerous features.

'Yes, it was . . . dear me . . . maybe twenty years ago now. She had a child, a baby with her. Newborn, as far as I could tell. And . . . well. She was a woman alone. I make no judgments, Mister Badger. Youth gets into trouble and there's nothing for it, no church or folk wisdom can sway them from their course. She was wise enough to know she could not keep a child and a roof over their heads at the same time. She had no family so she brought him to me, thinking that I would care for him in my loneliness and she would return from time to time to offer him the love of a mother. As it was . . . I did end up raising the boy, but I never saw her again. I know not what happened to her.'

'The child's name was Edward,' said Tim.

'Edward? No, she called him Thomas. And she asked that I use a different surname than hers. I suggested, of course, Atic. But she had another in mind.'

'God in Heaven,' Tim muttered. 'Was it . . . Brent?'

Miss Littleton gasped and he gave her a warning through his stern gaze.

'My goodness,' he said, flustered. 'Why . . . yes, it was. You have discovered much. She wanted something close to her own name, but wanted him to have his own identity. And he certainly had that – rather too much so.'

Tim flicked a glance at Littleton, whose desperate expression looked like she wanted to get a hold of a pencil about now. 'Was he a troublesome boy?' he asked.

'Oh my, yes. He grew up in the shop, worked in it for a while, and even enjoyed it in his youth, but as he grew older, he became restless, troubled. He knew I wasn't his father and he had questions I couldn't answer. He began to think I was lying to him. Poor soul. I couldn't convince him. He became more troubled. He began . . . well, to steal from me, and finally, he just left. I have seen nothing of him for these last five years.' He sat forward on the chair. 'Tell me, Mister Badger. Is he . . . is he still alive?'

'For now, he is. But he is in great trouble, wanted for murder.'

'Oh!' He fell back in his chair and, for a moment, Tim thought he'd fainted. But he was merely quiet, thinking his own solitary thoughts. At last, with fingers to his lips, he said, 'He couldn't have done it. He's a good boy at heart.'

'I don't think he done it, Mister Atic. That's why I'm trying to prove his innocence. Let me ask you one more thing about Mary Brennan. Could she have been using a different name? Might you know of one?'

'That's very peculiar that you should say. Several times over the years, I received anonymous coins in an envelope. I always wondered if it was from her. The last time I received one . . . it must have been a year ago because I still had a shop assistant then. He told me he knew the woman. She was a fortune teller at the last funfair that had come through town, a woman by the name of—'

'Josie Williams,' said Tim.

Littleton gasped again.

'Yes! That was the name. You said so before, didn't you? For a time, I thought she might be a friend of Mary Brennan's. But as time went on, I began to wonder if it wasn't her with a new name. Perhaps she was running from the father and did not wish for him to find the boy . . . or her.'

'I think that's exactly right, Mister Atic. You've filled in a lot of holes for me and my investigation. I'm much obliged to you.'

Atic suddenly shot out a hand and curled his fingers around Tim's wrist. 'You'll help him, won't you? You'll save him? Tell him he can come home to me. I do think of him as my son. If he needs money . . . if *you* need payment . . .'

'That won't be necessary.' Was he mad? But he couldn't bring himself to take money from this wretched old man. 'I will tell him, sir. But right now, I have to tie some loose threads together. You have been a tremendous help to me.'

'I'm so glad,' he said, lying back, eyes closed. He didn't move and Tim panicked. *Blimey! Is the codger dead?* But he was, in fact, snoring softly. Tim relaxed and straightened. When he glanced at Littleton, she had a gleam in her eye he didn't like.

He motioned for her to tiptoe away, but before he left the office, he grabbed the stuffed squirrel and left a shilling in its place on top of his calling card. He felt like a fool doing it. 'He wanted me to buy something . . .' he muttered in explanation.

They left by the back door, which he locked again, tucking the squirrel under his arm. Before she could speak, he spun on her, finger pointed into her face. 'You can't print none of that. Not yet.'

'I have the most amazing exclusive and you're telling me I can't use it?'

'Not just yet. Can't you see how this would compromise everything until we have all the facts? Do you want to be responsible for an innocent man hanging?'

'But this is evidence in his favor! Surely you can see that.'

'What I know, Miss Littleton, is that all the facts must be laid before us before he can truly be free of the hangman. You're forgetting we have to nab the real killer.'

'Tell me why Mary Brennan left a child with Mister Atic. Tell me why she now goes by the name of Josie Williams.'

'I will. In time, Miss Littleton. Blimey, haven't you listened to a damned thing I said all evening? Don't you trust me yet?'

She stilled. Clearly, she remembered, as did Tim, in a rush of heat to his face, how they had been entwined in the dark of Atic's shop. She seemed to be drawing closer, though Tim decided it was his imagination.

Wasn't it?

'I do trust you, Mister . . . Tim. Can you trust me?'

He hated to do it, but he gradually shook his head. 'I don't know, Miss . . . Ellsie. I'd like to.' He chewed on his lip and thought a moment. 'Come with me back to Dean Street. You and me and Watson can talk it through. Will you? You'll still get your exclusive. I promise.'

'Yes, Mister Badger. I will come with you.'

Now all they needed was a cab.

# TWENTY-TWO
## Watson

Even though he said he wouldn't, Ben waited up for Badger. *Of all the addle-pated things to do*, he thought, *why court that nosey reporter?* 'He's got a fatality about him, does Tim. Ready to kill this business before it's really begun. I'll kill him myself if he gives it all away to her . . .'

The sounds of the street door opening alerted him. He glanced at the clock on the mantel. It read quarter past one.

He rose, pulled tight the tie at his dressing gown, and readied to give him what for as the door unlocked. 'What hour do you call this?' he said, and then stilled, jaw loose.

There she stood, bold as brass on his threshold. He didn't even hear Badger's explanation. He just stared at her. That he would bring her here under their roof . . .

'Now, Ben,' he was saying when Ben's ears finally stopped ringing. 'I thought it was better to bring her here to talk it out rather than to let her go off and print the thing.'

'What are you talking about?'

'Good evening, Mister Watson,' she said, as genteel as you please.

He nodded to her but said nothing in response. Only pulled the top of his dressing gown tighter over his union suit.

'Sit down, Ben. Let me explain it. I figured a lot of it out tonight.'

Ben sat, barely registering that he'd done so. Badger waved around some sort of rat and Ben stopped him, pointing at the thing.

Badger laughed. 'Oh, this! It's just an ornament.' He tucked it next to the clock on the mantel.

Badger then explained about the music hall, and that he'd got an idea and took Miss Littleton to Atic's shop.

Ben jumped up. 'You what? Without *me*?'

'Honest to God, Ben. Sit down so we can talk about it.'

He sat again, but he felt his pulse pounding, hands curling into fists on the armrests.

Then Badger told some fool tale about breaking into Atic's shop – showing off, no doubt – and then discovering that Mary Brennan left a child with Atic who was . . .

'By Heaven,' he gasped. 'Thomas Brent? Our Thomas Brent? Quinn's heir, Thomas Brent?'

'Er . . . that last part I *didn't* tell Miss Littleton . . .' he said out of the side of his mouth.

When Ben glanced her way, her eyes were bright with possibility. They were both suddenly standing over her. 'You are not to print this,' said Ben in his sternest voice.

'I'll have to print it. It's my responsibility.'

'Yes, I agree.'

'Ben!' said Badger.

'To a *point*,' Ben clarified. 'But you can't go off willy-nilly printing *what* you like *when* you like. You have got to have some discretion, Miss Littleton. Don't you understand? If this gets out before all the facts can be given to the police, they may not be able to sort it properly, may not even believe it, and put the man on trial anyway. He won't have a chance if he goes to trial. You *must* keep it to yourself for now.'

'That's what I told her.'

She rolled her eyes and sat back in the chair.

Badger knelt beside her. 'Ellsie,' he said quietly.

*So it was Ellsie now?*

'Please. See reason. Trust me. Trust *us*, Watson and me.'

'It's no use, Tim,' Ben said. 'Can't you see she's used you from the start?'

'No, she hasn't. Awright, that first encounter when we had tea, but not tonight.' He looked at her forlornly. *Ah Tim. Did you trust her again?* 'Say it . . . wasn't that, Miss Littleton? We . . . we . . . had a good time, didn't we?'

She gazed at him. Ben couldn't tell from her blank expression just what was on her mind. 'We did have a good time,' she said. 'The best I've had in a long while. And I wasn't using you . . . this time. On my honor, Mister Badger.'

Badger looked as if he were trying to believe her, but his face had paled. *Poor Tim.* 'Then you still can't print it,' he said. 'We have to find out more.'

'Then you must *tell* me more. Make me part of your little club. You help me and I'll help you.'

'No.'

They both looked at Ben.

'This is all very pretty us all working together, but the fact of it is, Miss Littleton, I don't trust you.'

'Ben . . .'

'Shut it, Tim. You're too pixilated.'

'Who's pixilated?'

'*You* are! She's pixilated you.' And little wonder. Looking her over, she was a delightful dish in that tight-fitting gown that showed off her figure to the best advantage. That long neck, those genteel features. It was hardly surprising that Badger had fallen for it. Most men would have.

'Well,' she said, adjusting the hem of her opera gloves, 'I think you will find that the ship has sailed. I already know too much. And, short of mayhem, there's little you can do to stop me . . . Unless you agree to work *with* me.'

'Isn't that what we wanted all the time, Ben?'

'No, it isn't. We wanted her to stop printing lies about you and too much information to queer our investigation. But like she said, I don't suppose that – short of mayhem – we can do much about it now, thanks to your big mouth.'

'I resent that you said that,' said Badger, puffing himself up.

'Resent it or not, it's the truth. Now. Since you've got us at your mercy, what do you want, Miss Littleton?'

She stood, her face eager. 'I want to be in on it. I want to know what you know thus far. And, in the end, I promise to print not one word until you say so. Let *me* be your Boswell!'

'Our what?' croaked Badger.

'Like a Doctor Watson to the two of you. If I write up your investigations, I can make you both famous. Won't that help you to get more clients?'

Ben could see, even from where he was standing, the dazzle in Badger's eyes. 'Slow down, everyone. Let's all sit down, shall we?'

He knew he had to be the adult. Badger couldn't manage it – though he had a sharp mind, him figuring it all out about Mary Brennan and Thomas Brent, for instance. He had to admit, the man could do it when he put his mind to it. He just couldn't *act* like an adult.

They all sat, and both Badger and Littleton leaned forward in their seats.

'Awright. What you say is the most sensible solution, Miss Littleton. I don't like it, but it's our only course. So, this is what we know thus far . . .'

She whipped out a notebook and pencil from her little beaded purse and wrote quickly as he explained; how in the séance Quinn wanted to contact his old business partner about something he desperately wanted to find—

'And I got an idea about that,' Badger interrupted.

'Oh yes?' said Ben.

'Yes. What could it be but the identity of his son?'

'So Latimer somehow found out . . . And Brent working all this time in the man's household. And hating him.'

'That's dreadful,' muttered Littleton, eyes on her notebook, pencil working.

Ben squirmed a little uncomfortably in his chair. 'And that's why Josie Williams/Mary Brennan said what she said in the séance. A-T-I-C. To rile him up? A secret only she knew? That's evil that. But how did Latimer find out?'

Badger stuffed his hands in his trouser pockets. 'That's what we have to discover. And you know . . . I don't think he died of natural causes, like Smith said. I think someone killed him to stop him from telling Quinn.'

'That puts it back on Mary Brennan.'

'It does at that. We've got to tie her to it.'

'There's plenty of things that would look like natural causes,' said Ben. Now he was in his element. Chemistry. So many little poisons that wouldn't leave an obvious trace, especially for a man who was perhaps on his last legs anyway.

'But first,' said Littleton, 'we have to *find* Mary Brennan. How did she know Quinn needed to have a séance?'

They both looked at her. Badger smiled. It was in his eyes. The damned fool was falling for her.

'Yes, how *did* she know?'

Miss Littleton sat back in her chair, resting her notebook on her lap and gazing at the two of them in turn. 'I can now see how accomplished you both are. You really are good at this. I apologize all over again, Mister Badger, for having doubted you. And this time . . . I mean it.'

'I will take that apology, Miss Littleton,' he said, as he placed his hand to his heart with a little bow, 'as it seems genuinely sincere this time.'

The smile she gave him was enough to melt a block of ice. Ben rolled his eyes. His gaze fell to the clock again. And then that damned moth-eaten squirrel. 'It's late. Shouldn't Miss Littleton be going home now?'

She rose, stuffing her notebook and pencil back in her beaded bag that seemed far too small to contain them. She clutched something in her hand. 'You're right, Mister Watson. As further proof of my sincerity, I offer you both my card with my address.'

She presented it to Ben but Badger swooped in and snatched it first, reading it. He snapped the corner of the card with his finger. 'As I deduced.'

'Yes, you did. And now, gentlemen, if one of you would be so good as to fetch me a cab . . .'

Badger ran to the door. 'Back in a mo.'

The door closed behind him and they could hear him thump down the stairs. That left Ben and Littleton to regard one another.

'I'd appreciate it if you didn't break his heart,' he said, breaching the silence that had fallen between them.

The look of surprise on her face at his candidness was almost comical.

'Why . . . Mister Watson, I . . .'

He waved her off and strode to the fireplace. Taking up a poker, he jostled the coal through the grate. 'I like to speak plainly, miss. I know he's an easy mark, but it would be best for all around if you didn't toy with him.'

'I'll have you know I have no intention of—'

'Do spare me.' He watched the glow emerge from the coal, felt the warmth of the fireplace. He slammed the iron back in its stand. 'I can well see exactly what you're doing. He's flippant about it but deep down he's a sensitive soul and I'll not have you hurt him.'

He didn't look over his shoulder but instead felt her approach. Softly, she said, 'Mister Watson, I hope you can believe me when I say that I wouldn't hurt Tim Badger for the world. I . . . I truly got to know him tonight. And I can indeed see how sincere he is.'

'He's not in your social position. He's a lad from the slums of Shadwell. He'll never be in your social class. You can't expect him to be.'

She straightened. 'If there is one thing you must know about me, Mister Watson, it's this: I don't care a fig for social positions. You forget. I am a woman. And I've been told more often than I care to hear how I cannot do this or that, or go here or there, simply because I am a woman. And I am beginning to see just what some of these organized women's groups mean when they argue for their rights.'

Ben bristled at that. It wasn't something he was particularly fond of.

'I've had to fight for this job and fight to keep it. Fight to be taken seriously. Fight every time I go to interview men or women who don't think I am a real reporter. Fight for decent pay for myself. Fight even for a *desk* in the newsroom. And yes, I admit to playing coy games to get my stories. Using my "female wiles" as some have called it. And I justify it because it's necessary to do my job. But it doesn't mean I like doing it. Mister Badger is . . . he's a sweet man and intelligent and full of verve. And I like him. Yes, I do. I like him . . . perhaps more than is proper. But I promise to the best of my ability not to hurt him or break his heart, as you say. And that's the best guarantee that I can give you right now.'

They both fell silent again. They listened to the ticking of the clock, the coal crackle and fall through the grate. Until the woman broke the silence and spoke in a quiet, friendly fashion. 'Were *you* a Baker Street Irregular too?'

He sighed and watched the glowing coals. His eye flicked reluctantly toward the stuffed squirrel, giving a humorless chuckle as he folded his arms over his chest. 'No. I've had a lot of jobs, Miss Littleton – and none of this is for printing. That had better be clear.'

She nodded and listened with a solemn expression.

'Well . . . every one of my jobs has been good training for detecting, I can assure you. I was a milkman, a butcher, a barman, a roofer, a chimney sweep, a chemist's assistant and a funfair performer. And a blacksmith. And it was five years ago that I worked hard in that profession, and five years ago I first became acquainted with one Timothy Badger. He was fleeing from the law, as usual. Ran right across the roof of the stable I was working in, with rozzers hard on his tail, when he fell right through the roof. Fell right in front of me like some angel dropped him there. Course, he was no angel and neither was I. And for some reason, I hid him when the rozzers came through looking for him. And that was the beginning.'

'How extraordinary.'

'Tim has a way about him that makes people do for him. He's likable. And he took to me for some reason, and I've been ever grateful for that friendship. I'd hate to have it end because of some fool woman who don't know how to keep her trap shut.'

'Mister Watson, I give you my sincerest assurances—'

Before Ben could reply, Badger burst through the door, out of breath. 'Had to run all the way to Oxford Street to get it but he's waiting outside now . . .' He stilled and took them both in, trying to figure out what had been going on between them and suddenly not liking what he saw, if his particular frown aimed at Ben was anything to go by.

Miss Littleton moved forward. 'Then I will take my leave of you, gentlemen. And we shall talk again. I trust you will be investigating Stephen Latimer. I wonder if you'd mind if I talked to the Quinn household myself. Discreetly, of course.'

'Not at all,' said Badger.

At the same time Ben said, 'Out of the question.'

He and Badger squared off.

'Er . . . I'll leave the two of you to . . . to discuss it. Good night, then.' She brushed past Badger to get to the door. He looked away at last from Ben to open it.

'I'll see you off, Miss Littleton.'

Out he went, giving Ben a backwards scowl.

And by that, Ben knew for certain that they would never be rid of her.

# TWENTY-THREE
## Watson

He was up early and trudged into the drawing room just as Katie Murphy was laying out the breakfast things. He immediately straightened, adjusting his tie, his collar, and brushing down the sleeves of his tweed coat, as if he hadn't spent some time in his bedroom doing just that.

'Good morning, Mister Watson,' she said merrily.

'Oh, er, good morning, Miss . . . I mean Murphy.'

She tried to hide her smile by turning her head to grab the coffee pot. 'How about a cup of good, strong coffee this morning, sir?'

'Erm . . .' He fiddled with the serviette at his place at the table. 'You know, I don't think you should call me "sir." It don't feel right.'

'But it *is* right . . . sir.'

'But I'm not a man to be "sirred," if you get my meaning.'

She cocked her head to study him. He felt like a fly on the cheese. 'Well, if you consider that "sir" is a sign of respect, then I respect you, Mister Watson, for the work you're doing. Doesn't that deserve a "sir"?'

'But then calling you only by *your* surname doesn't seem respectful of *you*. I'd prefer to call you *Miss* Murphy, being more in the way that *I* respect you and your work.'

She blinked at him, saying nothing, which made him fiddle all the more with the silverware, the empty cup, the saucer.

'I mean,' he went on, 'it seems to me your work is just as important. With your excellent meals and keeping the place clean and all. And believe me, I've had enough of people surnaming me *without* respect, and I don't like to surname you when you should be a "Miss," which seems more respectful. See . . . see what I mean?'

A smile touched the edges of her mouth and she looked at him squarely. 'I can see that this vexes you.'

He gave a great exhale of breath. 'I never had no servants. It's me what's been the servant and it just don't sit well. If I can call you Miss Murphy, that would go a long way to making me more comfortable.'

'Well!' She put a hand to her cheek. 'My, my. Very well, Mister Watson. "Miss Murphy" it is. For you.' She gave him a final nod, spun on her heel and tromped out of the room, the ribbons on her cap flickering after her.

He sank into his chair and stared at the tablecloth. 'Blimey,' he whispered. Nothing had ever seemed as hard as that. Though . . . what he really wanted to call her was . . . 'Katie'. And he wanted to hear her call him 'Ben'. But he was much too wary of even suggesting it. Badger would call him a coward, but Mrs Kelly was right in that they shouldn't mix employer and employee. Look where it got poor Thomas Brent.

Badger came through his bedroom door, yawning loudly and stretching his arms up. He was in his waistcoat and shirtsleeves. Watson quickly motioned to him.

'What are you flapping at me about, Ben?'

'Put your coat on. This isn't no doss house.'

'What?'

'Miss Murphy will be coming back to serve the eggs,' he rasped.

'Oh. *Miss* Murphy, is it, now?'

'And *Ellsie* it was for *you* last night?'

Badger's lazy smile irritated. 'Well, it's just that—'

'Listen, mate, she's far out of your class. She's from Mayfair.'

'I know it. But look, Ben, if a lad like me can come from Shadwell and end up here on Dean Street, then only God knows just *where* I'll end up. Prime Minister, maybe.' He laughed and sat, pouring himself coffee before he shook out the serviette and tucked it into his collar, smoothing it out over his chest.

'Tim . . .'

Badger's face sobered slightly and he didn't look at Ben when he said, 'Just you worry over yourself, m'lad, and I'll worry over me.'

Before Ben could speak further, Murphy came through the door with two covered dishes of eggs and sausage on a tray. She set them up on the sideboard and then brought the toast in its rack to the table. 'Will there be anything else for you gentlemen?'

'Nothing for me, Murphy,' said Badger with his wide smile. 'What about you, Ben? Anything to tell *Miss* Murphy?'

Ben never lifted his scowl from Badger and gritted out, 'Nothing, thank you.'

She gave them both a quick glance and never even tried to hide her smirk when she turned and left them to it.

Ben admitted that Badger had a lot to be proud of, figuring out most of their case in one swoop. And he also had to admit that he himself might have been, perhaps, the tiniest bit jealous that Badger had done it with Ellsie Littleton instead of himself. But at least they were further along in the case and would surely meet the deadline that Inspector Hopkins had set for them.

He grabbed his plate and took it to the sideboard, loading it with scrambled eggs and kippers. 'Today we dive into what Stephen Latimer was all about.'

Badger stood beside him, shoveling all the rest of the eggs, sausage and blood pudding onto his own plate. 'And catch Mary Brennan, alias Josie Williams, if we can.'

'Do you want to split up?'

'Nah,' he said, spearing an entire sausage with his fork and biting off the end of the savory meat. A bit of grease trickled down the side of his mouth from his vigorous chewing, which he wiped away with the serviette. 'I'd rather work *with* you on it like the partners we are.' Ben raised his face and caught Badger's sincere expression. 'Don't think I don't know why you're so peeved at me.'

'Oh yes? And why is that?' Ben slurped his coffee and bit down on a bit of toast smothered in marmalade.

'Because I went and broke into Atic's without you. And I'm sorry for doing that. Truth to tell, I was . . . well. I was showing off a bit. Like you probably reckoned I was.'

Ben said nothing as he ate. Only raised his brows.

'And it was a ruddy stupid thing to do with a reporter. Strewth! I truly thought that at this point I could trust her. And that might be stupid too.'

Ben's brows continued to arch in the higher reaches of his forehead. The only sounds he made, however, were chewing and slurping.

'But working *with* her, her being our own Doctor Watson, so to speak.' He slapped Ben's shoulder. 'That sounds good, don't it? And if she finds out anything when she interviews the household today, that's one more clue we don't need to get on our own. I think this will work. Mutually beneficial to both parties.'

Watson finished his meal, pulled the serviette from his collar, and wiped his mouth with it. 'And you decided that all on your own, did you?'

Badger stilled, even stopped chewing, a wad of food bulging his cheek. He swallowed it hard and wiped his mouth. Sitting back, he stared at his colleague. 'Oh.'

'I thought we was in this together. Equals.'

'We are, Ben. Truly!'

'But here you are, making decisions that affect the both of us without consulting me.'

Badger shut his eyes. His cheeks burned red. 'Ah, I'm sorry, Ben. I just . . . just . . .'

'Didn't think.'

Ben left the table, tossing the serviette toward it, and strolled into the main part of the sitting room, first taking a few more calling cards and stuffing them into his waistcoat, scooping up a few coins from the carved box and dropping them into his coin purse, and then checking to see if he had enough cheroots and matches in his inside coat pocket, before, lastly, winding his pocket watch and setting it to the mantel clock . . . and shaking his head at the stuffed squirrel giving him a cock-eyed stare.

Badger was soon following him around the room, snatching his coat from off a chair where he had left it the night before and struggling to put it on. 'I'm sorry, Ben. It won't happen again.'

Watson ground to a halt and whirled around. 'Won't it? Because that seems to be your style, mate. You make me promises and then you break them. I'm just as invested in this venture as you are. I want to make it work. It ain't a lark to me. It's a vocation. Something that can better our situation. Together. It's a partnership. And if one of the partners goes off on his own without consulting the other, then surely there is tragedy ahead.'

'You're right, Ben. You're so right, and I won't do anything like it no more. I swear to you.'

Ben made for the front door and stopped again. 'You'd better keep your mind on it. And off skirts.'

'Now, Ben. Be reasonable.'

'It's just our whole lives on the line, is all. Think on it.'

Badger was suitably chastened as they made their way down the lane to Oxford Street where they could catch a green omnibus.

They paid their fare and rode, bouncing as it made its way over the cobbles. 'I was thinking,' said Badger, meekly. 'We should check up on Brent. He was in a bad way when I left him last.'

'That's a good idea.' Ben bounced with the 'bus. 'Do you think he has any inkling about Quinn?'

Badger's eyes darted here and there, looking for the street. 'Nah, how could he? Unless his mother told him.'

'It don't seem like something she'd tell him. Plus, she hasn't talked to the bloke in ages.'

They both agreed. Of course the 'bus wouldn't go to St Giles, so they had to get out close enough to it. They hopped off onto the nearest street and made their way there, leaping over puddles in the gutters and striding quickly along the cracked pavement.

'Did you kiss her?' Ben blurted.

Badger whipped his head about. 'Did I kiss . . . who?'

'Who d'ya think?'

Badger reddened, running his hand up the back of his neck. 'No, Ben, I didn't kiss her. Do you think she's a lass who'd let a bloke like me kiss her first thing?'

Badger seemed particularly agitated, as if he *had* been expecting it. Ben suddenly, unaccountably, felt bad for his friend.

'Tim, if you trifle with her, our reputation will be in peril.'

Badger hurried to keep pace. 'I didn't kiss her! She's not like these lasses down here. She's a lady.'

'Right you are. She *is* a lady. She's Lady Ellsie. She's the daughter of a baronet.'

'Pull the other one.'

He stopped and suddenly grabbed Badger's arm and swung him up against a house rail. 'Look, Tim, I took down the volume of *Who's Who* off the bookshelves this morning that Mister Holmes kindly left for us. She is the daughter of Sir Reginald Littleton, Baronet of March.'

Badger's mouth slowly fell open. 'No.'

'Yes. So . . . she's really a lady . . . though, strictly speaking, the children of a baronet have no titles. And she don't inherit the baronetcy. She's not a peer, not styled "Lady Ellsie" or some such,' he added. 'But *still*. You get my point.'

'She's really . . .' Badger stared at the ground, rubbing his face with his hand as if waking from a dream.

'She is. So get any notions out of your head now.'

'But . . . she talked to me like a . . . like a girl in a pub.'

'A girl with a job. Keep your mind on your own.'

Badger blew out a breath and adjusted his coat. 'Blimey. I wish you hadn't told me that.'

'I had to make you see clearly, mate. We've got a lot of work to do. Now let's get to it.'

The bells of St Giles-in-the-Fields church rang out. Ben supposed there were some old ladies who trudged to prayers every day, like nuns. Of course, some just went in to keep warm.

The slums of St Giles were a sad commentary on London life, for not too far away was prosperous Bloomsbury where Quinn had lived . . . and died. These old brick structures on this side of the church, painted with soot and grime, had been there since the early part of the century, and the landlords seemed uninterested in their investment, with no plans to improve them. And, by the smell of it, they didn't seem to have any intention of repairing the sewer either.

Badger said they were looking for a bootblack in front of a basement window, and it was Ben's dumb luck that he spied him first.

They made their way across the street, passing the bootblack's row of baubles and bits for sale on the sill. Badger took the lead and started down the steps when the bootblack stopped them.

'No one's down there that you'd be looking for.'

'What do you mean?' asked Badger. 'I've got a friend who lives down there.'

'Not anymore you don't. The coppers came and nicked him early this morning.'

# TWENTY-FOUR
## Badger

They strode at full tilt into Hopkins's office, with the sergeant from the desk running after them, shouting.

'It's all right, Sergeant,' said Hopkins, rising from his chair. The copper gave them the eye before he nodded to Hopkins and closed the door behind him. 'Won't you sit down?' said Hopkins, gesturing toward two chairs before his desk. The man seemed to favor brown tweed, for he always appeared to be garbed in it.

'Did you nick Brent?' Tim couldn't help himself and jumped right in, refusing to sit.

Hopkins sighed and sat himself behind his desk. 'Yes. We saw an opportunity and we grabbed it. There had been a complaint. We didn't know it was him at first.'

Tim sank to his chair. 'He didn't do it, Inspector.'

'And have you any evidence to the contrary?'

'Plenty!'

Watson put up a palm to slow him down. It annoyed Tim that he employed such techniques with him, but he reckoned, all in all, he was usually right. So he allowed Watson to address Hopkins first. 'We have come into quite an interesting chain of evidence, sir, that points to an entirely different culprit. But before we can discuss it with you,' he said, cutting off whatever Tim was about to say, 'we would like to talk to Brent.'

'All right. I'll allow it.' He got up from his desk and opened the door. 'Sergeant, these gents need to talk to Thomas Brent in his cell. Allow them all the time they need.'

The sergeant and his waxed mustache grumbled unintelligibly, but he grabbed his ring of keys and led the way into the cells.

They were taken down a long corridor with a curved ceiling, and door after door lining both walls on either side. Each heavy wooden door had a small grid of bars to view the prisoner, and the sergeant finally stopped at one and tapped on the grid with the key. 'Brent! Visitors.' He turned the key in the lock, got his copperstick ready, and opened the door.

Tim went through first. The white face of Brent looked up, eyes like hollows, despair slumping his body. Watson followed and the door was closed with a clunk of finality with the turn of the key.

'They got me,' was all he said.

Tim nodded. 'I'm sorry, Tom.'

Brent sat forlornly on the one steel frame bed with its straw-stuffed mattress. Its head was pushed up against a brick bench stretched along the entirety of the back wall, with a tiny window about ten feet above their heads that let in the only light in the four-by-eight cell.

Badger sat on the brick bench beside him. 'I should have checked on you sooner.'

'It's all for naught now.'

'No, it isn't. Look, Tom. We found out a great deal. Your mother was Mary Brennan, yes?'

Watson stood by solemnly, letting Tim do all the talking. He knew Brent seemed to be more comfortable talking to Tim.

Brent's sluggish gaze moved from one to the other. 'Yes.'

'And you was raised by Randolph Atic?'

'How'd you know that?'

'He's worried about you, by the way. He wants to help.'

Brent dropped his face in his hands. 'I haven't treated him very well. And he's been good to me, like my own father.'

Watson leaned against the cell wall and cleared his throat. 'He loves you like a father. And he believes you're innocent. Like we believe it.'

Tim rocked back against the wall, feeling the chill trickling down the brick from the window above. The cell was almost too small for a grown man. He remembered it well. 'You *are* innocent, ain't you, Tom?'

'Yes. Like I told you. He was a mean old bastard but I had no call to kill him.'

'Good to hear,' said Tim. 'Oh, and Tom, have you ever worked for a funfair or circus, or maybe a music hall?'

'What? No.'

'Do you know how to throw a knife?' Tim mimed it.

Brent looked from one to the other. 'Why would I know how to do that?'

'That's what we wanted to know.' Tim's eyes silently asked Watson if they should tell him.

Watson nodded.

'The thing of it is, Tom,' Tim went on, 'in the course of our investigating, we found out who your real father is.'

The man looked up. 'You . . . you did?'

'Yes. Turns out it's . . . well. Sorry, mate, but it's Horace Quinn himself.'

Brent sat silently, simply staring at the two of them a long time. 'What?' he croaked at last.

'Did you know, Tom?' asked Tim.

Brent shook his head, his face pale with shock.

Relieved, Tim went on. 'I know it ain't the best news, but the silver lining is this: you stand to inherit his house and goods. He's been looking for you, as it turns out.'

'Why are you telling me this now?'

'Because it's the truth,' Watson interjected. 'Ordinarily, this wouldn't help your case. But in this instance, we know who the murderer is. Erm . . .' He looked to Tim, and it was Tim who took up the story again with a deep sigh.

'Your mother worked in the Quinn household as the house-keeper a long time ago. Before Amelia Martin was ever hired. She and Quinn . . . well. As it happened, she fell pregnant . . . with you. She agreed to give up the baby to Quinn and pretend Mrs Quinn gave birth, and then she'd stay on as your nanny, see, and raise you. But . . .' He sighed again. 'That old bastard Quinn—'

'Easy now,' said Watson.

'Quinn broke his word, changed his mind and, after you were born, chucked her out. And so it seemed that . . . that Mary Brennan stole you and ran away. She might have killed Mrs Quinn.'

'She killed her?'

'I'm sorry, but it's looking that way. Everyone thought it was childbed fever for Mrs Quinn, but she wasn't the one giving birth. What else could it be?'

'How . . . how did she know Atic?'

'Before she got the job at Quinn's, she was a housemaid at the Atic place. She trusted him.'

'And left me there to rot.'

'Nah, mate. She left you there to someone who could care for you. She knew she couldn't.'

Tim watched him carefully. Brent remained dry-eyed, but it might be that he was in shock at it all. Finding out your mother was a murderer, your father was a lying bastard, and that you were an heir all at once would give any man pause.

Brent stayed as he was against the painted brick wall, taking it in.

'There's more,' said Tim. 'For years now, your mum went by a different name. Josie Williams. And it was her that did the séance . . . and it was her that killed Quinn.'

'My mother? That . . . that *Gypsy* woman . . . was my *mother*?'

'Yes. But . . . she ain't no Gypsy woman. She's an Irish woman.'

He and Watson waited, watching it all pass over Brent's face. He stared hard at the damp floor with its rusty square grate in the middle.

'So . . .' Watson straightened and pulled his hand from his trouser pocket. 'So we'll be trying to talk to Mary Brennan. We've encountered her twice but were not able to capture her. I'm afraid we must report this to Inspector Hopkins. But I don't think it will mean they'll release you just yet. But soon.'

'Look at it this way,' Tim added. 'You'll get fed regular here. And now you have hope of a quick release. You won't hang, Tom. That's a fact. And you'll be a well-off bloke when you get out. Because we'll tell the solicitor that we've found the long-lost heir.' *And we'll make our fee too*, he suddenly thought.

At that, Thomas Brent finally looked relieved. Badger realized he couldn't have remembered his mother either, having been surrendered to Atic when he was a newborn. So a father dead he didn't recall and a mother he'd never known down for murder. Inauspicious surely, but other men had it worse.

'I suppose you've earned your fee then. And if what you say is true, about me being a . . . an heir? I can afford it now.'

'We still have to capture Mary Brennan,' said Watson.

'My mother. Why did she kill Quinn? Or rather . . . why did she wait so long?'

'True, it seems she could have done it right away after leaving the house,' said Tim. But she reckoned, with a new name and a new place to live, he'd never find you. And he wouldn't have. But Quinn was trying to find out what Latimer's information was, and we reckon it was about who *you* were.'

'It was the only thing that seemed to matter to Quinn,' said Watson.

'And all this time,' said Brent with a hand to his forehead, 'I was right there, living in his household. And he treated me like a waster. What a mad story.'

'We'll have you out soon, Tom,' said Tim. 'That's what you need to hold on to.'

Still subdued, he didn't raise his head. 'I'm obliged to you, gentlemen.'

'Think nothin' of it,' said Tim. He elbowed Watson and the two of them called for the guard.

'That is an insane story,' said Hopkins once they'd told it again. The more Tim told it, the madder it seemed to him, too. They had to get their hands on Mary Brennan. But now all of Scotland Yard would be after her too. He hoped they'd get her alive.

'But do you believe it?' asked Watson.

Hopkins passed a hand over his mustache. 'I hate to say it, but I think I do.'

Tim puffed a bit. 'I don't suppose your lot investigated the death of Stephen Latimer?'

'Who's that?'

'Quinn's business partner. The reason he held the séance. He supposedly died of natural causes, on account of being sickly and malnourished.'

'We wouldn't usually investigate that, no. Best you find out if the man had a doctor.'

'That's good thinking, Inspector.'

'And the two of you came up with all this?'

'It's the method, I tell you, Inspector. My old guv's method of deduction. We're his protégés.'

'You are indeed. Well. We'll need to get this Mary Brennan, alias Josie Williams.'

'She's a slippery devil,' said Tim. 'Already tried to stab me as I lay sleeping. That was the dust-up you came to our lodgings about.'

'I see.'

Watson placed his hands behind his back and rocked on his heels. 'We reckon she also smothered Mrs Quinn, who was said to have died of childbed fever. But since she wasn't with child at all . . .'

'By Jove . . .' murmured Hopkins.

Badger smiled and popped his hat on his head. 'You'll need a nice thick file for this. Well, cheerio! We have a murderer to catch to tie it all up. Come on, Watson.'

Watson tipped his hat. 'Inspector.'

It was a good feeling leaving Scotland Yard without being pursued, with some respect under his belt, working *with* the coppers for a change, and being on the right side of the bars. He could certainly get used to this.

'How are we going to find out who Latimer's doctor was?' said Tim. 'Maybe there's someone near his house that knew?'

'Better still,' said Watson. 'Let's go to that solicitor. He might know of the doctor since he knew about his death early on.'

Smith welcomed them into his office. 'You have news for me, gentlemen?'

'We do,' said Tim. 'And we will have it for you soon. But we need more information. Did Stephen Latimer have a physician?'

'Yes. A Doctor Woodbridge. Elias Woodbridge, Regent Street.'

'Because we think Mister Latimer was murdered as well.'

'Good heavens!'

'But your heir is known to us. He's alive, and there's just a few complications to clear up before we can make him known to you.'

'That is splendid news! Splendid. I must say, you work quickly and efficiently. I will have no difficulty recommending Badger and Watson to others.'

Tim gave Watson a wide grin. 'We thank you very much, sir.'

'Upon revealing the heir's name, I will pay your fee.'

Tim rose. 'Then we'd best clear this up right away. Good day, Mister Smith.'

They both left the offices of the solicitor and stood on the pavement. 'You hear that, Ben?'

'I do. By God, this venture will rise, Tim!'

'Hard work, a little brain power, and Mister Holmes's methods, and we are on our way!'

He wanted to clap him in an embrace but, in the middle of the day, on the street as they were, he thought better of it. 'Come on. Let's get to Regent Street.'

They found the offices of Doctor Elias Woodbridge and waited with the other toff patients, those who didn't quite merit a house call. Much to his relief amongst the coughing and sniffling, they were allowed in first.

The doctor's office was a study in wood wainscoting, shelves filled with books, heavy green drapery at the tall windows, a marble fireplace with an arched silver grate, stuffed pheasants looking down from their high perches on corbels, and a leather-clad examination table with several brass floor lamps around it.

The man himself sported an impressive gray mustache that covered his entire upper lip and draped downward on either side of his mouth, with bushy eyebrows to match. A silver pince-nez sat on his bulbous nose with a black velvet tether attached to his coat's lapel.

'You are *private* detectives?' he asked, his scrutiny lingering over Watson in some disbelief, but unable to make a diagnosis from their appearance.

'Indeed, sir, we are,' said Tim. Watson was keeping tight-lipped, as he usually did in these circumstances. 'I am Timothy Badger and this is Benjamin Watson, my colleague. We are investigating one murder, sir, and possibly a second. I'll get right to the point, if I may. Do you recall your former patient, Stephen Latimer?'

The doctor's scrutinizing eyes ceased their ramble over them and instead fell into a blurred reminiscence. 'Indeed. The poor fellow. He was in a bad way. I was almost relieved for him.'

'Yes. But . . . though he was in a bad way, could he have been . . . er, *helped* along, shall we say?'

Tim didn't know what he expected from the doctor. He could have railed at them. Refused to believe anything other than his original report. Accused them of some sort of sensational conclusion.

Instead, the man sighed and sat back, removing the spectacles from his face. 'Well . . . I must confess that it did occur to me.'

Watson, likely caught by the man's cool demeanor, asked before Tim could, 'And why was that, sir?'

'When I was called in by his housekeeper, he was already gone, you see. I listened for his heartbeat, felt for a pulse, but he was, indeed, already deceased. And on examination I could find nothing untoward. It was a fact that he was malnourished and suffered from any number of ailments of poverty. How his housekeeper justified staying on . . . well. She was a good woman to cater to such a situation, out of Christian charity, no doubt. But. There was a peculiarity that I noted. Upon the side of his mouth, I found a damp feather, goose down. I didn't think much of it at the time. But later, when I did contemplate it, it crossed my mind that . . . someone . . . could have pressed his pillow to his face to suffocate him.'

'Blessed Lord,' murmured Watson.

'By Cripes,' Tim whispered. 'And, though this occurred to you, you did not think to report it to the Metropolitan Police?'

He shrugged. 'I didn't see the point. He had nothing to bequeath, no goods in the house, and he was soon to die at any rate due to a multiplicity of illnesses. What would be the point in bringing in a police inquiry?'

*Justice!* Tim wanted to shout. Even if it were his last day, a man needs the law to protect him. But upon measuring the stoic doctor, he did not judge it to be his duty to berate the man. What was done was done.

'Would you be willing to testify to your good opinion in court, sir?'

'Yes, should it come to that. I suppose it is my duty.'

'Thank you, sir. Do you think it was the housekeeper?'

'No. She was a loyal woman. She had family to return to. She had nothing to gain from it. And as I said, I deemed her to be a good Christian woman.'

'Thank you, again, Doctor Woodbridge. Here is our card should you have further questions. An Inspector Stanley Hopkins will call upon you at a later date.'

They bid their farewells and left his offices, walking along the damp pavement side by side. Watson remained quiet and thoughtful.

Tim took it for a long while – possibly a full minute – before he had to ask. 'What's on your mind, Ben?'

'I'd like to know why Mary Brennan killed Quinn, as we suspected.'

'Because he was a right bastard . . . though why had she waited so long?'

Watson pulled up his coat collar as a misty rain began to pelt their shoulders. It wasn't enough to clean the streets, and only made the pavement give off a muddy smell. 'If only we could nab her. She's a ghost herself, the way she disappears and reappears in the strangest of places.' He said nothing more, dropping into the solitude of his own thoughts. Tim said nothing either. He, too, was trying to work out why all this was being dredged up after something that happened twenty years ago.

The sun was fading behind a veil of fog rolling in from the Thames. It began shrouding the streets, drifting down from the rooftops, mingling with smoke and ash tumbling down from count-less chimneys. The lamplighters were busy on their ladders, lighting the street lamps. It seemed they were at it earlier and earlier, as the fog thickened ever more and the sunlight was stripped from the streets before the sun had a chance to set.

They arrived back to Dean Street and, in the dim lamplight, saw a shadowy figure lingering by their door.

Tim elbowed him and whispered, 'Ben, I think that's . . . it looks like . . .'

'It's Mary Brennan!' said Watson.

# TWENTY-FIVE
## Watson

B en was fully prepared to have Badger go after her when she ran, except . . . why was she waiting there if she didn't intend to speak to them?

'Mary Brennan!' he called out. It echoed hollowly on the gloomy street, devoid of human habitation, as if they were somehow transported to some drab goblin kingdom.

She turned to him, tensed, seeming ready to bolt, but didn't. She merely stood where she was, clutching the iron railing and breathing hard, puffing clouds of air into the cold mist. Once they were standing before her – Badger hanging back to give chase in whichever direction she ran – they could finally get a good look at her. It was Josie Williams, sure enough. Her eyes were like an animal's, darting here and there. She knew she was cornered, but she had put herself in that predicament. Ben sized up the situation.

'Shall we go in for some tea . . . so we can talk?'

She nodded, offering no argument. Ben presented her the stairs first, as if entertaining a lady of high rank. She clutched at her muddied skirts and raised them slightly to climb the steps. Watson then unlocked the door and led the way up the stairs with Badger bringing up the rear.

She certainly didn't smell like a grand lady, Ben observed. Probably living rough, frightened out of all her safe boltholes.

He turned up the gaslight when he entered their lodgings and offered her a seat by the hearth. Badger moved forward and stoked the fire. But it was Ben who rang the bell for the maid.

'Miss Murphy,' said Ben, without going silly at her presence for once, 'some tea for us, if you please.'

'Very good, Mister Watson.' She left without fuss. But he did notice that she didn't use 'sir'.

Badger stood by the fireplace fender, while Ben took a seat opposite Brennan, moving slowly and carefully so as not to startle her, as if she were a bird or a skittish cat. She seemed dirtier than the last time they had seen her on Drury Lane. She wrapped tight a flimsy shawl about her, her smudged and skeletal fingers digging into her arms.

No one said anything. They listened as the fire crackled over the sticks and settled to a warm flame in the coal. The rafters creaked. The occasional hansom clopped by on the street below.

They all turned at the thump on the stairs as Murphy pushed through the door with a tray. Without speaking, she left the tray on a table between the chairs, with three cups and saucers, a tea pot, a jug of milk, a sugar bowl and a plate of digestives.

'I'll be mother,' said Ben as he set to pouring milk and tea. 'Sugar, Miss Brennan?'

She nodded. He spooned in two, reckoning she might need it, and handed her the saucer.

She took it with trembling hands and drank. The warmth of it seemed to soothe and she set down a nearly empty cup. He filled it again.

'I must say,' he said, filling a cup for Badger and handing it to him, 'that we're a bit surprised to see you on our doorstep.'

'You ain't the only one,' she said, voice hoarse.

'We have been looking for you.'

'I saw in the paper that they arrested . . . my boy.'

Badger held his cup and saucer but didn't drink. 'As we told you might happen. So you admit to being Mary Brennan?'

'Isn't that why I'm here? I implore you, Mister Badger, Mister Watson. Don't let them hang him. He didn't do it.'

'Can you tell us about it? We've already spoken to Mister Atic.' Ben took up the plate of digestives and offered it to her. She took one, but he urged her to take more. She looked as if she needed the sustenance. Biting down on one and holding it between her teeth, she reached with her free hand and took a second.

Eating hastily, she snatched up the cup and drank. 'So you know a lot. Well, if you know that, then you know who the boy is.'

'Yes, Quinn's solicitor was most helpful in supplying that information.'

'Ah. Then the old bastard must have confided in him. Because *I* didn't tell nobody. I hope that old solicitor doesn't think it was some great love affair. It was ravishment, is what it was. He cornered me once in the kitchen when the missus was away. He was drunk, as he was many a day, and though I tried to fight him off, he was much stronger. And the next day, he went along as if nothing had happened. I kept my distance ever after. But it soon became obvious to me that I was in trouble.'

Ben was surprised she told it so matter-of-factly. But he supposed that women were stoic about the indignities that happened to them, perhaps had to be. He flashed on Miss Littleton's overtures about her constant fight for her place in the working world, and Watson felt a spark of empathy. Until . . .

'Did you kill Mrs Quinn?' he asked.

She raised her chin. 'Yes. She was going to keep my baby and call him her own. I was already grieving, the moment I handed him over to the nurse. But I settled it in my mind that I'd be there, I'd be his nanny and I'd be raising him, and someday I'd whisper to him that I was his real mam. But that was not to be. After Quinn – the bastard – made his pronouncement to me, I killed her, smothered her with her own pillow, and I stole him. And I'd have done it again in an eyeblink.'

'But what about Latimer?' asked Ben, setting down his cup. 'What happened there?'

She chuckled miserably. 'Stephen Latimer. He was Quinn's old business partner. A creature like himself, he was. But he was in a bad way. Just like everyone Quinn left in his wake. He saw me on the street one day and followed me, then cornered me in an alley. I didn't fear him because I had me knife and also because he looked like you could blow him over, he was that bad. But it wasn't violence he had in mind. It was blackmail.'

'Blackmail?' said Badger.

'Aye. He recognized me. He saw me at a funfair once, he said, telling fortunes. He recognized me from Quinn's household and put two and two together. And then he asked after me, and he discovered about Atic. I don't know how he knew, and when he saw me at the market stalls, he told me he'd tell Quinn if I didn't pay him.'

'What a scoundrel!' said Badger, truly affronted. Ben wanted to smile at him, he was that fond of the man. But he turned a serious expression toward Brennan instead.

'And what did you tell him?' he asked.

'That I'd get him the money. But I never had any intention of paying him.'

'You decided to kill him instead,' said Badger, sobering.

'Aye. I went to his house, saw the look of it all, and smothered him. He couldn't fight me. And I was fairly certain they wouldn't take it as murder.'

*What a cold-blooded creature*, Ben thought, watching her face for any signs of humanity. The only feelings she seemed to have were for her child. Ben's life hadn't been as hard as hers, or even Tim's for that matter, but he certainly lived among them in the slums, aware that a hard life meant facing certain hard facts. Men and women in the darker streets of London lived with a kill-or-be-killed brashness. He shuddered at the thought.

Tim had had it hard, without a mother or father looking after him. But it never seemed to affect his natural cheerfulness. Ben supposed it was because the man was one of action. He was always looking for the next job, be it legal or illegal.

He took a deep breath, laced his hands, and held them down between his thighs as he leaned toward her, giving her his most earnest expression. 'How did you come to do a séance at Quinn's?'

'That maid of his. She came one day to get her fortune told.' Ben recalled the rabbit's foot that Jenny Wilson would not let go of. A superstitious person such as that was bound to trust in fortune tellers, even though she had denied such. 'And she got to chatting, said that her master was desperate to find something or other that his dead business partner had wanted to give him,' she went on. 'Told me all about it, that it was Quinn and some old codger called Latimer, and by that I reckoned Latimer had sent him a letter, telling him he knew where his son was, and tapping him for a few pounds for that information. So I offered to do a séance for her. The lass didn't exactly jump at the chance at first but, after some thought, she seemed eager to do it. It was a lark at first for me. I could have told him anything and he would have gone on any number of wild-goose chases. And then I slipped in about Atic as my own joke. I . . . I . . .' She teared up, great drops of them welling in her eyes. One spilled over and made a wet line through the dirt on her cheek. It was the first time emotion had entered into her demeanor. 'I didn't even know me own son was sitting there right beside me till much later . . . from the papers. I hadn't known he'd taken a job in the very house in which he was born, working for his own wretched father . . . and neither of them knowin' it. Maybe it was the saints looking down, for I never wanted him to know that such a horrible devil sired him.'

She took a rag from her sleeve and wiped her eyes and nose.

'And that's why you killed him. To save your son.'

'That's the thing. I didn't. Oh, I had planned to. I crept into the house the night before I was to come. I knew the way, you see. I was surprised to find they had wallpapered over the door to the nursery. But I carefully cut it through. It was my escape. But then I thought, I could get from the sill in the nanny's room and clamber outside to get to the nursery sill, and leave by that room if I could get the light to go out. That would be even stealthier, I thought. And I practiced a few times that night, as quiet as can be. But I never got the chance. Someone else doused the light, and by that I knew what might be about to transpire. So I left by the adjoining door after all, and fled from the nursery down the back stairs. I didn't kill him, and I can't think that my boy did it either.'

Ben mentally punched a fist in the air. The mud on the sill! It *had* been part of a plan that was never used.

'But you knew how to throw a knife,' said Badger. 'Just like the throwing knives your compatriots had at the Traveller camp.'

'Aye, I know how to throw a knife. I threw one at you.'

'I *knew* you did it!' said Badger, jabbing a finger at her.

'It was the only one I had left. I'd lost the other one.'

Badger's face, so ready to accuse again, suddenly fell. 'Now *that* makes sense . . .'

'Never mind all that,' said Ben, shaking his head at Badger. He confronted Brennan again. 'By this confession, are you going to be turning yourself in?'

'Only if it will free my boy.'

Badger sighed. 'But . . . can't you see, Ben? It don't free him. Because Thomas could still have killed him. He had the opportunity.'

'But I'm telling you he couldn't!' she said, growing more agitated. 'He had no reason to. He didn't know about me or who I was. Or that Quinn was his father. Latimer didn't even know that it was "Edward Quinn" living under that very roof. Latimer only recognized me and probably wrote to Quinn saying as much, that *I* was still about and that I'd know where my boy was.'

Badger turned to her. 'But Thomas himself told us that Quinn was a cruel taskmaster. He cheated the man out of money that Quinn had promised him. He had just as much motive to kill Quinn as anyone else in that household. And whether he knew about Quinn or not, the prosecutor would claim that Thomas *did* know he was Quinn's heir, and killed him for the inheritance. That's a very strong motive.'

She shook her head vigorously. 'He can't have. He *can't* have. Even Atic never knew where he had ended up.' She suddenly pounced from her seat and grabbed Badger by his lapels. 'You *must* find the one who *did* do it! Save my boy!' Her eyes were wild. Her spittle landed on her chin.

Ben was suddenly behind her, taking her gently but firmly by the shoulders and pulling her away from Tim, setting her down again in her chair.

Badger had already recovered, absently smoothing down his lapels. 'We've got this all wrong. Don't you see, Ben? We got it wrong. If it's *not* Thomas, and I still don't think it was him . . . and it's not you,' he said, gesturing toward Brennan, 'then there's a *third* person to consider.'

Ben moved to stand beside Badger at the fireplace. 'How'd you mean we got it wrong? Well . . . if we are to believe Miss Brennan, here . . .'

'And we must believe her. *I* believe her.' He looked at her with a determined expression. Mary Brennan gazed back at him, eyes shining with gratitude.

Ben heaved a sigh of frustration. 'That leaves only two people in that room.'

'No,' said Badger, smacking his forehead. 'It leaves only one.'

# TWENTY-SIX
## Badger

'Where can we find you?' asked Tim. 'Will you be at the Traveller camp in Battersea?'

'No,' said Mary Brennan. Her lucidness seemed to have faltered and she gazed into the corner of the room. 'I've got nowhere to go.'

Tim exchanged a silent commiseration with Watson. 'You can . . . you can stay here for now. Let us talk to Mrs Kelly.'

Instead of ringing the bell for her, Tim opened their door and called out, 'Mrs Kelly! Are you here, Mrs Kelly?'

'What's the hullabaloo, Mister Badger?' She came from her flat, with the 'a' painted on the transom above her door, a feather duster in her hand. She turned at the newel post to look up the stairs.

'Can you give Miss Brennan here a little hospitality? If she can stay in your flat until we return . . .'

She stared at Brennan. 'In *my* flat?'

'Surely Mister Holmes explained that there might be some compromises here and there.'

She put the hand with the feather duster at her hip. 'He did say something of the sort,' she said reluctantly.

'Then this is one of those times. We thank you, Mrs Kelly.'

She glared at them the whole time as they led Mary Brennan down the stairs, even as Mrs Kelly rested her hand on the woman's shoulder. But Tim stopped them. 'Tell me one more thing, Miss Brennan. Did you lose that extra knife at the funfair, when you was doing fortune telling?'

'Yes. One day it was there, I had my punters, and then the next it was gone. Are you saying one of them pinched it?'

But he did not reply. He instead allowed Mrs Kelly to steer her through the door to her flat and close it behind them.

Tim rushed to the street door without even shutting up their flat at the top of the stairs, when Watson stopped him. 'Where are we going in such a rush, Tim?'

'We have to—'

'Mister Badger!'

Ellsie Littleton burst through the street door, forcing him to take a few steps back. Her shoulder seam was torn, her hair was in disarray where her hat had been pulled off, pins still stuck in her mussed tresses.

'Miss Littleton! He swooped up to her and didn't even stop to consider when his arm encircled her, hand at her back to ease her along to their stairs.

Up they went and through the door, where Tim seated her. Watson hurried to the sideboard and poured a glass of sherry, returning to her and offering it. She didn't bother sipping but tipped it back in one go. She clutched the empty glass to her chest and sighed deeply.

Kneeling beside her chair, Tim reached forth and touched her hand. 'Whatever happened, Miss Littleton?' It barely registered in the back of his mind that it was only a few days ago that he wouldn't exactly have minded if she had got into trouble from her meddling. But it was certainly not the case any longer.

She licked her lips of the sherry – something that froze Badger to the spot watching – until she seemed able to speak again.

'I went to the Quinn household, as I told you I was going to do,' she began. 'And I asked my questions. It started out relatively calm. I was as discreet as I could be, doing my best not to divulge all the information that the two of you had discovered, but I did pose the question: did they know that the child of Mister Quinn was in fact not from his wife; that it was the product of his association with the last housekeeper and that the child was stolen away? Well! I never expected such an uproar. Such . . . violence! Look at my dress. My hat!' She tugged at the already torn sleeve, tried to push her hair back into its careful coiffure, but it was far too late for that. 'I was so surprised at the vehemence that I immediately forgot the interview, and fought to free myself from that cursed house and ran and ran before my senses took over again and I hailed a cabby. I realize that, as a proper reporter, I should have stayed to discover why I was so railed at, but, frankly, I feared for my life.'

'I'm glad you didn't stay,' said Tim. 'I'm surprised that Mrs Martin allowed the maid to rail at you like that.'

'The maid?' She looked at each in turn. 'It wasn't the maid. It was Mrs Martin.'

'What?' Tim rolled it through his mind but couldn't fathom it. Buttoned-up, prune-faced Mrs Martin?

'At first, she was very quiet . . . listened stiffly, mind you, to what I was saying. But she suddenly exploded. She shot to her feet and came at me with her fingers like claws.' She made her fingers into claws to demonstrate. 'I've never seen anything like it, except in a madhouse.'

Tim glanced over at Watson. But Watson was looking at Tim as if they should both agree with Littleton, as if he expected it.

'But that don't make sense. We've got to get over there.' He rose and urged Watson to his feet. 'Er . . . Miss Littleton, you are free to stay as long as you like. And if you want tea or anything, simply ring that bell on the mantel.' They all glanced at the used tea things already sitting on the little table. 'Or . . . ask for fresh cups? We've got to go.'

'But where are you going?'

'We have to get to the Quinn household.'

She jumped up. 'I'm going with you!'

'No, Miss Littleton. I demand you stay here.'

'But I must report on the story.'

'You'll get it all from us later. Every word. You stay here, safe and sound.'

'Mister Badger—'

He grabbed her hands and shook them until she looked him in the eye. 'Ellsie,' he said quietly. His tender tone seized her attention at last. 'I don't want you to go. It ain't safe. We'll be back soon. Promise.'

He pressed her hands once more before releasing them. It was time to go and put this blasted thing to bed.

Tim pounded on the door to Quinn's house and Mrs Martin cast the door open with a mouth ready to berate when he walked her backwards into the foyer. 'You have some explaining to do, my good woman.'

For the first time, she seemed flustered. Her hair was not neatly pressed into a bun, but had pins hanging here and there on loose strands. She unsuccessfully tried to tap and tug it into place.

With shoulders uncharacteristically slumped, she wandered through the foyer and to the drawing room. They followed her and stood slightly apart, as if ready to grab her in whichever direction she sprinted. But that expectation was soon proved wrong. All the fight seemed to have gone out of her.

Tim was flummoxed. This was not what he expected. Not at all.

'You'd best make a clean breast of it,' said Watson gruffly. 'Why did you attack Miss Littleton?'

She clutched at her heart. Her cheeks colored and she looked away from Watson. 'I can't imagine . . . I never dreamed I'd . . .' She stifled a sob with her hand to her mouth. And then, as if remembering who she was, her spine straightened and she once again took on the manner of the staid housekeeper they expected her to be. 'I . . . I must apologize to that young woman. I never meant to hurt her. I don't know what came over me.'

'You can explain it to Scotland Yard,' said Watson, moving forward. 'It seems it was you. You who eagerly accepted a medium into this house to hold a séance.'

'I . . . what? You must be mad. That is the height of absurdity. I never did any such thing.'

'Ben . . .' said Tim.

But Watson went on, ignoring him. 'You plotted the murder of Horace Quinn. You made certain *you* sat next to him. You—'

'Hold, Ben.' Tim stared hard at Martin as she grew more frightened. This wasn't right. 'Let her explain herself to us first. I have questions about it myself.'

She swallowed hard. It rolled down her skinny neck that was revealed by the missing button of her high collar. She clutched her fingers together before her, as if this alone would keep her upright, keep her safe.

'I take it you are referring to the visit of Miss Littleton?' She swept her glance over them, and she nodded to herself. 'She came to the door, not more than an hour or so ago. She introduced herself as a reporter with *The Daily Chronicle*, which I thought at first was a very unfunny jest. But the more she spoke, I began to suspect that she was telling me the truth. When I finally listened to her words, I grew more and more appalled. She was insistent that a former housekeeper here – the one who preceded me – left because Mister Quinn . . .' She swallowed again and closed her eyes. 'It wasn't too hard to imagine. But that the housekeeper had planned on serving as the nanny of her own child while *Mrs* Quinn agreed to this deception . . . I have no words for my complete disgust on the matter.'

'I am very much afraid,' said Tim, 'that all of that is true, Mrs Martin. And now . . . I have to ask. Did Mister Quinn . . . did he ever approach *you* in an inappropriate manner?'

She breathed deeply. 'I wasn't always the spinster you see before you, Mister Badger. At one time, I could have been considered quite handsome. The "Mrs" is an honorific, you see. It is often bestowed upon women who choose to serve their betters in this capacity, forestalling their own life with a husband. I wore it with pride. And so, in my younger days – some twenty years ago when I came to this household, and being much more agreeable in face and form – an inebriated Horace Quinn *attempted*, mind you, such an inappropriate proposition. I was able with my wits – and a fireplace poker at hand – to disabuse him of the effort. He never tried such with me again.'

Tim cleared his throat. 'Well, Mrs Martin, I applaud your ingenuity. And aplomb.'

'Nothing to it. Some women are much weaker in their constitution and fall prey to men of his kind much too often. I was not to be one of them.'

'Then . . . why did you become upset with Miss Littleton's questions?'

'These situations were much too personal to discuss with a reporter, for her to spread the news far and wide and destroy the reputation of this household. After all, these things happened two decades ago. They cannot be allowed to affect the people who serve in this house now. It affects the reputation of myself, the housemaid, and . . .' She paused, no doubt thinking of Thomas Brent, whom everyone believed was the murderer.

'I understand your thinking,' said Tim, 'but you must also be made aware of this. The heir to Mister Quinn's estate was found. We found him.'

Watson, not to be bested by Tim's revelations, interrupted with, 'It's Thomas Brent himself. He is Quinn's long-lost son.'

Her surprise was certainly gratifying. Tim couldn't fault Ben for speaking up. They had both wanted to see her bested.

'That . . . that cannot be . . .' she sputtered.

'I'm afraid it's true,' said Watson. 'We got it right from the old housekeeper's mouth. And Thomas Brent did not kill Quinn. He has the right to inherit this house.'

Her eyes involuntarily scanned the walls, the rugs, the goods all around her. The realization that the man she had probably harshly ordered about was now the master was going to be hard to accept. It was all on her face.

'And since *he* didn't kill Quinn,' said Watson, stepping forward.

'Hold, Ben,' said Tim.

'For the last time, what do you mean, "hold"? We've got her.'

'No, we don't. Mrs Martin, did you kill Quinn?'

She shook her head. 'I certainly did not.'

'Even after he cheated you of your pension?'

With all dignity she raised her face. 'In all honesty, Mister Badger. There are ways for servants . . . to make do.'

Stealing from the master. Yes, he knew of servants who made up the difference between their salaries by taking food and selling it, even stealing trinkets from the household, valuable silver serving ware that was never used, and the like. That Mrs Martin felt she had to be reduced to that must have galled . . . but, of course, she must have felt it due compensation for ill-treatment. Tim couldn't fault her.

'Mrs Martin, where is Jenny Wilson now?'

She had pulled a kerchief from her sleeve and dabbed her nose with it. She seemed perplexed by the question. 'I . . . I imagine she is in the kitchen. Or perhaps her attic room.'

'What do we need with Jenny Wilson?' asked Watson.

'Don't you get it, Ben?' Tim strode to the bell rope and yanked on it. He waited.

Nothing happened.

He pulled on it again, but this time he waited only a moment before he stole to the back stairs and found himself in a darkened kitchen. She wasn't there.

He retreated to the servants' stair again and noticed a door to the back garden lying open. 'Ben!' he cried. 'She's scarpered!'

He didn't wait for his partner and flew out the door. He stood in the garden for a moment, allowing his eyes to adjust to the dark. There was a gate, he remembered, and he rushed for it. That, too, was hanging open. Now all he had to do was consider which way she would go.

He stopped, thought of Holmes's methods, and carefully backtracked into the damp garden. His eyes, adjusted now, scanned the mud and he spotted footsteps. Yes, they had to be hers. They were mostly the ball of her boots as she ran. But they weren't particularly deep, so no bag with her. Where would she go? Without her bag, without her things . . .

'Bloody hellfire! The river!'

# TWENTY-SEVEN
## Badger

Tim ran. It was a snaking way through the many curving roads to the Thames from Gower Street and he had no idea which way she'd go. But the straightest line would lead to Waterloo Bridge and that's where his feet took him.

Could he be right? About any of it? He knew Watson was displeased with the way he was proceeding. It would look to all the world – especially to Ellsie Littleton – that Mrs Martin was guilty. Her wild actions spoke of a desperate woman. But, as Mister Holmes was fond of saying, making conclusions before all the facts were presented was foolish. And so, he had remained *un*foolish. Or so he hoped.

All the evidence he could see pointed toward little Jenny Wilson. He saw it all, laid out in a line, from point to point to point. It wouldn't make sense to the ordinary eye. To a copper's eye, especially. And Watson – as smart as *he* was – was thinking too much like a copper. It was easier to scoop up a criminal in your net when you'd already decided on the easiest mark. But the easiest wasn't always the true culprit. Hadn't Mister Holmes proved that time and again?

He made it to the bridge and the lamplighters had done their job, with the glow of the lamps set all along the bridge's railings, shimmering their reflections in the dark Thames below.

And there! A lone figure standing at the rail. He slowed and softened his steps, getting as close as he dared before calling out breathlessly, 'Miss Jenny!'

She turned. Her face was white under the lamplight, her expression stark. She had planned nothing in her escape. She hadn't even worn a shawl, had no baggage, no shelter from the damp cold rolling up from the river. The only plan she seemed to have had was getting to the river . . . and ending her journey there.

'Jenny,' he said, coming closer. But when she climbed up onto the railing he halted. 'Don't! For the love of God, girl. Don't do it.'

'Why? Why should I not? So that the hangman can have me instead?'

'Ah. Well. It's like this. If you go without a confession written down good and proper, an innocent man will hang. Thomas Brent, for one.'

She had a genuine look of anguish as she bit her lip.

'He's the logical one, you see. And he didn't do it. As you well know.' He licked his lips. They were dry, even in all that damp fog descending around them. 'You liked Thomas, didn't you? He never did you any harm, did he?'

'He was polite and kind to me.'

'There now. You wouldn't see his life cut off like that, would you?'

'It . . . it wasn't as if I planned it . . .'

'Oh, I know,' he said, all the while steadily and slowly drawing closer. 'When you went to the fortune teller, you just saw the knife there.'

'It must have fallen out of her cloak. Beneath the table. I saw it. It was a strange one. It couldn't be taken for a kitchen knife. And I began to get the idea . . . because if I took a kitchen knife, it would be noticed missing.'

'That was clever, that.'

'And the master was desperate to get some sort of information that he knew his partner had. The master made the house miserable with his ranting and drink, and I was more than frightened that he'd . . .' She took a few shaky breaths. 'And I got to thinking about a séance, and maybe he'd like the idea, that he'd be just that desperate.'

'So you asked *him* . . . not Mrs Martin?'

'Oh no. I'd never have asked Mrs Martin. She'd never agree to it.'

'But that's not what you told the fortune teller.'

She bit her lip again. 'I wanted it to seem like the household wanted it. So that she would come.'

*Didn't plan it my arse, thought Badger.*

But he nodded to her, satisfied that his instincts had been right all along. 'When did you get the idea to use the knife?'

She looked off over the winding river with its many reflections of light from countless street lamps along the Embankment and on the distant bridges. It was ordinarily a lovely sight. He couldn't imagine what she was thinking as she gazed outward and then down to the black depths of the cold Thames.

'I don't know,' she said vaguely. 'A séance would be dark, you see. Dark and . . . the dark would hide me.' She kept looking along the river, watching the ripples and currents. 'Mrs Martin thinks she knows what happened between . . . between me and . . . and Mister Quinn. I told her what I could at the time. She thinks I fought him off. But I didn't. How I wish I had. But he was too strong. He . . . hurt me. I've been afraid of him ever since. I was afraid in the house the week before the séance, thinking something might happen.'

'Oh, dear lass. I'm so sorry.'

'Is every man like that, I wonder?'

'No. We're not. Thomas ain't like that either, is he?'

'Quinn never . . . he never even mentioned it again. Like it was nothing to him.'

'Men like that . . .' He almost said that they deserved to die. But in such cold blood? He couldn't say it. Couldn't believe it. But now, in the face of it, there was no use in moralizing. It would do Jenny Wilson no good.

'So you . . . took the knife. Kept it.'

'Yes. I had no plan. Until I got the idea for the séance. I looked at that Gypsy woman as she told my fortune and I got the idea in my head that Mister Quinn might do a séance and that medium must have read my mind and suggested it the same time I thought it. We were all to attend. I tried to sit next to the master but Mrs Martin pulled me to a seat beside *her* instead.'

'And you drained the oil from the overhead lamp ahead of time so's it would go out.'

'Yes.' She raised her face to him. 'You're clever.'

'And so are you. You waited for it to go out and then you jumped up and did the deed. How did you know just where he was? You might have stabbed someone innocent by mistake.'

'His smell. His pomade. It's strong. Stronger when . . . when he's all over you.' She rubbed her arms, making herself smaller. 'I'll never forget it as long as I live.' Her eyes moved again toward the inexorable Thames. 'Are you satisfied?' she asked with a tilt to her head. 'Can you now leave me to it?'

'But what about Thomas?'

'They'll think that old Gypsy woman done him in. It was her knife, after all.'

'But that's just it. It's a tangled story, that. You see . . . that old Gypsy woman was no Gypsy at all. Her name is Mary Brennan. And she was the housekeeper before even Mrs Martin's time. And Quinn attacked her as he attacked you. Only she fell into a family way. And she had the baby. And Quinn's wife couldn't, you see, so they told her they would pretend it was Mrs Quinn's and then they'd keep Mary on as the nanny. But Quinn changed his mind and chucked her out. So she stole the baby back instead.'

Horror spread across her features. He was almost sorry to have to tell her at all.

'And, as it turns out,' he went on, 'Thomas Brent . . . is that child. He never knew it. Never even knew that it was his very own mother at the séance, with murder in her own mind. But she didn't do it. And neither did Thomas. You have to set it right. My word won't amount to a farthing on it. It's only you who can make certain they are free.'

Her hand tightened on the rail, even as her feet twitched between the balusters.

He measured the distance between the two of them. He wasn't sure he could leap in time to catch her if she was determined. It was up to her now.

She cast her glance down to the Thames rushing below. 'He was always nice to me,' she whispered.

'Then don't let him die. Nor his mum.' Though she was certain to hang for those other two murders. But there was little point in sharing that just now.

Tim had never been so still in his life. He was afraid to breathe, lest he miss a chance to save her. Every muscle in his body tensed, ready. But as the time ticked by – and a small skiff appeared in the dark waters, its light bobbing ahead of it, illuminating little foamy waves at the bow – the girl's taut shoulders suddenly lowered and, slowly, she climbed down, as if it were the hardest thing she'd ever done. And likely, he thought, it was.

She wouldn't raise her gaze to him as she asked, 'Do you think God will forgive me?'

'Miss, I'm no vicar, but I don't think He'd mind you doing a good turn for an innocent man.'

She nodded. 'Then that's where we'll leave it.'

# TWENTY-EIGHT
## Watson

It was hours later when Ben finally tracked Badger to Scotland Yard. He found him sitting forlornly in Inspector Hopkins's office.

'Come in, Mister Watson,' said Hopkins good-naturedly. More softly, he said, inclining his head toward Badger, 'He's been here for some time.'

Ben stood over Badger until he finally looked up. 'Awright, Tim?'

He swallowed. 'I never really thought about the consequences. It was all just . . . not quite real before, I reckon. A puzzle, was all. I mean, when a murderer is brought in, you know it means the hangman. But now . . . I *know* the lass.'

'Ah.' He sat in the chair next to him and looked up to Hopkins. The inspector took the hint and walked quietly out of his own office.

'It's a sore thing, ain't it?' said Ben. 'Knowing.'

'It is.'

'But it's murder, Tim. Murder cannot go unpunished.'

As if he'd just thought of it – and maybe he had – he snapped his head toward Ben. 'Mary Brennan. We'll have to turn her in too!' He looked down at his hands, turning the palms up. 'More blood,' he murmured, as if seeing it there on his own hands.

'Mary Brennan hopped it. If the coppers are clever, they *might* be able to find her. But I have my doubts. If she's smart, she'll disappear in Ireland. Or maybe the continent. I doubt we'll see her like again. But we can tell Hopkins honestly that we had her, but she escaped.'

'Blimey, Ben.' He ran his fingers through his hair. Somewhere along the way, he'd lost his hat, or left it back in Soho.

'This is part of the trade, old son. This will always be the result of us catching them. It will always be the hangman.'

'I guess I just never thought it through.'

'Well, think it. And decide if this is the path you will take. And while you're thinking it, think on this. Maybe it's not so much the Quinns of the world that need justice, and he was a cold bastard and he's met his Maker and got his right Judgment. But the Thomas Brents of the world need it. And the Mrs Martins, for I was ready to cop her into the nick. Truth is needed. And we did find the truth. And if that is the path you want, and you're certain you want, I am your partner in it. I'm proud to be. Because I think I'd like a little more truth in the world myself. In this old town, at least.'

Badger clenched his hands and slowly nodded. 'There's honey in your words, Ben. And, God of Mercy, I want to believe you.'

He patted his friend's shoulder. 'In time, Tim.'

They sat for a while longer until Hopkins returned. And then Ben proceeded to fill in the gaps to the story that Badger hadn't been able to talk about.

It was late by the brief chimes of the mantel clock when they trudged back to their lodgings on Dean Street. The gas was low, so Ben turned it up and gasped, stopping dead, holding an arm protectively across Badger's chest as they stood in the doorway, protecting him from the shadow figure before them. But he needn't have worried.

'I see you solved your case,' said the graceful tones of the gaunt man with the wide forehead and receding hairline. He was smoking a pipe and, when he turned his head to face Ben, he pointed a sharp nose at him, eyes measuring. He looked just like the illustrations in *The Strand Magazine.*

'I take it that you are Mister Sherlock Holmes.'

'Indeed. And you are . . . *Mister* Watson.' He smiled around his pipe stem.

'Mister Holmes!' said Badger. And then he did what he had held back so bravely at the police station; he gave out a great sob and ended up turning himself to the wall and weeping into his arm.

Aghast, Ben tried to assuage him by patting his shoulders and whispering at his ear, 'It's Mister Holmes here to see *you*, Tim. Pull yourself together.'

Holmes merely watched, blowing smoke into the ceiling, where it drifted around him like a wreath. 'I have come for the both of you,' he said in a bland drawl. 'But that is neither here nor there. You may not realize it, Mister Badger, but I am fully aware of the tolls of solving crimes. As I told you before, I may have called it a game, I may have treated it often very *like* a game, but I am also always fully aware that it involves human lives. And this is the lesson *you* must learn. To do good in the world may involve some sacrifice. Sometimes it is the simple things. Allowing the police to take the credit for something *you* have solved, for instance. Or deciding whether it is right to let a killer go free. This will take a great deal of character . . . and I suspect that both you and your Watson have an abundance of that.'

He rose and, though Ben expected Holmes to go to Badger, he instead strode to the fireplace. Resting his foot on the fender, he stared down into the glowing coal, puffing on his pipe, and tucking his thumb into his waistcoat pocket. 'I came here to congratulate you on a job well done.'

Ben frowned. 'But . . . how did you know the case had come to its conclusion, sir?'

'I suspected it was coming to a head and that you and Mister Badger, together, would bring it to its conclusion about now. Also, I had heard from my current Baker Street Irregulars' – Badger raised his head – 'that you had gone with a suspect to Scotland Yard. You see, Badger, the cycle continues. Crime never stops; nor do I. Nor will you.'

Badger wiped his face with the sleeve of his coat and sniffed. 'No, sir, I will not.'

'Then you've decided. Good to hear!' He knocked the spent tobacco into the fireplace and tucked the pipe into his coat pocket. He swiveled to face them. 'It was a very good job, Badger, Watson. It took ingenuity and the judicious use of my methods. Yes, I see them in the results. Perhaps more use of them would have solved it sooner, but . . .' He waved his long-fingered hand in dismissal. 'You didn't guess. You must never guess.'

'Yes, sir. But . . . she'll hang. And one so young. And she was so hurt . . .'

'Yes. A great pity. But such is justice, Badger.'

'*Is* it justice, sir?'

'*Thou shalt not kill*, Mister Badger. There is no taking back a murder, you see. A murder is final, and so, too, should the punishment be thereof. Unless you aren't certain that she is the culprit.'

Badger stuffed his hands in his pockets, something Ben knew he never would have done in the man's presence had he been in his right mind. 'I was as certain as can be, well before she confessed it to me.'

'Quite right,' said Holmes. 'Well, there seems little else to discuss.' He approached Badger and offered his hand. Badger looked as if he'd rather be anywhere else but shaking the man's hand, but he took it gravely anyway. Holmes then offered his hand to Ben, but after shaking, Holmes didn't let it go. He pulled slightly and Ben stumbled forward, trying to hold back from completely falling over the man. 'Have you discovered what made that ghostly impression in the room; the "silky mist" spoken of, Mister Watson?'

How had he known about that? But Watson reckoned that Holmes was making sure he was apprised of all the facts of the case. Might have even talked to Hopkins behind their backs.

Ben stared into those eyes, brows slightly lowered, as Holmes leaned toward him in concentration. Was he trying to mesmerize him, like some music hall magician? He seemed perfectly capable of it. But Ben held himself steady, gripped the other's hand firmly, and looked him straight in the eye. He hadn't realized how nervous he would be, meeting the man at last. And he knew it was a test, so he thought carefully about what he had discovered and chose his words thoughtfully. 'I wonder how you knew about that, but I'll put that aside for now. Well, it wasn't just their imagination. When the light went out, Mary Brennan reckoned what it might be about, that murder was about to take place. She left the table and opened the secret partition door to the nursery. Opposite that wall was a mirror. The soft light from the window in that room cast what looked like a mist onto the mirror, causing the illusion of something there, which quickly dispersed when that passage door was closed again.

And, of course, by then, a murder *had* been committed and all in the room forgot about it.'

Holmes nodded and smiled, releasing Watson's hand. 'Very good. Well. It is all finished, then. Good night, gentlemen.'

He moved away from where they were standing to retrieve his hat and Ulster from the rack by the door, then left without further ado.

Badger heaved a great sigh. 'He's right. It's all done now.'

'I didn't expect that reaction from you,' said Ben sheepishly. Somehow, he felt he should have done something for his friend in that instance. But he still couldn't think of anything he might have done. He watched as Badger moved into the room and flopped down onto the chair Holmes had recently occupied. He let his arms drape over the sides.

'That's done it.'

'It has.'

'So she'll hang.'

'Best get used to that conclusion, Tim.'

'You're right. I had better.'

Ben removed his outer coat and hung it, along with his hat, on the rack. And to think that Sherlock Holmes had hung his own hat and coat on that very same rack . . . No, best not think that way. They were colleagues now. He'd told them they'd done a good job. Ben hoped Badger could enjoy their victory. Someday. And now that Brent was flush, he'd surely pay his full fee . . . and then some.

'What do you reckon, Tim?' he said, striding to the chair opposite his friend and falling onto the cushioned seat. 'Shall we be as famous as Mister Sherlock Holmes and Doctor John H. Watson?'

It was small at first, but there it was, a smile forming on Badger's face. 'I don't know about that. But a client or two out of it, once it hits the papers, won't go amiss. Oh!' He sat straight up. 'Miss Littleton!'

'I sent her home hours ago. But we'll send a message to her early in the morning to get her that exclusive. She'll have the whole story in any case. Our "Doctor Watson" indeed!'

'Well,' said Badger fondly, gazing at his friend, 'you can't have too many Watsons.'

# AFTERWORD

I have been a fan of the Holmes stories since my teen years. But I hadn't considered writing a pastiche until I had begun my research for my gas-lamp-steampunk fantasy series the Enchanter Chronicles trilogy. If it wasn't medieval, then my second interest in historical time periods was definitely the Victorian. Once I had gathered material and done some research for the paranormal series (even though it's a fantasy, I do like to get the *history* right), I became intrigued with the possibility of writing a Sherlock Holmes pastiche.

Now, there are pastiches and pastiches. Some rewrite Holmes and Watson completely. Some create relatives of the man to do their investigations and take off on their own stories. Some even involve dinosaurs, robots, or a cloned Sherlock Holmes into the twenty-second century.

This series is none of that.

I am by no means a Sherlock Holmes expert but I do like to do research. And when the idea came to me to write about one of his Baker Street Irregulars, all grown up and thinking he could be a private detective, too, with mixed results, I dove even deeper. I could have gone very serious and dramatic, but I decided that some comedy was more practical. After all, the Baker Street Irregulars were kids from the streets. Dr Watson describes them in *A Study in Scarlet* as 'half a dozen of the dirtiest and most ragged street Arabs that ever I clapped eyes on.' To which Holmes remarked, 'There's more work to be got out of one of those little beggars than out of a dozen of the force.' These were fellows who could barely read and write, from the poorest of the poor, and that's why they made perfect spies because no one would take note of them. And if one of them had notions above his station and felt he was clever enough, bold enough, and could figure it out, he, too, could be a detective for hire. Especially with the help of a very clever man who had lots of experience in a variety of jobs, including that of a chemist. I loved writing from Badger and Watson's perspective, how they'd figure out the mystery without the benefit of Holmes's education, how they'd work their way through a case with their wits alone, trying to use Holmes's methods, faltering in that, and getting into a spot of trouble along the way. And how Mister Holmes would feel obliged to help them because he was amused by their audaciousness. It's going to be great fun.

Now, a word about Inspector Stanley Hopkins. I chose to include him in the series because he was one of the few inspectors who truly admired Holmes and his methods, and tried, though sometimes failed, to employ them properly. Just as Tim discovers, it isn't as easy as it looks. And, as Dr Watson says in 'The Adventure of Black Peter,' 'Holmes had high hopes, while he [Hopkins] in turn professed the admiration and respect of a pupil for the scientific methods of the famous amateur.' But mistakes were made, as Tim makes his own, and Holmes was not satisfied with the performance of the Scotland Yard inspector in the same story: 'Stanley Hopkins's methods do not commend themselves to me. I am disappointed in Stanley Hopkins. I had hoped for better things from him. One should always look for a possible alternative and provide against it. It is the first rule of criminal investigation.' I suspect Hopkins got better at it, as will Tim and Ben. With time.

As for Ellsie Moira Littleton, is she too modern for her time period? Not in the least. There were already female reporters employed by a few of London's many newspapers at the time this series is set. And it was only a scant few years later that the Suffragette movement began taking shape in England. Ellsie was raised in privilege, but she seems to have an enduring need to help social justice causes, though she doesn't yet have the vocabulary for such.

And finally, it's such a pleasure to pen the Great Man himself, a man who also warred with notions of caste. It probably helped him to understand each level of society as he moved among the lower classes in disguise and playing his roles.

But look at me. I'm talking about him as if he were a real person. To many, he was and still is, a living person. People still write to Sherlock Holmes. But in Conan Doyle's era, 221 Baker Street didn't exist. Street numbers on Baker Street didn't even go up to the 200s. However, in the 1930s, London converted their street numbering system and Baker Street finally had its 221 . . . but the address was the headquarters of Abbey National Building Society, a bank. From the 1940s, they dutifully forwarded the letters they received for Holmes to the Conan Doyle family, and later to the Holmes Collection at the Marylebone Public Library. After a while the bank, being good sports, decided to hire and set up a 'personal secretary to the detective' to answer correspondence themselves. And then, in the 1990s when there finally was a Sherlock Holmes Museum on Baker Street, the museum owners naturally assumed *they* would get the mail to answer, but the bank was steadfast that *they* would continue. Appeals were even sent by the museum to the Doyle estate, but they didn't seem to want anything to do with it, not being keen that people should believe Holmes was a real person with a real address, despite the fact that he probably would have been dead for the last seventy-plus years. The dispute ended when the bank gave up their building and the museum could finally take over the correspondence. Whew! All for a letter on Holmes's stationery with the return address of 221b Baker Street upon it. I guess, thinking about it, I wouldn't mind having one of those letters myself.

I hope you enjoyed this novel as much as I enjoyed writing it. If you did like it, please consider reviewing it.

We'll see Badger and Watson again in their next outing as a mummy-unwrapping party goes awry when the partygoers make a grisly discovery in *The Mummy of Mayfair*.

You can see all my other novels at JeriWesterson.com. Happy reading!